MY FIRST MY LAST MY ONLY

DENISE CARBO

This novel is entirely a work of fiction. The names, characters, and incidents portrayed in it are the work of the author's imagination.

ISBN digital: 9781734872903

ISBN paperback: 9781734872910

This book is dedicated to my grandmother, Mimi. I spent many summers and holidays at her home on a lake in New Hampshire. I cherish those memories. They are the inspiration for the Granite Cove series.

CHAPTER 1

"Are you avoiding me?"

The smooth timbred voice jolts through me, drops of sticky orange mimosa from my glass splash on the back of my hand. *Hell yes, I'm avoiding you!*

I turn and plaster a smile on my face. "Of course not, why would you think that?"

I can't bring myself to meet his gaze so I stare over his right shoulder at all the attendees of my mother's Memorial Day party milling about behind him in the foyer and living room.

"You leave the room every time I enter."

Yup, absolutely. "Total coincidence."

"How are you Franny?"

Uh, let's see...my stomach is churning so hard I just might throw up. "I'm fine, and you?"

"Good. I'm happy to be back in Granite Cove. Maybe we can get together and revisit some of our favorite spots."

I blink several times as if my eyes have somehow gained the ability to change moments of reality like the remote on a TV flips through different channels.

"Sure, we could do that." *Never gonna happen.*

"Oh Mitch, there you are, there are a few people dying to meet you." My mother casts a questioning glare in my direction before smiling up at him, hooking his arm through hers, and directing him back towards the living room.

Yes mother, spirit away your precious guest of honor before your wayward daughter does something to embarrass you.

I take the opportunity to dart from the dining room, through the butler's pantry, and into the kitchen. It's swarming with catering staff so I push through the swinging door into the living room and out the first set of French doors onto the patio.

My father is holding court to the left. A guffaw from one of the men surrounding him is followed by a few chuckles. I can guess the story he's telling, the time he sliced a golf ball into the trees and a squirrel mistook it for a rather large nut and absconded with it into the woods. He tells the same one at every Memorial Day party, an annual tradition that, if I'm not mistaken, every single one of the people standing around him listening have heard. Yet they're avid listeners. Grant Dawson has a natural charm which draws people in. He could probably recite a grocery list and people would still find it witty.

I did not inherit his ability.

The breeze off the lake cools my overheated skin. I pray it will stop the nervous perspiration threatening to show through my black Maxi dress.

A group of women, contemporaries of my mother's, occupy one of the patio tables to the right. I edge closer. Perhaps if I stand a couple of feet away, I can appear to be part of the conversation, but not close enough that any of them will expect me to join in.

A discreet glance at my watch reveals I have another half hour before I can safely make an escape. Over the years I've gotten it down to a science. Attendance at these gatherings is mandatory, but if I stay for a minimum of an hour, my mother will let me make excuses to depart with little more than a frown and a raised eyebrow. Oh yes, and the sigh of disappointment, mustn't forget that.

Raising the fluted glass, I do no more than wet my lips with the orange bubbly decadence of the mimosa. My mother shoved the glass at me upon my arrival with the admonishment to "go mingle." Arguing is pointless, and it gives me something to do with my hands.

In my peripheral vision, I spot a familiar dark head exiting the far set of French doors near my father.

I dart back through the doors closest to me.

Regardless of my mother's schedule, the party is over for me. I'll slip through the kitchen and escape upstairs.

I arrive at the swinging door just as a tingle squirms down my spine.

"Francine." Those throaty cultured tones freeze me in place as if I were five years old instead of twenty-five.

The hesitation costs me dearly.

The door slams into my forehead, halting my progress. The smack of the door shudders through my body and sends me stumbling backwards into Vanessa Michaels, the bane of my entire childhood.

My mimosa sails into her face and she lets out a startled shriek. Luckily, just the liquid since the glass is still clenched in one fist of my spiraling arms as I frantically try to regain my balance.

The horrified gaze of the server standing in the now open kitchen doorway catches mine as I find purchase by crashing into an immovable object.

A soft grunt echoes above my head.

Strong hands grip my arms. Mitch's shoulder cushions the back of my head. I blink stupidly, staring up into his big baby blues.

His grin reveals perfectly straight white teeth. "Nice to see some things haven't changed."

"For God's sake, Francine!" Mother grabs me, wrenching me upright. Her hands dig into my upper arms, her perfume engulfs me, and the coppery tang of blood touches my tongue when I lick my lips.

Snatching the empty glass from my fist and handing it to a server hovering behind her, she glowers at me and then pastes on a smile and faces the guest of honor.

"I am so terribly sorry Mitch. Are you injured?" She clutches both her hands to her chest and stares at him beseechingly.

Granted, I am not what anyone might describe as petite or even—*wince, wince*—lightweight, but I hardly think I could have caused much damage to him either.

"I'm fine Ms. Dawson."

"Oh, call me Elaine, please." She places a hand on his arm and lets it linger on his bicep.

Vanessa grabs the napkin the wary server offers her and dabs at her face and chest. Personally, I only spot the streaks of liquid creating a few tracks through her heavily made-up face. She's only dabbing her chest to call attention to it. After all, she has it on full display. The blue sundress can barely contain it all.

"Francine take Vanessa upstairs, so she may clean up." Mother gives me a pointed glare when I don't immediately hop to do her bidding.

Must I? This promises to be even more unpleasant than the room full of people openly gawking at my latest disaster. I enter the kitchen through the now propped open door, hoping Vanessa won't follow but knowing she will.

I glue my gaze to the pristine white tile floor as I trudge past the caterer and lone server in the kitchen, both valiantly attempting to appear busy and not stare at the spectacle. The tantalizing aroma of hot coffee tempts me to detour for a cup, but the lurking presence behind me and the threat of my mother's continued disappointment prompts me to exit the kitchen.

The click of Vanessa's heels follows me into the foyer and up the wide curved staircase. Halting next to the guestroom with an attached bathroom, I stand to the side and let her enter first. The hostile scowl she shoots me makes me want to run down the hall to my bedroom and hide behind the locked door.

Instead, I let out a tremendous sigh and follow behind her. "I'm sorry Vanessa. Is there anything I can do to help?" Stopping next to one of the twin beds covered in a silver duvet, I wrap my arms around my waist. Lavender from the dish of potpourri my mother displayed on the dresser scents the room. It's supposed to be calming, isn't it? I take a deep breath.

Pausing on the threshold to the bathroom, Vanessa pivots and glares at me with disdain. "Only you would humiliate me in front of Mitch Atwater! If I didn't know better, I'd think you did it on purpose, not just a result of your klutzy behavior. Really *Fanny*, if I were you, I wouldn't even go out in public. Your poor parents must be mortified by you."

I do an inner eye roll lest she see the nickname still bothers me. I suppose she continues to call me Fanny as a reminder of her superiority and my relegation to the undesirables section of humanity. Flouncing into the bathroom, she yanks a tissue out of the box on the counter and dabs at her face.

With a pointed glare at my reflection in the mirror, she tosses the tissue in the garbage next to the vanity and grabs another. "Why are you still standing there? Leave!"

My shoulders flinch. "I *am* sorry," I whisper as I leave the room, shutting the door behind me.

Trudging down the hall in the opposite direction, I spare a quick glance at the stairway hoping to find it empty. Once I assure it is, I pick up my pace to just shy of a jog to reach my bedroom before I encounter anyone else.

My head is throbbing.

Shutting and locking my door, I lean back against it closing my eyes.

Mitch Atwater is back in Granite Cove.

CHAPTER 2

Pushing off the door, I trudge into my bathroom holding my aching head and inspect my forehead in the mirror over the sink. A lump is already forming with a cut in the middle. A drop of crusty blood has oozed out and left a streak against my pale skin. Frizzy strands of hair escape the tight bun I painstakingly stuffed them into this morning. I look like I stuck my finger in a light socket and got zapped. Funny enough, I've done that before. More than once.

My hair has a mind of its own. I either wear it in a bun or braid to tame its wild tendencies. I chopped it off once thinking it might help. It did not. I looked like Little Orphan Annie on steroids.

My hair is orange, not red, not auburn, orange and frizzy. I keep it long hoping to weigh it down. My mother and sister are both blondes. My father's hair was dark before it changed silver. Someone might think I was adopted unless they saw the photos of my great grandmother, Eloise.

I wet a green washcloth with cold water and hold it to my head. Pain lashes my forehead. I wince and plop down on the closed toilet seat.

I'm now stuck in my room until the party ends, which won't be for hours yet.

Mitch's presence only puts a small wrinkle into my plans. Actually, not even that. His arrival is insignificant.

I'd only learned of his return upon my arrival at the party when my mother informed me with glee that her guest of honor was the award-winning movie director, Mitch Atwater.

My first thought had been to run for the hills. My second was to run to the closest salon for a complete makeover and to the nearest store for a killer outfit. Neither happened, instead my mother dragged me into the party.

No matter, I survived our encounter and it's doubtful I'll see him again. Granite Cove may be a small town, but its population is large enough that I don't know all the residents and those I do I hardly run into every day.

Standing, I toss the washcloth in the sink and wander into my bedroom to sit down on the four-poster bed. I rub the black jersey material of my dress between my fingers. The dichotomy of me wearing black and my mother white does not escape me. I wear this dress because it's comfortable and if I spill anything on it, it's unlikely to show. The dress covers me from the modest neckline to the tops of my black gladiator sandals.

I grab my phone off the nightstand to check my messages and emails. Mother doesn't allow family members to have their phones at her parties. Probably because we could use them as an excuse to escape if we claimed a dire emergency. Not that she'd accept that ploy from me.

No voicemails and the only new emails I received are advertisements. Somehow I must have gotten on a list somewhere for every type of junk mail there is. One is an ad for sexy singles in my area. I could actually use that one.

Ugh. I drop back on the bed.

Why hasn't Mr. Brick gotten back to me? I sent him a fair offer to buy the building. We've discussed it several times since I started renting the space for The Sweet Spot, and I finally saved up enough money.

Buying the building is not only the first step in my new life plan, it's the key ingredient everything else hinges on. I buy the building, move into the apartment above the bakery, and finally get a life. Once I have my own place, I can focus on getting a social life and maybe even a love life.

The same pale gray bedroom furniture I've had since I was a child mocks me from every direction. A fancy prison which keeps me under my parents' rule and prevents me from living the life I want to live. My chest tightens and the air in the room grows suffocating. I need to get out of here, right now.

I scramble off the bed and stand there debating my options.

The gaiety of the party seeps through the floorboards. I can't waltz down the front staircase without being seen and subjected to a retelling of my latest antics, which will no doubt lead to a laundry list of my most embarrassing moments. I could, however, use the back stairs attached to the balcony in my parents' room which leads to the side of the house. Yes, there's a chance I'll be spotted, but the odds of a clean getaway are much better than my only other option.

There's the tree outside my sister's bedroom but the image that pops into my head of me hanging upside down from a branch with my dress over my head and my lady parts showing for the world to see or the one with me sprawled on the ground with broken bones savagely nixes that idea.

I tiptoe towards my bedroom door. Then I stop and roll my eyes. Not only can no one see or hear me in my bedroom, but it is utterly ridiculous to be sneaking around my own parents' house as if I'm going to commit a great caper.

I unlock the door and peek around it. There's no sign of Vanessa. One encounter with her was more than enough, thank you very much. I slide out of my room, shutting the door behind me, and stride over to my parents' room.

The door opens soundlessly, but I still listen in case one of my parents has snuck up here for a moment or if a partygoer or two has decided to use the room for some nefarious reason. Ascertaining I'm alone, I shut the door and peer around the room. A king-size canopy bed dominates the room parallel to the French doors which open onto the balcony overlooking the lake.

The French door refuses to budge so I lodge my shoulder against it and give it a shove. It opens with a shudder and a bang as it swings wide and bounces against the house. I freeze on the threshold. Someone surely heard and is peering up from the patio to see who made the noise.

I'm not going back to my room, so I shuffle onto the balcony and gently close the door. It rattles into place despite my efforts to be quiet. I gingerly walk to the stairs, keeping to the side of the balcony next to the house in case someone is looking up.

A peek over the railing at the top of the stairs shows me a clear path along the side of the house.

To avoid any prying eyes from the front of the house, I traipse down the stairs and cut across the lawn into the neighbor's yard. I jog around to the front of the house and into the next neighbor's yard to reach the sidewalk.

I stride across the manicured lawn, a dog barks at me, and I quicken my pace. The neighbors won't mind, they're at the party, but that doesn't mean I want to be bitten by a dog guarding their territory against trespassers.

After a brief jaunt up the road to the walking path that loops around the park, I let out a deep breath.

The escape is a success.

I amble along the park path to the shore of the lake where I slide onto one of the wooden benches lining the walkway. A sigh of relief escapes me, and a bit of a smug smile.

May is still early for boating season to populate the lake, but the spring air is warm enough for a few brave dedicated boaters to drag their vessels out of winter storage and traverse the choppy water. Several towns share the massive lake. Granite Cove isn't the largest, but it's not the smallest either.

A shadow appears on the ground at my feet, and I glance over my shoulder as Mitch eases onto the bench beside me. His light blue gaze focuses on my forehead and he winces. "Ouch, that must hurt."

Craptastic! So much for no one noticing my great escape.

The corner of his mouth lifts. "Did you get a concussion?" Peering into my eyes, he shakes his head. "Your eyes don't appear dilated."

I turn my head and stare at the lake. "Are you a doctor now?"

"Nope, played one once though. Does that count?"

A smile twitches at my lips, but I refuse to let it go. I remember the film and his costar he was rumored to have had a torrid affair with. My impulse to smile disappears.

"How have you been, Franny?"

His deep voice sends a shiver over my skin that has nothing to do with the weather. I scrunch my nose and stare at up at the cloudless blue sky. How have I been? Pretty much the same, unfortunately, but I can't say that, so I shrug instead.

"What brings you back to Granite Cove?" I suppose I can make polite chitchat. Besides, part of me is curious to know his answer.

His silence prompts me to peek at his profile. He's staring out over the lake. There are a pair of white sailboats moored nearby bobbing along on the water. Farther out, a motorboat speeds by. Nothing really to capture his attention.

"I guess I needed a change. I was happy here once."

Yeah, so was I.

"A change from what?"

He drapes an arm over the back of the bench and rests his ankle on the opposite knee. "The short answer is life in general. The long answer is probably best for another time."

I scoot farther away on the bench and cross my legs. "Sounds complicated."

"Life usually is, isn't it?"

A constant minefield of missteps and regret. I tap my dangling foot and cross my arms over my abdomen.

But that's all going to change. My plan is firmly in place and life will be great. Positivity is my new theme. While I waited in the doctor's office, I read a magazine full of self-help articles which inspired my life makeover. I even drew up a vision board with pictures of people having fun and couples in love. Perhaps I should have pilfered the magazine so I could reread it when my motivation was sagging. Like now.

Who am I kidding? I've never stolen anything in my life.

"What about you?"

I glance in his direction without meeting his gaze. "What about me?"

"What's going on in your life? Husband? Kids?"

Nope and nope.

A sailboat glides by with a bright white sail. I bite my lip and squint up at the sun. "I own a bakery in town, The Sweet Spot."

"I know. I bought the building."

My building? He bought my building?

I lurch to my feet only to sink back to the bench.

"What's wrong?"

He places his hand over mine gripping the edge of the bench. I stare at the contrast of his darker skin over my pale white freckled hand. I pull my hand away and tuck them both under my legs. "Mr. Brick sold you the building?"

He leans forward to rest his elbows on his knees with hands clasped in between. "Was that the name of the owner? My lawyer handled the sale. He set up a corporation, so my name doesn't show up on the documents. It's just a business thing."

A business thing? No wonder Mr. Brick has been avoiding my calls and attempts to negotiate buying the building. He already sold it.

Tears threaten, but I swallow them back. I lift my hand to rub at the pain gathering in my chest, but I drop it back and press harder against the bench. The wood digs into my palms.

What does he need the building for? Is he going to kick me out at the end of my lease and turn it into a trendy restaurant or something? Isn't that what celebrities do, open restaurants?

Although, not here in Granite Cove. The town is not exactly a hot spot, or even close to one. The nearest airport is over an hour away. Even the closest highway is a half hour's drive. We're tucked into

New Hampshire's lakes region, surrounded by green hills and blue skies.

What am I going to do? If he does intend to kick me out, I need to find another building. If he doesn't, then do I go on renting and living with my parents? Either scenario makes me nauseated.

Water laps against the rocks. The paved walking and bike path winds along the shore of the lake on this side of the park. It intersects with the sidewalk that lines the town docks in the center of the cove. For the first time in my memory I'm wishing for someone to stroll by and interrupt us. Surely one of his fans has tracked him down. Perhaps even my mother wondering where her guest of honor has disappeared to?

I'd run if I thought my legs would hold me. My muscles are shaky.

He bought my building.

"If it's the rent you're worried about, I'm not going to change it on you."

I'm biting my tongue so hard I'm surprised I haven't chomped it off. Tears prick my eyes and I blink them back as fast as I can. I stare out towards the lake but honestly, I see nothing but my own misery.

"Franny?"

I open my mouth to snap, "What?" but smash my lips together instead and grip the bench tighter. What does he want from me? Oh right, he mentioned not changing the rent.

"That's good…" My voice cracks, so I clear my throat and try again. "That's good to know."

Pain squeezes my stomach. Loosening my grip on the bench, I hold my hands protectively over my abdomen. It's done that more and more. With my luck, it's an ulcer.

Damn it! The building was mine. He stole it out from under me. How could he do that? How could Mr. Brick do that? I should have had papers drawn up. All I have is his verbal promise to sell when he was ready. Another harsh lesson learned. Never trust anyone on their word alone. Get it in writing. Business 101.

I guess the handful of business management courses I took in college before I dropped out to pursue my culinary aspirations didn't stick. I can picture the roll of my mother's eyes and the ensuing lecture on not only making bad business decisions but the never-ending admonishments over the wasted college tuition money they spent on my freshman and sophomore years. My father will shake his head sadly and then change the subject. If it hadn't been for the small inheritance I received from my grandmother I would never have been able to afford culinary school. My parents refused to pay for it. If I rebuffed the college of their choice, they wouldn't cover the costs.

"You sure you don't need a doctor to look at your head?"

A quick shake of my head elicits a wince of pain. It hurts, but my heart hurts more.

"I don't remember you being this quiet."

I can sense him staring at me, but I keep my gaze fixed on the path at my feet. I wasn't shy or silent with him, not when it was just the two of us, which it was the majority of the time.

"That was a long time ago." I stand. "I have to go."

I don't wait for a response from him. I'm too shattered to care.

My dream and plan are destroyed.

I stride down the path with no destination in mind. Mitch has broken my heart. Again.

CHAPTER 3

The predawn sky twinkles with stars, and distant lights shine from across the lake. My reflection stares back at me from the large window at the back of the bakery kitchen.

I spent my entire day off yesterday bemoaning my fate and cursing Mitch's return. Sometime after I reached the bottom of the pint of ice cream, it occurred to me that my plan wasn't completely sunk. Yes, it had been torpedoed, and it was listing to its side, but it was still afloat.

The building was sold. His offer must have been far above mine for Mr. Brick to accept, so making an offer to Mitch was pointless. I don't have the money. He did say that my rent wouldn't change.

I am finding the positive amidst the wreckage.

It would mean I needed to continue renting instead of buying, but I can do that. What I can't do is continue living in my parents' house.

My new plan is to contact Mitch, or even better his lawyer, to rent the apartment upstairs. Not ideal, but it still accomplishes my end goal.

I shake my head and shoulders to clear my mind and focus on the task at hand, preparing all the baked goods to fill the shelves of my bakery when we open in two hours.

Cinnamon infuses the air from the muffins baking in one of the ovens lining the outside wall to my left. I check on bread dough rising on the counters in the middle of the room and the bagels cooling on the movable racks lined up by the front wall.

The solitude makes it one of my favorite times of day. It's just me in my kitchen creating the day's offerings.

I finish making the danishes and prepare them for the ovens. Once the muffins finish baking, the danishes will go in.

By the time the breads have risen and are ready to go into the oven, streaks of pink and peach appear over the horizon. I step back from the counter and smile. This is why I do most of my preparations on this marble counter under the window, so I can witness the sunrise over the lake. The ribbons of color lengthen and brighten as the ball of orange and yellow rises over the water, casting its light and reflecting on the calm surface.

Nature's splendor always has a way of bringing joy and peace to my world. I enjoy the view a moment more, wash my hands, and move over to the smaller counter area in the kitchen reserved for making the allergy free options I have available for my customers.

Sally arrives while I am filling the glass display cases in the front of the bakery with product.

"Good morning, Sally."

"Mornin'." She shuffles between the countertop height display cases into the kitchen and returns with a tray of muffins. Sally knows the procedure and does well with the customers. Having lived and worked in town most of her life means she knows most of the clientele. She regales me with the latest accomplishments of the handful of grandkids she has while we work in tandem to prepare for opening.

At six on the dot Sally unlocks the front door and flips the sign to open from closed with a quick twist of her wrist. She fills the napkin holders on the two small, circular tables under the front window while I do a last scan of the beverage area on the left to make sure the machines are on and brewing and I fill all the accoutrements.

Customers trickle in, and I slip back into the kitchen to decorate the cupcakes and specialty cakes. Besides the few I always have on hand for the spontaneous customer, I also take special orders for different occasions, including weddings. That part of my business has been steadily increasing and I hope to focus more on it, but now that is up in the air as well.

The eight o'clock morning rush arrives, and Sally needs me out front to fill orders. I smile and nod while taking orders and handing over cash and receipts. People tend not to linger and chat when they are on their way to work and standing in line for their first cup of coffee of the day.

Sally rings up one of the coffee travel mugs emblazoned with my logo for The Sweet Spot, a black oval and pink lettering.

I am about to slip back into the kitchen when the bell over the door rings, signaling another customer. Monica Frasier moseys in, another long-time resident of Granite Cove. Sally is still with a customer, so I remain at the counter while Monica approaches with a smile. Her nut-brown hair is straight as a pin and secured at her nape with a black barrette. Her gray suit jacket and skirt are form fitting, but not revealingly tight. She teaches at the Elementary School.

"Good morning, Franny. It's shaping up to be a beautiful day isn't it?"

"Looks that way. What can I get for you today?"

"Oh well…let's see." She glances over the tops of her black-framed glasses at the contents of the display cases. "Everything looks wonderful and so tempting. How about one of those cinnamon muffins? And a chai tea please."

I put her muffin in one of the white bags with my logo on the top and start her tea. Monica follows me to the beverage area. I give her a brief smile and wonder if she will add to her order. She wanders over to the display case on the far right filled with the specialty cakes, tarts, and pies.

"You really are quite talented Franny. Every time I attempt to bake, something goes horribly wrong."

"Thank you, but really it's a matter of following the recipe to the letter. It's like a science experiment, the measurements have to be exact."

"That explains it then. Science was not one of my strengths. I'll take that chocolate cheesecake too please. It's perfect for my book club meeting tonight."

Monica hands me her debit card. I slide the tea and muffin across the counter and box up the cheesecake.

She slips her black purse back up her arm to her shoulder, stacks the bag on top of the box, and places the cup next to them in an orderly fashion. "Would you like to come? We discuss the book a bit, of course, but it's really just a chance to get together chat and have wine and cake."

My response is automatic. "Thanks, but I can't." Handing her the receipt and card, I smile absently. "Enjoy."

Tucking the receipt and card in her purse and picking up her purchases, she gives me a faint smile. "Maybe next time. Thank you."

Monica leaves and I turn towards the kitchen. Sally stands in the archway with her arms folded across her ample middle scrunching up the black apron, so the pink lettering of The Sweet Spot figures prominently across her bosom. A scowl crosses her face.

Uh oh what faux pas did I manage to do now? Sally never appears to care if she is my employee, she acts as if it's her duty to instruct or chastise me when she deems it necessary. I guess it's an old habit from being my teacher in school.

"That's the third time I've heard you refuse her invitation. What's so all-fired important you can't attend?"

"I have business matters to take care of."

"Uh, huh. You need to get your priorities straight missy. People need to come first. I never see or hear about you socializing with anyone. You keep rebuffing offers of friendship and you will end up alone."

Friendship? "Monica was just asking to be polite."

Sally rolls her eyes. "I know the difference between being polite and a sincere invitation. She's a sweet girl. I remember her in school always helping and organizing groups. Even spent her lunch hour a time or two tutoring someone in English. I know because she used my classroom to do it." Planting her hands on her hips and stretching the black apron taught, she leans toward me. "She didn't spend her lunchtime hiding in the girl's bathroom."

Ouch, direct hit. Yup, that was me. And here I thought no one had noticed.

"You're still hiding."

Hell yeah, I'm hiding! It's better this way. I've been burned one too many times thank you very much. I open my mouth to defend myself, but I can't think of a thing to say. Maybe Monica *was* extending a genuine invitation and maybe I was clueless about it. She had been a couple years ahead of me in school, closer to my sister's age than mine. It never occurred to me she was offering friendship.

Damn it. Being more social and making friends was one of the steps of my new plan. I'm failing all over the place.

Sally brushes by me and pats me on the shoulder when the door chimes and another customer walks in. "Think on it."

I shuffle towards the kitchen to do just that when a shiver dances down my spine.

"Morning Franny. The delicious aromas wafting up through the floor dragged me out of bed."

Heat envelops my face and I can't get the image of Mitch in bed out of my head. His dark locks on a white pillow. His long, muscled form on display.

Swallowing hard and pasting a smile on my face I spin around and pray he thinks my face is red from the ovens or something. "Good morning Mitch. What can I get for you?"

A white tank top highlights his well-defined arms. I guess I shouldn't be surprised. He's a former actor and current member of the Hollywood elite. Isn't it a requirement of some sort for them to be in stellar physical shape? His black jogging shorts hang loose on his frame, but I still glimpse a very toned thigh.

I'm totally checking him out while he's checking out the bakery.

Inwardly groaning, I drag my gaze back up to his face and keep it glued there while I patiently wait for his decision. Mitch is heartbreak wrapped in a handsome package. I'm not opening it again. In fact, I'm securing it with duct tape. No, a chain and padlock.

I spot Sally puttering with one of the displays out of the corner of my eye and glance in her direction to see if she caught my ogling.

Despite being old enough to be his grandmother, Sally is regarding Mitch covetously. A slight smile even graces her lips. My mouth drops open when she catches me watching her and gives me a wink and a nod. I can't hold back the short snort of laughter that escapes me.

I look back at Mitch, clearing my throat as I do. Let him think I had a tickle in my throat or something.

Mitch smiles and I blink at him stupidly for a few seconds. Damn, yes, he's a great looking man. Hell, he's downright gorgeous. But that's not it. He smiles with his whole face, dimples pop out, impossibly white teeth grin, and blue eyes twinkle. Even the tiny wrinkles at the corners of his eyes are sexy.

Holy cow! No wonder he was a teenage heartthrob. My heart is throbbing pretty hard right now.

"Any recommendations?"

"Um…well…the muffins are popular, but I guess it depends on what you're in the mood for."

Wait a minute, he said he smelled them from bed? What bed?

A sinking sensation invades my body. "Are you living in the apartment upstairs?"

"Didn't I tell you I bought the building the other day?"

"Yeah, but not that you would be living here."

"Is that a problem?"

Yes!

So much for my dream still being afloat, it's hull is deluged by water and taking a nosedive to the bottom of the sea like the Titanic.

"Franny, I told you the terms of your agreement aren't going to change."

"Yes, I know. You surprised me, that's all."

"I'm looking forward to living over the bakery and waking up to an ambrosia of scents I can follow downstairs to sample a few of your treats. If you tell me you sell good coffee too, I'll be in heaven."

I take a deep breath and try not to wince at the lash of pain whipping my abdomen or the tears threatening to fall.

"Yes, we sell an assortment of coffee choices. It's been voted best in the village two years running by the Granite Cove Gazette, the local paper." Normally I'm not one to brag, but I'm damn proud of that and hope to extend that accolade to include best on the lake, then to the Lakes Region, and why not, best in the whole state of New Hampshire. Of course, now my future and the future of The Sweet Spot is up in the air.

"Must be good then."

I peek at him to judge if he's being sarcastic or sincere. He smiles at me when he catches my gaze. Granted, it's not an Oscar or anything, but people around here aren't exactly known for trying new things, they tend to stick with what works and not rock the boat. There had been plenty of concerned warnings I would fail, my own family's included.

"I guess you will have to try it yourself and see."

"I'm going for a run, so I'll stick with a black coffee and one of those bagels with everything on it, but I'll take a couple of the muffins for later."

That explains the outfit. The women of Granite Cove are likely to adjust their schedules to get a peek or two at him running. I can just see tomorrow's headlines now. "Woman causes an accident watching local celebrity instead of the road."

"Do you want the bagel toasted with cream cheese?"

"Yeah, do you have chive cream cheese?"

"Yes."

Sally moves behind me to get his coffee while I grab his bagel from one of the baskets on the wall holding the assortments of baked breads.

I glance in his direction and away and run my tongue along the inside of my teeth.

I need to finish his order. "What muffins do you want?"

"Blueberry."

I bag two muffins while Sally takes the bagel to toast and put cream cheese on it.

"Do you work until closing?"

"Yup. If the bakery is open, I'm here." Even when it's not, I'm often here.

"Here you go." Sally hands him the bagel and coffee while I step to the side and wipe down the already clean counter.

I sense his gaze on me, but I refuse to look up.

So much for my plan. So much for being able to avoid Mitch. He's living right upstairs and will likely be frequenting the bakery.

"See you later, Franny."

I raise my hand in a feeble wave and dash to the kitchen when he opens the door to leave.

Slapping my hands down on the marble counter, I stare at the lake. Gasps of air tighten my chest and throat. Tears fill and overflow my eyes and the view of the lake grows blurry.

What the hell am I going to do now?

My dream is dead and buried.

There's no positive spin I can put on this.

Did he do this on purpose? Is he playing some sort of game? Why would he buy my building? It wasn't even listed for sale. If it was just for a business decision, wouldn't any other building do?

Is he trying to ruin my life?

The bastard!

CHAPTER 4

Setting the alarm and locking the back door behind me, I take a deep breath of fresh air and peek up the back stairs to Mitch's apartment. I'm forcing myself to call it that now, hoping it will help me get used to the fact that my dream of owning the building and living in the apartment is over. Kind of like when you rip a band aid off instead of peeling it slowly.

There is a plaintive meow and a nudge against my calf. I smile down at the large orange cat. "Mr. Pudding, what are you doing here?"

I glance at my watch and bend down to scratch him behind the ears while he winds in between my legs. Mrs. Roberts will worry if her cat isn't home for dinnertime.

Mrs. Roberts has to be close to eighty, if not older. I'm not sure of her exact age, she was old when I was a kid and not the old kids believe anyone over the age of thirty to be. I mean the white hair, slow gait, and reverent tone everyone addresses her with kind of old.

Scooping Mr. Pudding up into my arms, I waltz down the alleyway toward her house up the street. It'll add more time to my walk home, but I'm not in a hurry. I have no plans, unless you count a silent meal with my parents, if they're home, or a quiet dinner alone.

The cat settles into my arms and starts to purr. I'm beginning to believe he might do this on purpose. It's not the first time he's shown up at my door at closing and I've carried him home. Are cats cunning enough to orchestrate a free ride? I wouldn't know since I've never owned one myself, or any pet. Animals aren't allowed in my parents' house. Mother claims she's allergic but having never witnessed her even sneeze around an animal, I suspect she simply doesn't like them.

One more reason to get a place of my own, like I need additional motives.

Using the crosswalk to the left of the bakery, I stroll up the sidewalk to her white Victorian house with the sunny yellow door and wide front porch.

The ping of the doorbell echoes back after I press the button. A moment later, Mrs. Roberts opens the door and smiles when she spots her cat in my arms. Her snow-white hair is in a loose bun on top of her head. Her ankle length plum colored dress is crisply ironed. I don't recall ever seeing her in pants of any kind. Mr. Pudding leaps from my arms and sashays down the hall to the kitchen reinforcing my opinion he wanted me to carry him home.

"Thank you, Franny. I put out his dinner a few moments ago and it worried me when he didn't come to the door when I called. Come in. Come in." She shuffles back and holds the door open. "I still have some of those delightful meringues you brought me last week. Would you like some?"

Meringues aren't much more than egg whites and sugar. I make a batch every couple of weeks and bring them to her because they're a favorite of hers and keep well as long as they're in an airtight container.

"No thank you. How are you Mrs. Roberts?"

"Oh, fine, fine. At my age each day is a blessing when it is routine and pain free." I follow her to the kitchen.

Mr. Pudding is devouring the food in his dish.

Glancing around the small kitchen, I search for any evidence of a meal for her in preparation. When I don't spot one, I frown. I've seen her freezer packed with frozen dinners before.

Mrs. Roberts rests a hand on top of the stove next to a cherry red tea kettle. "Would you like tea?"

"I'll get it. Why don't you have a seat?"

She lowers herself into one of the chairs at the round table. Mr. Pudding jumps into her lap and curls himself into a ball.

Once I fill the tea kettle and set it on the stove to heat, I get her a teacup from the cabinets flanking the window over the sink.

"The meringues are in that cabinet there."

I open the cabinet she points to, and locate the familiar white ceramic hinged jar she keeps the cookies in. There are a few boxes of pasta in the cabinet nestled in among various jars and boxes.

"How about I whip you up spaghetti for dinner?"

Her eyes perk up and she smiles. "Only if you will join me dear. I was planning on having one of those Salisbury steak dinners from the freezer, but spaghetti sounds so much more appealing."

"I'd love to." I putter about, grabbing a pot and other ingredients to prepare a meal for the two of us. I know where most items are from previous visits.

She doesn't have any family nearby, at least none she's ever mentioned, or I've seen.

Once the steam blows from the tea kettle, I pour the hot water over a tea bag and place her cup on the table.

"Agatha and Steven are having a baby."

"That's exciting." I've only spoken to the couple who rent the apartment upstairs in passing. They're both in their late twenties, not too much older than me. A baby. Wow, I can't even contemplate the thought of having a child yet. Of course, first I would need someone in my life to father that baby.

"Yes, Agatha showed me this black and white picture with squiggles all over it and said it was a picture of the baby inside her womb. I didn't tell her I couldn't see a baby."

Chuckling, I add the pasta to the boiling water.

"I think it will be awhile before it looks like a baby. When is she due?"

"Some time in the winter, I suspect. They didn't mention any plans to leave, but I'm not sure how much longer they'll want to stay now they're starting a family."

I glance over my shoulder and peruse her expression to see if she's worried about them moving out and leaving her without a tenant and the help and companionship I'm sure she's grown accustomed to. They're the third tenants she's had since I started coming here.

She pats her sleeping cat while staring out the window over the sink.

I gather the olive oil, herbs, and a can of tomatoes I find to make a quick topping for the spaghetti. I'm sure she'll be able to find another tenant if they do move out. Her house is part of the village and prime real estate.

Her house is steps from my bakery. I could rent the apartment now that my plans are kaput.

"Well if they do move out, you could rent it to me."

I keep my back to her and hold my breath during the momentary silence. I whisk the ingredients together and wait for her response.

"What happened to your plans to buy your bakery's building?"

Mrs. Roberts is the only one I've confided in about my dream to own the building and move into the apartment.

"Mr. Brick sold it to someone else."

"That weasel!"

A bark of laughter escapes me, and I glance at her. She's scowling and Mr. Pudding raises his head as if to see what disturbed his mistress.

"I agree, but there's nothing I can do about it, so I need to make new plans." Thankful she doesn't chastise me over not having an agreement in writing to purchase the building, I stir the spaghetti and grab two bowls to serve it in once it's ready.

"What do the new owners plan to do with it?"

"He said it was just business, whatever that means. He said he's not raising the rent or changing my lease, but he's living in the apartment."

"You've talked to the new owner?"

"Yes, Mitch Atwater bought it."

Not sure whether she knows who he is, I peek over at her while I grab two forks from the drawer.

"I heard he was back in town. Daisy Howard chewed my ear off about him the last time I stopped into the store to get my groceries."

After draining the spaghetti and mixing in the sauce, I put a serving in each bowl and carry them to the table.

"How do you feel about him being back?"

I plop into the chair and stare at her. What does she know?

"Pop those eyes of yours back into your head missy. I may be old, but I'm not blind or feeble minded. I know you two have a history."

"History is all it is. It was a long time ago and he means nothing to me now."

After I'd calmed down and could think rationally, I realized how unlikely it was that Mitch had hatched an evil plot to ruin my life. I doubt I even crossed his mind when he decided to come back to Granite Cove. I might have been a slight blip of a memory but nothing more.

The pungent olive oil and tender pasta slide down my throat as the rich scent of parmesan fills my nostrils. I sense her gaze on me, but I concentrate on my food. Hopefully she'll drop the conversation.

"Did I ever tell you about my late husband?"

I pause with a forkful of pasta hovering over my dish. I knew she was a widow, but that was it. "No."

She leans back against her chair with a sigh. "He was a charmer. I had stars in my eyes from the first day I met him. He was several years younger than me. Quite scandalous in those days."

A smile teases my lips imagining her young and in love.

"My parents were both long gone by then. They left me this house." She gazes out the window, but I think it's the past she really sees.

She waves her hand in the air. "We were married within months. I had been well on my way to becoming a spinster so I saw no point in waiting. He was a travelling salesman and would be gone weeks, and sometimes months at a time."

"You must have been lonely."

"I was." She nods. "I was, but I was also used to being alone. I liked to say he had a wandering soul."

Leaning forward, she raises her eyebrows and frowns. "It sounded more romantic. The truth is he liked to have this as a base to come back to when he was tired. I would be waiting here with open arms every time. He would stay awhile, but that itch would get him and he would be gone again."

She takes a tissue from its place tucked in her sleeve and dabs at her nose. "Some men aren't born to stay in one place for long. Things might have been different if we were able to have kids, but it wasn't meant to be. Looking back, it was probably for the best."

Because he travelled so much? Wouldn't a child have been a comfort to her being left alone so much?

A long drawn out sigh escapes her. She raises her chin and turns her gaze back to me. "He was a thief."

My eyes just about pop out of my head.

She nods and wipes a finger along the edge of the table.

"What do you mean?" Does she mean metaphorically, like he stole her heart?

"Exactly what I said, he was a thief. When he was away, he was stealing and robbing. Oh he still sold things from time to time to keep up appearances, but his real profession was crime."

Wow!

I can't think of a single thing to say. Mrs. Roberts was married to a thief. Did she know all along? No, I can't believe that. She wouldn't condone something illegal. Although people did things for love they wouldn't normally do all the time.

"I got suspicious when his clothes kept getting fancier and he started bringing me jewelry. I thought maybe his sales must have picked up, but he was always complaining how bad they were. So I did a little snooping in his briefcase and suitcase. I checked his jacket pockets. There were receipts from places different from where he was supposed to be. At first I thought it was a sign he was unfaithful."

"That must have been so awful for you."

"It was. I thought my heart would break into a million tiny pieces and never heal again. But then I got mad."

"Understandable. You felt betrayed."

"Oh, I was. I kept digging. He was unfaithful. I found notes from other women, but I also found newspaper articles."

She folds her hands over her stomach and nods. "The fool kept clippings of his crimes. I compared the receipts and the newspapers. They all matched."

"What did you do? Did you confront him? Was he caught?"

I would have heard about this if he was, wouldn't I? I mean she's been a widow for as long as I've known her, and this may have all happened before I was even born, but surely someone would have mentioned Mrs. Robert's husband was a criminal if they knew.

"Yes, he was caught, but no, I didn't confront him. I was too afraid. He wasn't the man I thought he was. Fear kept me silent. Fear and shame. Shame I didn't really know who he was or what he was capable of. Shame that I let him fool me."

"I don't blame you a bit for being scared, but you shouldn't feel ashamed. He was the criminal, not you."

She smiles wanly.

"So he got caught?"

"Oh yes, he went to prison. They arrested him out in California."

He must have died in prison. What a story. Does no one know what happened to Mr. Roberts since he was arrested so far away? It wasn't like the internet age back then when everyone knows everything about you because they can look it up online. I've been visiting her for over ten years and had no idea.

"I'm telling you this story for a reason, child. To make sure you understand you always have choices even when you believe you don't."

"What do you mean?"

"Don't let fear blind you to all the options which might present themselves. There's always a path to take. It might not be the one you were hoping for, but it will still get the job done. After all, it's the end result that matters."

Umm…okay. Is she trying to tell me staying at my parents' house might not be a terrible thing? Because it most definitely is.

Or perhaps she means I need to find another solution.

"Charming men can hide a black heart."

Woah, is she talking about Mitch?

"If you mean Mitch, I told you he's in my past, not my future."

"I don't know what that young man is up to. I only want you to be careful and not be blinded by his good looks and charisma."

"No worries there, Mrs. Roberts. I am totally focused on my bakery and finding a new place to live." I bring the dishes over to the sink, rinse them out, and set them in the dishwasher. Leaning back against the counter, I fold my arms across my waist.

"Which brings me back to finding a solution to your problem."

Is she going to offer me the apartment? It's not a bad solution. It's convenient. I've never seen it, but at this point I'm not in a position to be too picky.

"Do you know why my husband went to prison in California?"

"Uh, no. I assumed because that is where he was arrested."

"Yes, but there were plenty of other states he committed crimes in. Right here in New Hampshire for one."

She leverages herself up using the table. "No my dear, he was arrested there because I wanted him as far away from me as possible."

"I don't understand." I doubt the justice system would take the wife of a criminal's preferences into account.

"I didn't have the gumption to confront him personally, but I couldn't tolerate letting his foul deeds go unpunished. Nor did I want anyone to know about my shame. So I gathered together all the evidence I could detailing his crimes in California and sent them anonymously to a police station there."

She walks over and rests a hand on my shoulder. "I found an option I could live with."

CHAPTER 5

"It needs work, but it's on the lower end of your budget."

Needs work? A massive understatement.

I stuff my hands in the front pockets of my shorts and lean to the side to look underneath the counter. A layer of grime coats everything. It's an old diner with a standard setup of a long counter with stools, booths lining the outer perimeter, and there's a pass-through to the kitchen accessed by a swinging door on the right.

The overall square footage is roughly the same as my bakery, but it's flip-flopped. The kitchen is narrow, and the public space is the largest. It would require a total gut and renovation. There's nothing I would salvage in the kitchen. Grease is caked on all the appliances and cabinets.

The building is in the newer part of town, outside the village.

I hate everything about it.

Sighing, I face my realtor, Bill Bovier. He is one of three realtors in town. Vanessa, of course, is not an option. I'd rather run down the middle of Main Street stark naked than ask her for help.

Okay, that might be extreme. But they both rank the same.

Lisa Johnson, an older woman, is on vacation. I chose Bill by default.

"It's not going to work for me."

"Okay, I have another building to show you in Granite Cove and there are more options if you're willing to consider properties outside town."

I'm not ready to give up on Granite Cove, but I need to see what's available to make an informed decision. If I will move my bakery or continue renting. Only one thing is certain, I need to move out of my parents' house.

"Let's look at the other building and you can email me information on others in the area and I'll decide if I want to see them."

Tugging his handkerchief from his pocket, he blows his nose. Bill informed me of his allergies when I met him at his office this morning, announcing it like an appliance that comes with a warning label. He stuffs it back into the pocket of his beige pants which are riding dangerously low under his prominent stomach. A brown leather belt is helping the pants defy gravity. That and the constant yank he gives them.

"I'll do that. You sure this can't work for you?"

"One hundred percent." The renovations alone would blow my budget.

Nodding, he frowns and takes one last look around. My confidence in his ability to find me what I'm looking for is rather low at the moment. It wasn't all that high to begin with, but after seeing this place my options appear scarce.

I stand next to the passenger side of his white sedan and wait while he locks up. He unlocks the doors and opens the driver side door while I climb into the passenger seat. Glancing over, all I see is his stomach and the row of buttons bisecting it. The sound of him blowing his nose once again resonates over the top of the car.

He climbs in and drives out of the parking lot. The one positive thing I see about this diner is the ample parking.

"Now this next one will require a little imagination."

This one didn't?

"It's by the train tracks. It was a store a few times, and before that a house."

The train tracks meant outside the village again. The old depot, now defunct, was turned into a group of stores. There were a few nice buildings over there which might not be too bad, but it still wasn't the village.

"Next to the depot?"

"No, this is farther up the tracks on the outskirts of town."

Ugh, even worse. The farther away from the village we go meant the less foot traffic I would get patronizing my bakery.

I had taken Mrs. Roberts advice and come up with a list of different scenarios and options to salvage my plan. Option one: continue renting in my current location but find a modest house to buy. Option two: buy a new building with living space and move my bakery. Option three: continue living with my parents to save up more and buy the building from Mitch at whatever exorbitant price he wants.

Each choice had pros and cons, mostly concerning my meager budget. The third wasn't really viable because my life plan hinged on getting out of my parents' house. I only consider it because I want to be thorough.

Curiosity had gotten the better of me, and in the middle of figuring out ways to get my plan back on course, I looked up Mr. Roberts on the internet. I tried anyway. I guess the name is too common and I don't have enough information about him, like first name, specific crimes, the dates involved, his age, the town or city he was arrested in.

The more I thought about her story, the more amazed I became. The sheer gumption she had to not only turn her husband in but do it in such a way as to ensure he would be far away from her.

I want to be that strong and smart.

He pulls into a loose gravel driveway and I glance at him to see if maybe he got lost and is turning around.

Bill puts the car in park and stares at the only structure in sight.

It's an old barn.

With a giant hole in the roof.

There has to be a mistake because… it's a barn. How could this be a former store, or especially a home?

"Ready to take a look?"

"It's a barn."

"That was probably one of its uses back in the day, but most recently it was an antique store. There's a bathroom."

Oh goody.

I should at least look at it and not make rash judgements.

The gaping hole is a problem. The lack of windows and large barn doors appearing to be the only entrance are also problems.

"Is there a kitchen?"

He said it was a home once, so there should be a kitchen, right?

"No, but it's a wide-open space for you to design your dream kitchen."

Closing my eyes, I rest my head back against the seat. These are my two options, a grimy diner and a barn.

"You could turn the loft area into a living space for yourself. It has a lot of potential."

I heft a giant sigh and climb out of the car. "Let's go look."

After much prying and pulling on the doors, he gets us inside.

It's even worse than I imagined.

Stray furniture is strewn about the large open space. A small square shaped room is tucked into the back corner. I assume it's the bathroom. There's a ladder disappearing into the ceiling next to it. The loft area? No stairs to access it, but a ladder.

Bill walks over to a table with two chairs. He upends one chair and sits down. "You have a look around." He waves towards the ladder.

I meander around the debris laden floor and peer up the ladder. I can see water damage on the ceiling above and it's not even near the hole in the roof.

A sharp squeal sounds behind me and I whirl around.

Bill is standing on top of the chair he was just sitting on with his hands clutched to his chest in fright.

I follow his gaze to see an oversized rat disappearing into a hole in the floor.

Ugh.

That's it, I'm done.

As I walk back towards Bill still hyperventilating on the chair, a crack splits the air and he goes tumbling down when the chair crumbles beneath him.

I run over to help, but he is already scrambling up with his gaze fixed on the hole the rat disappeared into. He moves quickly for a man his age and size.

"Are you all right?"

He nods. His face is pale and there's a sheen of sweat covering his forehead.

Please don't let him have a heart attack or stroke.

"It won't work."

After giving me a swift nod he turns and heads for the door.

When I exit, he's already in the car mopping his forehead with a tissue.

Okay then, my realtor has a strong aversion to rats. They don't bother me, unless they're in my home or bakery. That's a no go.

I climb into the passenger side and glance at him to make sure he's okay.

"All right, I'll keep looking. I have a few homes to show you. You said you were also interested in seeing standalone houses."

Back to business, I guess.

My budget for a house is small. If I keep renting the space for my bakery, it doesn't leave much room for a mortgage payment on a house.

"Let's see them."

Bill drives back into town and shows me a duplex, a cape on the outskirts of town, and a bungalow not too far from the village.

The duplex is an automatic negative for me. A trio of dogs on the other half of the building barked the entire time we looked at it and I also don't want to take on the added responsibility of managing the rental. The cape is the largest. Two bedrooms and a bathroom upstairs and a half bath, kitchen, living room, and dining room downstairs all set on two acres of property. What am I going to do with all that land? It will require maintenance and I don't have the money in my budget to hire someone so it will mean I have to mow the lawn, trim the bushes, and whatever comprises lawn care.

Standing in the center of the bungalow, I fold my arms over my waist. It's small, the smallest option he has shown me. There's only one bedroom, a bathroom, living area, and a galley kitchen. It's also the most expensive option because it's right outside the village. I could still walk to the bakery. It's at the top of my budget.

Wandering back into the bedroom, I gaze out the back window. The yard is fenced in with a chest high white fence, it surrounds the property on three sides. A large Maple tree sits in the center. I could get a dog, or a cat, or both.

Bill peeks in the doorway. "What's the verdict?"

"It could work, but it's expensive."

"We could make an offer, see if they bite."

The lawn is manageable, even I could mow it. I could plant flowers along the front walk too.

If I do this, then it means keeping The Sweet Spot where it is and not having to endure all that moving my bakery would entail.

Rubbing my forehead, I glance around the room at the wooden floors and the large closet.

"Make the offer."

CHAPTER 6

The hunter green kayak glides over the smooth as glass water with the occasional help from the swipe of my paddle. Other than walking to and from the bakery when the weather allows, it's my one form of exercise during the warmer months. Granted, on days like today it doesn't take much exertion to skim along my favorite route around the edge of the lake. It's more of a lazy meandering, enjoying the view.

Bill called and told me they didn't accept my offer on the bungalow. I was careful not to dwell too much on the house or make plans so I wouldn't be disappointed if it didn't go through like I still am over my building.

It didn't work. I'm still disappointed.

He's going to continue looking for both commercial options for the bakery and residential.

The docks are bustling with people and boats. *The Dorian John,* the mammoth white ferry that traverses the lake, stopping at the three busiest towns, is filling up with people for the dinner cruise. A horn announces its imminent departure. It's more of a tourist boat than a form of transportation. During the summer, the ferry makes four cruises per day. Two are strictly a brief stop at each town, one in the morning and one in the afternoon. Then there are a lunch and a dinner one which give longer, more leisurely tours of the lake. I took it once as a kid, but never again. My parents live on the lake and have always had a boat, first at the marina then at our house, so there was never any need or desire to take the ferry.

There's a slight chill to the late afternoon air. Luckily, I wore a sweatshirt and the light life vest adds a layer of protection from the wind.

Two older men in a small fishing boat bob along the shore with their rods and lines cast towards the rocks. Returning their nod and wave, I steer the kayak around the tip of the peninsula leaving the village behind. Houses dot the shore. Two kids play in the yard of one of the houses with a small beagle running along beside them. Their giggles carry clear as a bell over the water and I smile.

A splash and the telltale circle left behind on the surface from a fish jumping occurs a few yards to my left. Perhaps the fish is escaping the fishermen I passed by, or more likely, it's chasing after a tasty bug for its dinner.

The tiny cove ahead is my destination. I always drift around daydreaming for a while then I'll spin around for the return trip.

I love this cove and the century old behemoth of a house that stands watch over it. Once the summerhouse of a wealthy family, it's been empty for as long as I can remember. The faded white shingles and dark green shutters hang askew in places. The grounds are overgrown with weeds and untrimmed trees and bushes in desperate need of attention, but I can still picture ladies and gentlemen sashaying along the pathways from a more elegant time.

Gliding past the giant gray boulders guarding the entrance to the cove, the house comes into view and I smile. The dock has long since disintegrated or washed away so I usually just bob along the shore. I've explored the grounds a time or two and furtively peeked inside hoping a caretaker isn't present to run me off. It's fun to fantasize over the house, but I don't want to get caught trespassing.

A loud banging rents my peaceful reflections from my mind. I jump and wobble back and forth for a moment in the kayak. I regain my balance and search the area, but I can't identify where it's coming from. An echo across the lake making it sound closer than it is?

The banging resumes.

Nope, it's coming from the house. Pushing away from the shore with the paddle, I steer the kayak farther along past the towering pine trees so I can see the other side of the house.

A shirtless man is standing on a ladder hammering something. His back is tan, lean, and muscled. I get rather caught up in the view, so I set the paddle on the edges of the kayak and enjoy the show.

It appears he might be fixing a shutter but what do I know about carpentry? Is a descendant fixing up the place? Did someone else buy it? A slight pang pinches my chest. In the back of my mind I dreamed of buying it and fixing it up one day, but it's just a fantasy. I could never afford this place. It will be nice to see it fixed up if that's what they're doing. It would be horrible if someone bought the land and tore it down to build a modern eyesore in its place.

The man stretches and yanks on a shutter. The flex of muscles draws my gaze downwards towards a well-rounded derriere encased in denim.

Wait a minute, I recognize that butt. Well, what I mean is, I ogled that butt in my bakery a week ago. My gaze skyrockets back up. Yup, the chestnut brown hair teasing the nape of his neck is the same. That's Mitch on that ladder.

Sucking in a breath, I can only conclude one thing his presence signifies. He bought the house. My house. Just like he bought the building housing my bakery. I guess he's putting down roots here in Granite Cove. Perhaps he means to stay this time around.

He descends the ladder and I fumble for the paddle to get the hell out of here before he sees me.

Instead of grabbing the paddle, I knock it into the water with a plop.

The paddle is floating free beside me in the lake. I huff a breath and snatch at the end closest to me but only succeed in pushing it under the water.

It pops back to the surface, but now a few feet farther away.

I lunge forward but it's too far away.

Damn it!

I cup my hand and use it as a paddle to get closer, so I can snag the oar. There, I've almost got it. My fingers trail along the tip of the wooden handle only to thrust it farther away.

No!

Lurching awkwardly, I stretch as far as I can.

Like a slow-motion reel of old black and white comedic film, the kayak wobbles, then rocks, then ice-cold water douses my face and body as it loses its attempt to balance out my lopsided weight and rolls over.

I submerge under water with a loud splash and a mouth full of lake water. I clamp my lips together.

My life vest automatically inflates once it touches the water.

I find purchase on the rocky bottom and I come up sputtering.

"I thought those were unflippable."

Mitch is wading into the water grinning at me.

I shove my dripping hair out of my eyes and grimace. So much for getting away unseen. "Yeah, well, it probably is to everyone but me."

His chuckle reverberates from somewhere above my head as I search the water for the recalcitrant paddle and now my kayak.

"Looking for this?" He's holding the paddle in his grip and the kayak is bumping against the rocky shore behind him.

"Come on. Let's get you out of the icy water. You're shivering."

It isn't until he says it, I realize I am. Next, I'll probably turn Smurf blue. I grasp the hand he extends toward me as I trudge through the shallow water. Walking in water wearing a swimsuit is one thing. Trying to do it in jeans, sneakers, a sweatshirt, and inflated life vest is something altogether different.

His hand is warm and strong and I latch onto it, letting him help tug me to shore. I let go once I'm standing on solid ground and wrap my arms around my midriff. Mitch grabs the end of the kayak, hauls it up onto the shore so it won't float away, and puts the paddle inside it.

I stare at the kayak. Can I get in it and make it back to my parents' house before freezing to death? Which is worse, dying of embarrassment or cold?

Mitch wraps his arm around my shoulders and gives my arm a quick rub. "Let's get inside. You need to change into dry clothes. It may be June, but that water is as cold as ice."

Okay, it might be a slight exaggeration. I'm not likely to freeze to death but my skin is pebbled like one of my mother's handbags. Shivers are rattling my bones and my teeth might chatter any moment. No one in their right mind will intentionally swim in the lake for another few weeks. Of course, no one has ever said I am in my right mind. People have stated the exact opposite on many occasions, however.

We step onto the brick pathway leading to the house. Someone has tried to pluck the weeds growing between the bricks, but the path is still in need of repair. A damaged or missing brick mars the curved pathway every few feet. Clumps of naturalized Daylilies tower above the weeds along the meandering path. In a few weeks' time their buds will open and a sea of orange and yellow will fill the lawn.

My water-logged sneakers squish with each step I take, sending a cold surge between my toes. I try not to lean into his side, but the man is radiating serious warmth and the temptation to snuggle in and grab some of it for myself is overwhelming.

Instead, I look at my surroundings. The grass around the house is mowed. Fresh areas of dirt and stumps mark the spots where someone removed overgrown trees and shrubs. Hedges nestle against one another in varying shapes. They haven't been trimmed in a long time, but I can see the remnants of gardens.

He directs me up a wide set of steps onto the blue stone patio which stretches almost the entire length of the house and towards a set of French doors. "The house is being renovated, so it's in quite a disarray. Watch your step."

Stepping inside, I blink so my eyes will adjust from being outside. A cavernous room greets my gaze. I understand what he means when I notice the walls opened to bare the inside wires and wood, and piles of debris in the middle of the room.

"Wait here for just a minute while I grab something for you to wear. I have a few items here since this is where I spend most of my days."

Mitch jogs off to the left and disappears beyond an archway. Removing the life vest, I step farther into the room rubbing my frigid arms. A granite fireplace with an ornate wooden mantel is centered on the right wall. I hope he isn't planning to destroy it. There's a musty smell in the air from disuse, and construction dust coats everything.

Reappearing with a bundle of gray and black in his arms, he holds them out. "It's a sweatshirt, sweatpants, and T-shirt. Pretty much all I've got here. They'll probably hang on you but at least they're clean and dry."

He's donned a navy-blue T-shirt and jeans himself. Looking away, I try not to mourn the loss of seeing his bare chest. I take the clothes from him with a smile. "Thanks." I refuse to comment on how they might fit. I'm no petite little flower. More like an orange headed giraffe.

I doubt they'll be hanging on me. A few days after my eighteenth birthday I had a physical and my doctor told me I was no longer considered overweight. I almost hugged her. I'll never be dainty. It's just not in my genes.

"You can change around that corner. There's a powder room still intact."

Nodding, I trudge off with the dry clothes held out in front of me so they won't get wet from the sodden clothes dripping from my frame. Intricate crown molding at the top and base of the walls decorates the wide hallway he directed me down. There are several closed white wooden doors with crystal doorknobs I'm itching to peek behind farther along the hall, but the first door is open, and it's the powder room he mentioned. It's sweet how he used the old-fashioned term for it.

Tiny white hexagon shaped tiles dot the floor with little black accents sprinkled throughout. Peeling floral wallpaper covers the walls. A counter spans the length of one wall with a white porcelain sink in the center. Cascading ribbons mold the sink from top to bottom. A shiny brass faucet with the spout and handles shaped into swans perches over the sink.

After placing the dry clothes on the counter, I shut the door and peel my wet clothes from my body as quickly as I can and drop them onto the floor with my wet shoes. Shivers race over me as I dress in his dry clothes. My bra and panties are soaked and resting in the pile on the floor, so I must go without.

Let's face it, I can get by without a bra just fine if I were only more daring. Zipping the black sweatshirt all the way to the top I glance down at my attire. The light gray pants are baggy, and a little long, but I won't be tripping over the hem nor am I worried about them falling for being too loose.

Dark wood etched with flowers frames the mirror over the sink stretching the length of the counter. My reflection stares back at me in horror.

Not only have I lost my baseball cap somewhere in the lake, but there are wet weeds sticking out of my orange hair. Leave it to me to carry the lake's plant life home with me.

CHAPTER 7

The all over blush of embarrassment raises my body temperature a few more degrees. Between that and the dry clothes I am no longer shivering. I pluck out the weeds and stuff my unruly hair into a bun on top of my head. Thankfully the water is working, and even warm, so I wash the best I can using the sink. I stoop, collect my clothes, take a deep breath, and open the door.

Mitch is waiting in the hallway leaning against the wall. I grab the door jamb to prevent another awkward fall.

"I was debating whether to knock to see if you were okay." He pushes off from the wall and holds out a plastic bag. "I found this for your wet things."

"Thanks." I take the bag from him, stuff my clothes into it, and clutch the bundle to my chest. I look back up at him.

He stands with his thumbs hooked in the front pockets of his jeans. "You good?"

"I'm fine. Most importantly, dry."

His smile sends flutters in my chest. I grind my back teeth together. His smile has caused that reaction in me for much longer than I care to admit. Casting my gaze away from him, I tilt my head to the side to peer down the hallway I'm longing to explore.

"Want a tour?"

"I'd love one." The words slip out of my mouth and I wince. I should head home as quickly as possible. "If it's not too much trouble." Curiosity wins out. This might be my only chance to see the house I've been dreaming of exploring for years.

"No trouble at all." He strolls by me. My gaze drops and I can't help but appreciate the view as he moves past me along the hall. The worn denim cups his well-shaped butt.

So sue me, I'm only human. Besides looking at and appreciating what God gave him shouldn't get me in too much trouble.

Especially when he can't see me doing it.

"You coming?" He glances over his shoulder at me still lounging in the doorway.

"Hmm... oh of course." Please don't let him be aware I was ogling him behind his back. Although he must be accustomed to women's covetous looks considering it was once part of his profession. A particular advertisement comes to mind where he posed for a famous designer. He was on the beach in a tight swimsuit and nothing else but a pair of lowered sunglasses, his intense blue eyes gazing over the top. The ad was for the sunglasses, but I can't recall a single thing about them.

I trail behind him and drag my gaze from admiring him to admiring the house. We step through a wide archway into a giant foyer with a marble floor and curved grand stairway. My mouth drops open.

"The place needs a ton of work, but when I walked into this room, I knew I had to have it. They don't build houses like this anymore."

Wood paneling lines the two-story walls and ceiling. A gigantic crystal chandelier hangs from a chain centered in an ornate ceiling medallion in the middle of the coffered ceiling. "It's spectacular. All the times I fantasized about this place I never imagined it was this magnificent."

"You fantasized about this place?"

I said that out loud? "Um... well... yeah."

His grin ratchets up a few notches. I might not have believed it possible, but damn the man's smile really can melt hearts. His hand is resting on the carved wooden banister which depicts a vine of roses winding up its base. The woodwork is stunning and intricate. How many hours of labor were required to create this masterpiece?

"Then I must give you the grand tour. Come on, wait until you see the view from upstairs. They haven't worked up there yet, so you still get a strong impression of its turn of the last century charm."

He takes the stairs two at a time and I can't help but smile at his enthusiasm. I'd feel the same way if the house was mine.

Large wooden double doors stand at the top of the stairs. A hallway stretches in either direction with multiple doors off each one culminating in floor to ceiling windows at either end allowing light to pour in.

He opens the doors to reveal an enormous master bedroom. A fireplace is centered on the wall to the left flanked by two open doors. I can see that they're both closets. Mitch strides in front of me and across the room to a set of French doors which open onto a wide balcony. He has to lean against the door and give it a shove to get it to open.

A loud creak sounds before it swings open with a flourish. Mitch steps to the side and holds open the door. "The balcony is safe and sound, I promise."

Stepping past him, I can't help but inhale sharply when a faint scent teases my nose. A masculine mixture of wood shavings, exertion, and him—it's an aphrodisiac I want more of.

Metal scrolled railings at waist level edge the balcony which extends the length of the second floor, but it's the view that captures my attention. From up here, the lake shimmers for miles. The sun is setting and layers of pink and lavender stretch across the horizon.

A few of the many islands inhabiting the lake are visible. Some are little more than a stand of trees and rocks. Others are several acres with houses on them. What it is like to live on an island? You can't just hop in your car and go to the store. You have to hop in your boat and then your car unless you want to do all your shopping in the village. It must take an organized soul. A few of the houses are year round so travel gets even more precarious and requires careful planning. I'm not sure I'd enjoy being trapped on the island until the ice is thick enough for snowmobiles. When I run out of something, I want it immediately, not at the whim of the weather. What happens if there is an emergency and someone needs immediate medical care? It's doubtful a helicopter could find a place to land on the tree clustered islands.

Mitch leans on the balcony next to me and we both silently enjoy the panoramic view. The mountains surrounding the lake are thick with evergreens. A few houses peek out of the trees on the hill tops, but mostly unspoiled nature fills the vista.

The air cools and a breeze tickles a lock of hair curling behind my ear. I sense his gaze on me, so I veer back towards the inside of the house.

I lose count of the number of bedrooms he shows me on the second floor. There's something unique found in each, whether it be a stained-glass window, a window seat, a quiet alcove, or built in bunk beds in a room meant for kids. Back downstairs, I follow him from room to room as he points out the house's treasures and explains the renovations he has planned.

To my everlasting relief, he plans to maintain the house's grand history. He appreciates its value. My fears he may have purchased it for the land alone are unfounded. Other than asking a question here and there concerning the renovations, I'm relatively silent throughout the tour. The deep timbre of his voice lulls me into a relaxed state. No wonder he was such a successful actor.

"Have I bored you to tears?"

I owlishly blink at him as we stand facing each other in the formal dining room. "No, not at all. I can't tell you how happy I am that you plan to keep all the wonderful elements of the house intact. The house has far surpassed the limits of my imaginings." I peek towards a swinging door on the side of the room. "Honestly, I'm dying to see the rest of the place, especially the kitchen."

"Coming right up." He pushes through the swinging glass door to reveal a butler's pantry filled with cabinets and a prep area and sink. It opens into what could easily hold at least three of my parents' kitchen and their kitchen is large.

My gaze flits around the room. Where to start? I want to take it all in and start opening cabinets and peering into drawers, but I clench my hands together behind my back instead and stroll around the room.

"As you can see, the contractors haven't started in here. I have yet to approve the final layout for the kitchen. Something isn't quite right. Would you like to look at the architect's plans sometime and give me your professional opinion?"

I stare at him and desperately hope he isn't kidding. Oh, what I could do with this space.

"From your expression, I'll take that as a yes?"

Am I drooling? I close my mouth and smile. "I would love to."

"Great, it's a date then."

A date? Did he say date? Yes, he did, but he didn't mean *date* date. He meant it as an appointment of sorts, not the man-woman thing.

Okay, when he offered for me to look at the plans, I envisioned I would take them with me and make notes and hand them back. Nowhere did my imaginings include Mitch being with me while I added my opinions about his kitchen.

Get it together Franny.

"I don't know about you, but I'm starved. How about we get a pizza or something on the ride home?"

He's planning on giving me a ride home? "Oh, that's not necessary. I've got the kayak and all. I should head back."

"Have you looked outside? It's dark. You can't kayak home."

"It's no big deal. I'll stick close to shore."

"Franny, it's not safe. You have no lights on the kayak. Boats won't be able to see you. Not to mention, the temperature is dropping. I'll drive you home and we can make arrangements to pick up your kayak."

One side of my brain knows he is correct, but the other part is busy trying to come up with excuses. I can use my phone for light. But it had been in my pants pocket when I fell into the lake. I haven't thought to check if it even still functions.

He's renovating this house and bought my building. My intention to avoid him is not working, and I admit it wasn't all that feasible once I found out he was living in the apartment over my bakery.

The past needs to remain in the past.

My new life plan is all about moving forward. I can't do that if I dwell on ancient history and allow it to influence my actions and choices in the present.

"A ride home would be great, thanks."

He leads the way to the front of the house where a blue pickup truck is parked on the circular driveway. I look around for the sports car or luxury sedan I expect Mitch to own, but he strides toward the truck.

When am I going to stop making assumptions about him or anyone else? Time and experience keep showing me I usually make the wrong ones. Am I missing the female intuition thingy people are always talking about, or is mine asleep on the job? I'd like to have a word with my guardian angel as well. Then again, maybe mine is so overworked making sure I don't kill myself with all the accidents I somehow end up in the middle of.

A sharp piece of gravel bites into my bare foot and I wince. I prance my way along the rest of the path and over to the truck where Mitch is waiting.

"I didn't think about your bare feet. I'm sorry."

"Not your fault. I'm the one who decided to take a swim in the lake with my shoes on."

"So you planned that little swim?"

I return his smile with a wry one of my own. "Planning had nothing to do with it. It was more like the result of the absence of planning."

Mitch chuckles as he holds open the passenger door for me and I haul myself up into the truck and shove the plastic bag with my things on the floor next to my bare feet. Looking up, I stare at the large stone fountain in the center of the loop. A sailboat crests a stone wave.

Mitch walks around the front of the truck, climbs into the driver's seat, and starts the truck. A moment passes before I realize we aren't going anywhere.

I glance at him and he quirks one side of his mouth up. "I don't know where you live."

"Oh." Damn, now I have to admit I still live with my parents. Either that or have him drop me off down the street at a random house and hope he never finds out it wasn't mine.

Forcing a tight smile to my lips, I mumble, "I still live with my parents." Lying isn't the answer. For one, I suck at it. I was always caught as a kid. And two, he lives in town now, he is bound to find out eventually. The town isn't that big, and everyone tends to know everyone else's business.

New vehicle smell permeates the cab of the truck. The seats are a soft, tan leather. He presses a button on the dash and heat permeates from the top and bottom warming my back and legs. I snuggle back against them and luxuriate in the warmth.

My car is secondhand, maybe third or fourth hand, a basic sedan with none of the extras. With my strict budget, frills like heated seats, or even adjustable ones are off the list. My driver's seat has been stuck in the same position since I bought it. A few buttons on the side tease me with the option of movement, but I've resigned myself to accept they are there just for show.

"Are you warm enough? I can raise the heat."

"No, I'm good, thanks. Can I take this heated seat home with me? I might sleep in it if it were mine. It's more comfortable than my bed."

Ugh, stop talking Franny.

"I might have napped in the truck last week, but don't tell anyone. I'm not used to the physical labor of construction. Working out in a gym is a lot different from working in the sun all day on neglected grounds."

"Your secret is safe with me."

The blinking neon open sign of Joe's Pizzeria flashes when Mitch drives into the parking lot. "They still sell pizza by the slice?"

"Um... yeah." Joe's is in an old Federal style building. The first floor is the restaurant and the second is a bar. The attic is split into a pair of apartments accessed by two sets of stairs on either side of the building. Maybe one of them is available for me to rent.

Mitch jumps out of the parked truck and strides to the front door. He did say he was hungry before we left. Thankfully he doesn't appear to expect me to follow him inside. There is no way I am going in public dressed in his sweatpants and hoodie. Especially with no bra and no shoes. Ha, they wouldn't allow me in with no shoes, anyway. I have the perfect excuse, not that he even asked.

The parking lot is full of cars. Is he being mobbed inside by everyone who's dazzled by the new celebrity in town? The only celebrity, unless you count Annabelle Carpenter. Her claim to fame is the three appearances she made on the local news show as the resident expert on a local bird. She holds court at the library after each appearance and puts up flyers all around town. Mitch might attain her level of celebrity, but then again, to the older generation he might not.

He steps out of the restaurant smiling at Maria, one of the waitresses, who trails behind him chatting away. She used to live in one of the apartments above the restaurant, I'm not sure if she still does. About three years behind me in school, she was a popular girl, a cheerleader. Maria holds the glass door open with one hand and props the other on her hip. Short black hair swings against her jawline as she tilts her head and winks at him. Dangly earrings rest against her cheek and a nose ring flashes in the overhead light.

A slight temptation to crack the window and eavesdrop on what they are saying grips me. I glance at the controls and roll my eyes. They're electric and he has the keys.

Mitch strides across the parking lot to the truck.

I watch Maria to see if she will linger in the doorway and if she will recognize me when the interior lights come on when he opens the door. Will she be surprised? Will she gossip about it? Do I care?

Of course I do, I'm human and insecure. I fervently wish I didn't give a rat's ass what other people think about me, but it has been ingrained in me since birth to behave and not shame my parents. I've failed at this family doctrine more times than I care to count.

She flounces back into the restaurant before Mitch opens the door, so I guess I'll never know the answers.

He climbs into the truck carrying a large pizza box and a thin plastic bag with two bottles of water, plates, and napkins inside. "They had a whole pizza ready, so I grabbed it." He shuts the door and looks at me. "You eat pizza, right? I guess I should've asked. You're not allergic or anything?"

A loud grumbling echoes in the truck's cab emanating from my stomach.

"Should I take that as a yes?" Mitch laughs while I wince and try not to sink down in the seat.

He hands me a paper plate, napkin, and water bottle and opens the pizza box. The aroma of hot pizza wafts from the box and my mouth waters.

"Thank you." I accept the pizza slice he holds out with a smile. It smells delicious and I know from experience it will taste just as good.

Taking a bite, I close my eyes and savor the combination of seasoned Italian sauce, thin crust, and gobs of cheese melting in my mouth. A string of cheese hangs between the pizza and my mouth on the second bite and slaps me in the chin when it releases. Sauce speckles the sleeve of the borrowed hoodie. Cringing, I vow to spray with stain removal as soon as I get home. I always keep a stash of the stuff in my bathroom and at the bakery.

I cave and take a second piece. Mitch gestures with his pizza to the side of the restaurant. "Look familiar?"

Two young teenage boys stand on the sidewalk digging through their jean pockets and counting out whatever cash they scrounged up.

A chuckle slips from me. "Yes, it does." We had collected cans and bottles wherever we could find them a couple of times to exchange for the deposit money and then we used the cash to get a couple slices of pizza.

I had received a small allowance every week from my parents, but I don't think Mitch did because he never had any money.

"Do you remember that time we were looking for cans and

thought we'd come across the mother load when we found that tree with the cans stuck on the ends of the branches?"

Mitch's laughter rings out in the truck. "That old guy appeared out of his garage shaking a fist at us and yelling we were destroying his art."

"How were we supposed to know cans stuck on a tree branch was art?"

"Damn, I had forgotten about that."

"Me too. Seeing the kids made me remember it." Not really. I had always remembered it.

It reminds me I have no cash on me and no way to reimburse him for the pizza. I'll have to pay him back later.

"So, tell me what's changed in the past decade? The town seems busier than I remember."

"Well it is the start of tourist season. The summer people are arriving." Mitch's parents had once been part of that group. They lived here only in the summer and left in the fall. Many of the locals rely on the income generated by the summer people. "I guess there are probably more of them. They built a condominium development on the other side of town a few years ago. It's still the same Granite Cove though. Hanson's Grocery is still around. Do you remember we used to get a root beer and bubblegum there all the time?"

"Sure do. And what were those chocolate cake things they had there called?"

"Whoopie pies."

"Those were good. They still make those?"

"No, Mrs. Simpson used to make them, but she moved to Pennsylvania to be with her grandkids a few years ago. I bake them in the bakery from time to time."

"My mouth is watering just thinking about them."

"Well, I suppose I could make them this week."

We reminisce over our summer adventures, one tale after another. The last one has tears leaking out of the corners of Mitch's eyes as he laughs. My eyes are watering too, but it isn't from laughter. Not that I will let him know.

We had gone raspberry picking and most of the berries had ended up in our stomachs rather than the containers we carried. I had tripped over a tree root in the ground and lay sprawled on the grass with raspberries all over me. The juice had stained my skin and clothes. Not all the stains on my pants were from the raspberries, however. Unbeknown to me, my entrance to womanhood had arrived that day.

After I had left Mitch, I had been on my way home when I ran into Vanessa and her friends. They had laughed hysterically pointing at my pants in horrific delight. I had run home in tears. Their torment had continued once we returned to school in the fall. Not a happy memory for me.

"I suppose I should get you home." He starts the truck and drives out of the parking lot while I gaze out the passenger window trying not to let the memories drag me down.

Colonial and Federal style buildings line the main street of the village. They were private homes at one time, but now they are stores and other various businesses. He drives past the small-town green which divides the old part of town commonly referred to as the village and the newer part of town that developed as the town grew and sprawled out. A large octagonal gazebo occupies the center and a war memorial statue presides over the pointy triangle end at the intersection of Main Street and Town Street. Flowers and neatly trimmed bushes surround each structure and are dotted throughout the green along with benches. Lights strung throughout cast a luminous glow over the entire area.

"Today was your day off, so the bakery is open tomorrow, right? I've been missing your coffee. I may be going through withdrawal."

I glance at his profile and smile. "I told you I make good coffee. The bakery is open Wednesday through Sunday."

"Award-winning, I know. I see why. Those muffins are spectacular too."

"I told you I would bake whoopie pies for you, didn't I? I guess now I'll have to make those for you tomorrow since you rescued me and bought me pizza."

He grins. "Interesting name choice, whoopie pie."

"I didn't name them. They're named that because kids exclaimed, *whoopie* when they got them as a treat. I believe it predates any different connotation on the name you might be referring to."

"Are you blushing Franny?"

Damn it. My cheeks heat even more after he points it out.

"The bane of fair skin and freckles."

"It's cute. The blush itself and that someone saying *whoopie* makes you blush."

Rolling my eyes, I grab my bag of stuff from the floor as he enters my parents' driveway and parks. "It's not the word, it's what you were implying."

"What did you think I was implying?"

"You know very well what you were implying."

"Yeah, I do, but I want to hear you say it. The word is sex, Franny. Come on, say it."

"What are you, twelve?" I open my door and climb out.

"Chicken."

I puff out a breath and stare at his grinning face. Glancing around behind me at my parent's house, I turn back to him and whisper, "Sex, there are you satisfied now?"

"Not particularly."

I stare at him gazing back at me. What did he mean by that?

"Yeah, well, thanks again for everything. Goodnight." I back away and shut the door.

Mitch lowers the passenger window. "Goodnight Franny. I'll be dreaming of your whoopie pies. Don't disappoint me."

CHAPTER 8

"I was hoping you would stop by today. My jar is empty. I must have eaten all the meringues and forgotten."

Mrs. Roberts sits on her front porch in one of the wooden rocking chairs. I often find her here people watching. She told me it's one of her favorite pastimes.

"I brought over a double batch this time so you shouldn't run out for a while." I hold up the box and smile.

She pats the arm of the chair next to hers. "Come visit for a spell."

I sit down, open the box, and offer her the meringues. She peers into the box and selects one. Her eyes close as she bites into it. Nothing makes me happier than seeing someone enjoy my creations.

"Delicious as always, my dear. Thank you."

"My pleasure."

We rock in silence for several minutes. I had a busy day at the bakery today and it's nice to sit and enjoy the silence.

"What's new with your bakery? Is your young man going to sell you the building? I'm afraid I won't be able to rent you the apartment. Agatha told me they plan to stay."

I tilt my head in her direction. "He's not my young man and I haven't asked him to sell me the building because I can't come close to whatever he must have paid for Mr. Brick to go behind my back like that. I had a realtor show me places for sale, but nothing has panned out yet."

"Maybe you should make him your young man again and then he'll sell you the building for what you can afford, or even give it you."

A snort of laughter escapes me before I can choke it back. "Mrs. Roberts!"

"What? People have done much worse. Besides, it's not like it would be distasteful to spend time with him again, would it? I remember I time when the two of you were inseparable."

"That was a lifetime ago, and I'm not that deceitful."

"Hardly a lifetime. When you get to be my age, a handful of years passes in the blink of an eye." She reaches over and pats my hand. "You're too honest to deceive someone, but a little charm never hurts. It's when charm is all there is when the true harm occurs. There has to be substance."

Was she referring to her husband? I want to ask her about him, but I don't want to bring up any painful memories.

"Why didn't you ever marry again?"

"At my age?"

"After your husband went to prison."

"My dear, I didn't divorce my husband. I should have, but I let fear guide me. I didn't know how he would react. He insisted on his innocence and I pretended to believe him. Perhaps if I had divorced him when he went to prison, he wouldn't have shown up like a bad penny when they released him early for good behavior."

My shocked intake of breath draws her gaze.

"Oh yes, I hadn't seen the last of Charlie Roberts. He walked in the front door as bold as you please one day."

"What did you do?"

"I waited. It was only a matter of time before he continued his old ways. I'm not sure if he suspected I was the one to turn him in or not, but he got better at hiding any criminal activity."

"You weren't scared? I mean he was living with you, right? Or was he gone a lot again?"

"Terrified. He still disappeared from time to time, but he would come back."

"Did he ever hurt you?" The thought of her being at his mercy made my stomach roll over.

"Not physically. That wasn't Charlie's style. He lied and manipulated to get his way."

"I'm so sorry you had to endure that. I can't imagine how you managed."

"I had a goal that's how. I knew it was only a matter of time before I would find evidence of his foul deeds, but then I got too impatient."

I pull my feet up on the chair and wrap my arms around my knees. "What happened?"

"See, I wasn't able to locate anything incriminating, but what I found out was that he was being unfaithful with several women."

"Oh my."

"Oh yes. And he was using the money my parents had left me to do it since he wasn't working."

"It's a wonder you didn't kill him!"

Oh Lord, she didn't, did she?

"The thought crossed my mind a time or two. I bear my share of guilt for what I did and the consequences."

Mrs. Roberts sighs and sets her chair to rocking again. "I got angry and I told the women about each other. Anonymously, of course. I mailed them letters."

What would I have done? Would I have confronted him and all his women, or quietly divorced him? I'd like to think I had the strength to face them all and tell them what I thought of them, but I've never been the angry tirade type.

"I pray on that decision often. Never do anything in anger, Franny."

Mrs. Roberts uses the arms of the chairs to push to a stand and grabs her cane leaning against the railing. She picks up the box of meringues and shuffles towards the door.

"I'm going to take a little nap. Thank you for stopping by."

"I...goodbye, Mrs. Roberts."

I wait until she goes inside and I hear the lock turn before heading down the stairs of the porch. What had happened when she told the women about each other?

Now that I had a first name and knew he came back to town, I could search the internet for more information. Something had happened that made her feel guilty.

I cross the street and take the alleyway between my bakery and the sporting goods store next door. The alleyway leads to the sidewalk along the docks and to the park near my parents' house.

The park isn't crowded. A family is having a picnic on the grass. I step off the path to let an elderly couple walk by hand in hand.

A woof sounds behind me. I turn and glance over my shoulder. A giant dog barrels towards me. I glance around. His leash is dangling down his side. He's escaped his owner.

The dog stops in front of me, jumps up, and puts his paws on my chest. I step back and lift my arms to counterbalance his weight, but he weighs a ton.

Down I go.

The grass tickles my arms as I lay there staring up at the treetops. A rough wet tongue licks my face.

"Waldo!"

I peek through my hands trying to block my face from another swipe of the tongue. "Are you Waldo?"

Woof! Woof!

"I'm so sorry! Are you okay?"

A young woman with deep brown hair streaked with blonde pulls Waldo back a few steps by his collar and picks up the leash.

"I'm fine."

Sitting, I rest my arms on my drawn-up knees, not ready to stand just yet.

"Honestly, he never does this. He got away from me when I was untangling his legs from the leash. He took off before I could grab him."

Waldo butts against my shoulder and I laugh and rub his head.

"It's nice to meet you Waldo, but your technique could use polishing."

The woman laughs and holds out her hand as I haul myself up from the ground. "I'm Kelly."

"Franny."

Her white jeans are immaculate despite chasing after her dog. I would be covered in grass stains, dirt, fur, and God only knows what else.

"I am so sorry."

"Don't worry about it." I pat the brown furry head that comes up to my waist as he sits on the grass. "What kind of dog is he?"

"A Great Dane. He's a sweetheart and must really like you. He's not usually so boisterous about it."

Just my luck, a male suddenly finds me irresistible and he's a dog.

CHAPTER 9

After saying goodbye to Kelly and Waldo, and once again assuring her I am fine, I stroll over to my favorite spot in the park, my bench. It's not really my bench but I like to think of it that way. I sit down, tilt my head back, and close my eyes. The late afternoon sun warms my face and a light breeze ruffles my hair. The waves lap against the shore. A boat engine rumbles across the lake in the distance. Ah, peace and tranquility, it doesn't get much better than this.

Leaves rustle nearby. Opening my eyes, I spot a squirrel dashing up a tree. It leaps from branch to branch somehow balancing and gripping the wood. The end of the branch sways and then bounces as another gray squirrel joins in the fun. Their tiny legs carry them up and down the tree trunks and zipping along the branches.

Laughter bubbles out of me.

"Talking to yourself is one thing, but laughing? That might be cause for concern. Care to let me in on the joke?"

Mitch is leaning on the back of the bench smiling at me. Sunglasses hide his eyes. A black hoodie and jeans camouflage his toned form and I'm momentarily disappointed until I notice how the worn denim cups his attributes.

"The squirrels were entertaining me."

He slides onto the bench and rests his arm along the back behind my shoulders.

"I went by your house to return your kayak. No one was home, so I left it by the boathouse."

I look down at the ground and grimace. How could I forget to arrange to pick it up?

"You didn't have to do that. I'm sorry, I should have taken care of it."

"There's nothing to apologize for. It wasn't a big deal."

Glancing at his face to judge if he is serious or only being polite, I smile when he appears sincere. "Thank you."

Mitch nods and scans the lake. "So what are you doing here? Besides watching the squirrels?"

I shrug. "I like to stop on my way home from the bakery and relax for a bit."

"It's a peaceful spot." He taps my leg. "What happened here?"

I glance down at the grass stains and dirt decorating my pants. "I had a run in with an ardent admirer."

His eyebrows raise and lower. "Care to elaborate?"

"Not particularly." I sigh and roll my eyes when he continues to frown at me.

"It was a dog, okay?"

He laughs and leans back against the bench stretching his legs out in front of him.

"What are you doing here?" And what is with the sunglasses and hoodie? Is he hiding from fans?

"I needed some fresh air, so I took a walk. I've been out at the house all day with the contractors."

"Are you hiding from someone?" I point to his get up.

His mouth quirks up on the side and he removes the sunglasses and hangs them on the collar of his black T-shirt after unzipping the hoodie.

"I spotted a guy with a camera in town earlier and got a little paranoid he was looking for me. It's probably just a tourist or something."

"Does it happen a lot? People chasing you around for a photograph?"

"Not so much anymore." He shrugs. "I'm sure I overreacted. I guess I got in the habit of avoiding paparazzi from before."

"Before?"

"When I was acting and when I was with Margeaux, it was a common occurrence."

So, he's not with his supermodel girlfriend anymore. Is that the reason he moved to Granite Cove?

I've read the headlines of the tabloids while standing in line at the grocery store. And I may have clicked on an entertainment article a time or two when it popped up on my web browser. Not that I will admit any of that to Mitch.

"I would hate being followed around all the time. How did you stand it?"

A derisive laugh emanates from him and he runs his fingers through his hair. "Not well, which is probably why I jumped to conclusions. Let's talk about something more palatable, like when are you going to make those whoopie pies for me?"

"I already have a batch made ready for tomorrow."

He grins and puts his arm back along the bench behind me.

"I'll be there bright and early as usual. Save some for me."

"Will do." I stare out at the lake. A woman paddles by on a paddle-board. I always wanted to try one of those, but balance isn't exactly my forte.

"That looks like fun, ever try one?"

"I don't think I'm equipped with the skills needed."

"How hard can it be? Do they rent them next door to the bakery? We should try it."

I dart a sideways glance at his profile. He wants to hang out and be buddies again like nothing has changed.

I gave up on my plan to avoid him, but friends? He was my best friend once.

Moving forward, right?

"When it gets a little warmer. I'm not ready for another dip in the lake and I know that will happen when I try to stand on one of those and balance it in the water."

He chuckles. "Okay, we'll wait a couple of weeks. I want to take a drive around the lake sometime too and see what's changed and what has stayed the same."

"It's been awhile since I've driven around the lake. I've gone in either direction but not all the way around and I wasn't sightseeing."

"Then that's something else to add to our list of things to do this summer. How about Mt. Washington? I've never been. My parents and I never got around to taking many sightseeing trips."

A list? We were making a list of things to do together.

"I drove up to the top once and I'll never drive it again. I could probably handle riding as a passenger as long as you don't mind me covering my eyes half the time."

"That bad?"

"I don't care for heights and I care even less about trying to stay on a narrow road with cars coming at you and a sheer drop out the window. The view from the top is killer though. You can see for miles in every direction if the wind doesn't knock you down."

Mitch laughs. "Where's your adventurous spirit? You used to be the first to suggest something daring, like climbing a tree or exploring an old barn."

He's right. I wasn't so afraid back then, not when we were together, anyway. Was it age and experience that taught me to be cautious? Or is it fear preventing me from taking chances and enjoying the process?

"I don't know. Maybe I was waiting for you to come back and explore with me."

Ugh, I did not just say that out loud.

My hands are sandwiched between my legs and the bench. I'm cringing inside and looking everywhere but in his direction.

"I think I've been waiting too."

"You've been all over the world making movies."

"Not necessarily waiting to explore, but something was missing."

Deep brown locks of hair flutter against his forehead and my fingers itch to comb it back. Is he saying he was missing me? Am I reading too much into his words?

He smiles. "I'm keeping Mt. Washington on our list. We will find your adventurous spirit again."

"Okay, deal. We should also add a trip to Portsmouth while we are it."

"I agree, I've been meaning to check it out. What else should we put on the list?"

"I don't know, but I'm drawing the line at climbing trees just so you understand. Those days are in the past. I can't afford any broken bones."

"Duly noted. How about hiking?"

"I can do hiking."

"Renting a couple of quads to go exploring with?"

"Four solid wheels not requiring me to balance? Yeah, I'll try that too."

Mitch laughs. "It'll be safe, I promise."

"What's the most adventurous thing you've ever done?"

Mitch crosses his legs at the ankles. His fingers behind me fiddle with my hair. "Probably scuba diving in Australia with sharks."

I gape at him. "Why on earth would you do that?"

"That was pretty much my mother's reaction too." He shrugs one shoulder. "It didn't scare me. The scariest thing I've ever done was to stop accepting acting gigs and get someone to give me a shot at directing."

"You didn't think anyone would give you a chance?"

"I had to prove myself first. I directed a few television episodes in exchange for a cameo and then moved onto bigger projects from there. What about you? What's the scariest thing you ever did?"

"Nothing I've ever done compares to swimming with sharks, but the scariest for me was telling my parents I was dropping out of college to go to culinary school."

"How did they take it?"

A rough laugh escapes me. "Not well."

"But you still did it."

"I didn't see it as a choice. It was something I needed to do."

"Having sampled your genius, I would have to agree." Mitch stands and stretches. "Come on, I'll walk you home."

"You don't have to do that."

"It's getting dark. The sun is going down."

"There's still a while before it gets dark. I live in the opposite direction of you and I make the walk almost every day."

"Which doesn't comfort me. It means someone could learn your routine. Don't you watch the news?"

I stand and shake my head. "No, I don't. It's too depressing. Besides, this is Granite Cove, not Los Angeles."

"Bad things can happen in small towns too. You shouldn't walk alone after dark at the very least."

We stroll along next to each other on the path. There's still at least an hour until dark, plenty of time for me to get home safe and sound, but I'm not going to argue anymore if he wants to walk me home. It means I can linger a little longer in his company.

"Your parents must have come around about culinary school especially after you opened the bakery."

Not so much.

"It's not what they wanted for me. My mother envisioned something a little more glamorous, I think."

"Doing what you love is the key to happiness."

We reach the end of the park and turn down the sidewalk of the residential section. Familiar colonials and a few capes line the street all with manicured lawns. American flags wave from poles and porches.

Has the bakery led to my happiness? It's the only thing that has brought me any joy lately. I've closed myself off from everything else and instead of hiding in the girl's bathroom, I'm now hiding in my bakery.

"You've gotten quiet."

"Sorry, my mind was wandering."

"Anything you want to share?"

"No." I'm not ready to confess something that personal yet.

"Okay, fair enough, how about telling me who the woman with the binoculars in the window of that widow's walk up there is?"

Chuckling, I peek up at the white house we are approaching. Sure enough there is a pair of binoculars trained in our direction.

"That would be Mrs. Summers. She likes to sit up there and watch everyone. Don't worry, she's harmless. She doesn't go out much. I think she's agoraphobic."

"Okay, does she live in that big house alone? Is there someone to look out for her?"

"She has a husband, a retired doctor. He plays golf with my father. They have grown kids I believe, but I've never met them."

I wave to her as we pass by and she waves back. She'll go on her porch, but I've never seen her in town. I've stopped and chatted with her a few times over the years when she sat in the rocker on her covered porch.

"Do you know everyone in town? I mean I guess that's part of the charm of a small town, right? Knowing your neighbors?"

"I don't know everyone. Granite Cove isn't that small, but I've lived here all my life so there are a lot of familiar faces. It can be comforting or unsettling depending on how you look at it. Many of them have known me since I was a kid so they know my life story, good and bad."

"What's bad? Tell me your deep dark secrets."

I stop at my parents' driveway.

"We're here. You'll have to wait to learn my secrets."

A smirk appears on his handsome face. "I'll tell you mine if you tell me yours."

Temptation tightens my skin. What secrets does he have to share?

Rubbing my upper arms, I glance at a crack in the pavement. I'm not ready to share any of my secrets with him. I doubt we will ever share that level of trust again.

"Goodnight Franny, we can save the secrets for another time."

"'Night."

He waits until I go in the house before turning and walking back the way we came.

I watch him from the living room window until he disappears out of sight. My fingers rest against the windowpane. My breath leaves a little circle of condensation.

I draw a heart and smile.

Silly, something a teenager would do.

I wipe the heart away.

I'm not a teenager anymore.

CHAPTER 10

Mitch stands just outside the bakery, surrounded by a group of women. His schedule is now known, as well as his temporary living arrangements above the bakery, and he is often mobbed before and after his morning run. Business has picked up for me as a result, so I can hardly complain.

The whoopie pies I made for him earlier this week were such a hit I added them to the daily menu. I'm sure some are buying them because Mitch always does, but a sale is still a sale no matter the reason. I'm experimenting with variations, red velvet with a cream cheese filling, peanut butter mousse sandwiched between the chocolate cakes, and a vanilla espresso cake with mocha frosting in the middle.

"Let me offer you a little friendly advice, Fanny."

How had I not noticed Vanessa's arrival? She leans toward me over the counter. I am still standing by the coffee station after helping a customer. Sally is busy helping another customer. A waft of flowery perfume tickles my nose as a smirk tilts the edges of Vanessa's glossy red lips.

"You're embarrassing yourself by mooning over Mitch Atwater. He is way out of your league." Her gaze rakes me from top to bottom.

"You're not even on the same planet as him."

Mooning? Was I mooning? Okay, yes, I was momentarily gazing out my store window at him and the women surrounding him, but I wouldn't call that mooning.

Vanessa fluffs her black hair over her shoulder and places a hand on her flat abdomen. The royal blue silky blouse she is wearing is unbuttoned to reveal a great deal of cleavage.

Experience has taught me it is better not to engage her at all, so I simply gaze back at her while valiantly trying to wash all emotion from my face. If she scents weakness, she will move in for the kill, like a wolf circling its prey. Her comments have already drawn enough blood, I don't want to give her ammunition to draw more.

"Is there anything I can help you with Vanessa? Coffee? Muffin?"

"No, I don't drink caffeine or eat sweets. They're not healthy. I prefer to keep my body in tip top shape." Her gaze drops to scan my body, lingering on my hips.

Well then what the hell are you doing in my bakery? Oh yes, you're here to insult me. Haven't had my dose in a while, she's been slacking I guess and felt the need to rectify it.

Real subtle, Vanessa. I suppose I should be thankful she has shortened her nickname for me from Fatty Fanny to just Fanny, but I'm not. I'm guessing the only reason is it would reflect badly on her if she used the childish moniker.

Biting my tongue at the reply I'd rather give, I remind myself I am a business owner and I mustn't insult the customers. Or throw a pie in her face.

The front door opens, and my gaze darts up desperately hoping for a reprieve from Vanessa. Mitch walks in smiling.

"You should learn to be less obvious with your interest." Apparently, she's not done with her insults this morning.

"Interest in what?"

I see the entrance to the kitchen in my peripheral vision. What would happen if I turned and ran? Mitch heard her comment. She might tell him she caught me mooning over him. I remain in place and fantasize about gagging her with the towel I'm twisting in my hands.

"Oh Mitch, hello, I didn't see you there."

She bats her false eyelashes at him and giving him what she must think is a coy smile, but it resembles a shark moving in for the kill.

"I was just trying to give Fanny here some friendly advice on a certain crush she has on someone."

Please someone save me! A small emergency or natural disaster would be welcome right about now.

Mitch's gaze snags mine and I give him a weak smile. I can't tell what he is thinking behind those blue eyes, but the smile he came in with disappeared. He glances down at Vanessa.

"I'm sure *Franny* does just fine without your advice." His emphasis on my name makes it clear he picked up on her misuse of my name and he doesn't approve.

My white knight.

"Oh, this is a small town and we like to help each other out here. Isn't that right?" Vanessa scrutinizes me and I glare right back. Was she seriously expecting me to bail her out?

Knowing she could still do more damage and embarrass me further, I force a tight smile to my lips. "Small towns have a way of doing that." That is the extent of my help.

She titters and places her hand on Mitch's shoulder. Her red fingernails stand out starkly against his white T-shirt.

"Mitch, I'd love to show you around our little town to welcome you to Granite Cove."

Say no, please say no. The thought of Mitch and Vanessa spending time together in any way makes me ill.

"Thanks, but I've been here before." He steps to the side and angles his body away from her so that her hand drops from his shoulder.

Vanessa props her hand on her hip. Her smile falters, but she tosses her hair and keeps the smile plastered on her face. "Oh, well then, if you change your mind, I own the real estate office just up the street."

Mitch nods and Vanessa sashays out the door. That very well may have been the first time Vanessa has ever been rejected before. At least it is the first one I have ever witnessed. And yes, I am petty enough to appreciate it and oh so thankful I would not have to endure watching Mitch and Vanessa together.

"I'm guessing she's not a friend of yours?"

Snorting rather indelicately, I clap a hand to my mouth and then drop it. "No, more like mortal enemy from the first day of school."

Mitch folds his arms along the top of the case and leans closer. "So, who's the guy you're interested in?"

The breath stutters in my chest and visions of me turning blue while I panic trying to come up with an answer that won't humiliate me flash through my mind. Honesty is out of the question.

I can't tell him Vanessa was referring to him. Even though she was way off base. I am not crushing on Mitch. Just because I may admire the way he looks doesn't mean my heart is involved.

I will never make that mistake again.

I NEED A NAME AND FAST.

A familiar truck drives by the window.

"Bobby Calvert." I whisper the name and glance over at Sally and the customer she is chatting with to make sure no one overheard. Everyone in town knows Bobby Calvert. He grew up in town, the same as me, and owns a landscaping business. I should have chosen someone more obscure, or better yet, had the sense to make someone up.

Mitch straightens and folds his arms over his chest. "Tell me about him."

Oh dear Lord, this is why I don't lie. It just gets deeper and deeper.

"Franny I'll be back in a minute. Meredith just bought a bunch of plants. She's going to show them to me in her car." Sally walks around the counter, removing her apron and folding it as she goes. She drops it on top of the counter before she and Meredith stroll outside, leaving me alone with Mitch.

There goes my excuse not to elaborate. I suppose I should be thankful there won't be any witnesses to my downfall. Whether it is a downfall for the sin of lying or because I am about to humiliate myself, I'm not quite sure. Probably both in my case.

The door closes behind them and I peek back at Mitch, he's still staring at me expectantly.

"What do you want to know?" And why? Why does he care who I have an interest in any way?

"Who is he? What does he do? Does he live here in town?"

Frowning, I debate how to answer him. I don't want to give him any more information than I already have. What if he meets Bobby?

The ramifications of a single lie are suddenly mind blowing.

"I'd rather not talk about this, okay? What do you care anyway? And please don't tell anyone!"

"By that I take it he doesn't know?"

I roll my eyes at him and scrub the counter with the mangled towel still clutched in my hands. "No genius, he doesn't know, and I don't want him to."

"Why not? How are you going to find out if he returns your feelings, or if he's even worthy of your interest?"

My hand stops in mid swipe. *Worthy of my interest?*

"We're friends, aren't we? Friends help each other out."

What on earth does that mean?

Sally returns and I take that as a signal to escape. "I have stuff to do." I scramble for the kitchen, fervently hoping absence will make him forget the subject forever.

No such luck.

He follows me into the kitchen. "I have an idea."

I spin around and gawk at him. Why wouldn't he drop this?

"You can't be back here."

Mitch looks around the kitchen. "Why not?"

My arms flap. "Because, it's for employees only. Health code and all that. Shoo."

Folding his arms over his chest, he rests a shoulder against a cooler. "I own the building, remember?"

Crap! How could I forget that?

"Listen to my plan and stop hyperventilating."

I close my eyes and mouth and then waltz over to the sink to wash my hands. I wasn't hyperventilating. Slightly panicking, maybe.

If I have to listen to whatever plan he has, then I will bake something. Baking soothes me. Besides, I am still working. Not all of us are so rich we can laze around coming up with ridiculous plans about nonexistent romantic interests.

Defensive much? Yes. I am.

"Friend that I am, I'm willing to help you catch the interest of this guy."

God help me!

I gather ingredients to make a cake.

"Making a guy jealous is guaranteed to catch his interest."

"Wait, what?"

"If he sees you're attracted to someone else, then you'll grab his attention."

"That's ridiculous." Isn't it? That doesn't really work.

"Trust me."

"And just who am I supposed to pretend to be interested in?"

"Me." The measuring cup full of flour slips from my nerveless fingers and hits the counter with a smack sending up a cloud of white dust.

Oh God!

The room wavers and I slap my palms flat on the counter and wait for the vertigo to pass. I look up. He's reclining against the cooler watching me.

I've been struck dumb. Did he just suggest I show an interest in him?

"You'll be helping me out too."

"I will?"

"Yeah, if people think we're an item, then the women will stop trying to ambush me all the time. One followed me up to my apartment. I had to shut the door in her face, because she wouldn't go away. I was half afraid she'd still be there the next morning."

Ah, there's the catch. He needs a make-believe girlfriend.

And he is choosing me?

Mitch saunters over to the opposite side of the counter I'm working at and places both his hands flat on the surface facing me. "I'll teach you everything you need to know to catch this guy."

I remeasure the flour and then the rest of the dry ingredients. "Like what?"

"I understand how guys think, obviously."

Not so obvious. I'm a woman and I never know what other women are thinking.

"What's the harm?"

Oh I don't know, I will be in a fake relationship with a guy I used to believe I was in love with to make the guy I picked out of thin air interested in me. How could that possibly go wrong?

CHAPTER 11

As closing time approaches my gaze strays to the clock more and more. Mitch left this morning with the parting comment we would get together today after work to put our plan into action. Our plan? My plan is to avoid the humiliation of him finding out that Vanessa thought I was mooning over him. His plan is to avoid the multitudes of women chasing him around and help me make my imaginary crush jealous.

How do I let myself get into these messes?

Olivia wanders back into the kitchen and catches me staring at the clock. Her light blonde hair is secured in her customary ponytail. Not a stray hair in sight. I've just finished wrangling my hair back into submission, so I admire the way hers appears to effortlessly behave. She's a year or two older than me, yet her fresh scrubbed face makes her easily pass for a teenager despite being the mother of twin school-age boys.

"It's closing time. I flipped the sign and locked up."

I nod and smile letting her believe I was watching the clock anticipating closing time, not dreading it with every fiber of my being. Okay, not every fiber, there are one or two that are anticipating being in Mitch's company.

And that might be even scarier.

She looks around the clean kitchen. "Anything I can do to help clean up and get ready for tomorrow?"

One of the many things about Olivia that make her such a great employee, she is always willing to help out more. She doesn't clock out when the clock strikes five o'clock even though she has things to do. Her mother babysits her sons for the hour from the time they get off the bus until she arrives home. They're identical, and I still can't tell them apart despite the multitude of times they've been to the bakery.

Besides, I already scrubbed the kitchen and prepared everything. Usually I linger for another hour or two after closing, enjoying the quiet time in my bakery, but not today. Today, I have everything done and now I am glancing at the back door instead of the clock.

"I'm all set. Thanks Olivia. Go enjoy those adorable twins of yours."

She laughs as she removes her apron and smooths her navy-blue sundress sprinkled with tiny white flowers. "They're adorable all right. They're also a handful. I love them to pieces, but sometimes I want to hide in the closet from them. Then of course I'd have to deal with whatever mayhem they got into while I was hiding."

"I can only imagine."

"Feel free to come over sometime and witness them in action. We can sit on the back porch with a glass of wine and watch them wreak terror and destruction."

The smile and shrug are ready to escape when I catch myself remembering Sally's comments concerning hiding.

"You know, I'd enjoy that."

Olivia's surprise is clear by her widened eyes, and I wonder if I chose the wrong time to take a chance that someone is making a genuine offer of friendship rather than being polite.

A grin stretches across her face.

"How about today? Ryan is taking the boys to Little League practice tonight so we would have time to ourselves."

Olivia and her ex-husband seem to have such an amicable relationship. I wondered if they might reconcile, but the divorce finalized over a year ago. They are one of the few divorced couples I know who remained friends.

"I can't tonight. I have plans, but I would like to get together." Afraid those plans were on the verge of pounding down the steps to knock on the back door any moment, I gaze between the door and Olivia. I'm not ready to come up with an explanation yet.

"Tomorrow?"

"Yes, that sounds great."

"Perfect!" Olivia heads toward the back door. "I'll see you tomorrow." She glances over her shoulder as she turns the handle. "No canceling, I will hold you to it."

Smiling, I hold a hand over my heart. "No canceling, I promise. You'll have to tell me what treats to bring for them. They like those giant cookies, don't they?"

"Yes, they do, but we'll save those for after dinner as a bribe to behave. Parenting is all about bribery and negotiation." Poking her head back in the door, she holds a finger to her lips. "Don't tell my mother, she would be appalled."

I laugh as Olivia walks out the door. Her car is most likely parked in the parking lot down the street. I reserve the few spots in front for customers, and the building has no additional parking. It isn't ideal, but to keep the small-town charm and the old building, you have to accept the lack of parking space nearby.

That's one of the reasons I walk to work as often as possible. It takes a bit of time from my parents' house on the other side of town, but it gives me exercise too. The sporting goods store next door and I, along with the tavern, and the souvenir shop all share the parking lot in front of the docks. The businesses across the street have their own parking lot behind the buildings.

The outside stairs creak. I freeze in place and then spin around, looking for something to do. I don't want to appear as if I was just standing around waiting for him, even though that is exactly what I was doing.

I pace to the end of the counter and back and then twirl back, placing my palms flat on the smooth surface. *Get a grip!*

A single knock on the back door, the handle turns, and there he is.

Dark gray pants and a lavender polo show off his fit body and my palms itch to touch. I rub the outside of my thighs instead. Lavender is my favorite color.

I don't have to look down to see my tan Capris and blue peasant blouse hardly compare to his stylishly put together appearance, but at least I'm not wearing borrowed sweatpants and a hoodie this time.

Removing my apron, I keep my gaze firmly planted at my feet. Nerves are clamoring inside me. This is insane. Should I come clean and tell him I am not interested in Bobby? Then what? Tell him who Vanessa was really talking about? Or come up with another lie and dig myself in even deeper?

"I thought we'd try dinner at the old renovated mill. I heard the food there is good, but if you'd prefer somewhere else, we can go there instead."

"We're going to dinner?"

A smile quirks his full lips and I drag my gaze back up to meet his.

"Yes, our plan, remember? You keep the women at bay, and I help you snag the interest of your Biff or Bud or whatever his name is."

"Ah, right, I just didn't realize it involved dinner."

"How else are we going to let people know we're an item if we're not seen together in public?"

An item? Forget butterflies, elephants are dancing in my stomach.

Dial it back a notch, Francine. It's all make-believe. And does he really believe this will fool anyone? No one will believe we're an item. His last girlfriend was a supermodel.

My mood plummets into despair.

This is ridiculous. I have to come clean.

"You have something against dinner?"

"No, of course not."

"Good, then let's get going."

Mitch walks over and grabs my hand. I nearly jump onto the counter in surprise.

He glances down at me with one dark eyebrow cocked up. "Problem?"

"No, no problem." I shake my head and trail after him with my gaze glued on our entwined hands. *Tell him the truth before this goes too far!*

"Oh wait, I need my purse." I let go of his hand, jog over to my desk, grab my small purse, and check to make sure my phone and keys are inside.

After locking the door, I peek up at him for direction. He takes ahold of my hand again and a pleasant warmth spreads through me.

I'm going straight to hell.

"Since it's so close, I thought we'd walk, but if you prefer, we can drive. You're probably tired after being on your feet all day."

The Mill, appropriately named because of its former function, is only a couple blocks away on the river that feeds into the lake.

"I'm fine. I walk to and from work anyway, so I'm used to walking."

We stroll along the alleyway hand in hand.

We'll go to dinner and chat about old times a little, and then I'll casually explain the mix up. Vanessa was just being her catty self and stirring up trouble, and I was embarrassed and panicked like I tend to do around her. No harm done. It was all a silly misunderstanding.

Of course, it makes me sound like a total twit.

He's bound to ask why I lied. Why I didn't just say she was mistaken?

Ugh!

No wonder my love life is nonexistent. I suck at dating. Hell, I am a complete failure.

During my freshman year of college, I went on a date with a boy named Johnny. We had been assigned to the same study team for class. I thought he was interested in me, but it turned out he was interested in a lot of girls and seeing how many he could get into bed.

My sophomore year my roommate cajoled me into a double date with her, her boyfriend, and his brother by telling me how wonderful he was. What she didn't tell me was she asked me because she knew I wasn't his type. She wanted him for herself. I walked into the dorm room to find them in bed together. I dropped out of college not long after to attend culinary school.

Then there was a blind date my mother pressured me into with an acquaintance's son. A very pleasant evening with a nice man who preferred other men.

After that final fiasco, I concentrated all my efforts on my bakery.

Turning right onto the sidewalk, we head towards the center of the village. We will need to cross the street and take a left to get to the restaurant.

I expect someone to stop us any moment asking me what I am doing with Mitch or better yet what he is doing with me, but other than the occasional stare no one pays us any mind. We pause on the bridge spanning the narrow river which flows into the lake to let a group of people pass by. A mama duck and her babies are bobbing in the water. I smile at the adorable sight.

"We'll have to bring bread back with us from dinner."

Nodding, I gaze up at him with a smile. There's a sign over by the docks that warns against feeding the ducks, but people ignore it mostly.

Arriving at the restaurant, the poor hostess almost trips over her own feet when she spots Mitch. I can relate and smile to reassure her, but she's not paying me any attention. Her dazzled gaze is stuck on Mitch. She escorts us to a quiet table next to a large window with a view of the river without any incidents.

The sound of water trickling over the working water wheel outside the building provides a soothing background. Half walls and tall potted plants give the illusion of privacy around the room filled with square tables adorned in black tablecloths. A flickering flame dances inside the narrow hurricane lamp in the center of the table.

"The rustic charm of this restaurant reminds me of a place I visited in Croatia. It was in a tiny village up in the mountains. Did you ever get a chance to travel like you talked about?"

Glancing down at the menu, I shake my head. "No, I've never ventured out of the United States." Actually, I've never been out of

New England, but I am not volunteering that tidbit. "You must have traveled all over the world."

"I've done a fair amount going on location or promoting a movie. There are still plenty of places I'd like to see."

"What are some of your favorites?"

"I was in this film in Italy. I got to travel all over the country, from Rome, Florence, Venice, and the Amalfi coast. Beautiful architecture and scenery everywhere."

"You enjoy architecture, don't you? You talked about it during the tour of your house too."

"In another life I might have been an architect. Every place I've visited I've taken a tour of the landmark buildings or if one wasn't available, I've bought tour books and guided myself."

The waiter stops at our table and introduces himself. If he recognizes Mitch, he doesn't mention it or let it show. I order a chicken and rice dish while Mitch orders a steak and baked potato.

Mitch rests his hands on the table and smiles. "So, no traveling the world yet. What about the sailboat you used to talk about?"

"You witnessed my prowess with the kayak. You really think I should attempt learning to sail?"

His grin widens as he laughs out loud. Heads turn to stare and linger.

Our conversation is interrupted a few times by people stopping at the table for an autograph or picture, or just to say hello. Each time Mitch handles it well with a genuine smile and a charming quip while he poses for the picture or signs a napkin.

The meals arrive and the conversation naturally segues into his career after talking with fans of his movies. I learn a lot about the amount of work that goes on behind the scenes to accomplish the couple of hours that are actually seen. It is clear he prefers being behind the camera rather than in front of it.

When the waiter brings the bill, I wait until he walks away, then I lean over and whisper, "I insist on paying."

"No." Mitch ignores me and slides his credit card into the folder.

"Mitch." It seems only fair I pay for the meal. It is my turn. He bought the pizza. At the very least, we should split the bill. It's not a real date.

He leans over to me, so we are nose to nose. "We're supposed to be dating, remember? Are you trying to damage my reputation by letting people think I'm a cheapskate?"

I hear his words, but I am having a tough time processing them. His eyes are inches from mine and so is his mouth.

Swallowing hard, I lean back in my chair.

The waiter arrives and takes the folder with the bill and Mitch's credit card. I gulp a few swallows of my water and look anywhere but at Mitch.

By the time the waiter returns with his card, I calm my jumping pulse and hopefully not give away how his nearness affected me.

Obviously, I need to get out more. It's an integral part of my new me plan for a reason. Part of having a social life is dating. I'm only reacting to Mitch because...well he's gorgeous, yes, and we have a history.

I'd probably react to any handsome guy that paid me a little attention right now. If I don't find someone soon, I'll be relegated into spinsterhood.

Maybe I *should* let Mitch teach me about dating.

It's not like it would hurt anyone if I let the charade continue. He needs someone to play his girlfriend to keep women away. Why not me? I'm sure he suggested it because he knows I won't blur the lines and start thinking it's real or do something stupid like fall in love with him.

CHAPTER 12

A familiar dark head catches my gaze and I lean over the sink to peer out the window. I recognize Mitch's stride, but I only see a glimpse before he disappears. Jogging to the window over the counter for a better view, I press my nose against the glass and search the public docks where I saw him.

There.

He's carrying a box across the parking lot and down onto the docks.

What's he doing? Did he rent a boat?

Is he bringing supplies to his house?

No, that doesn't make any sense. There's no dock at his house, and why would he use a boat to transport anything when his truck is much more convenient?

Mitch walks back up the steps empty handed and disappears out of view once again.

Short of walking outside, there's no way I can see what he's doing.

Once again, he strides into view carrying another box.

An older woman with steel gray short hair walks behind him toting a bag in each hand.

Who is she?

He must be helping her, but with what?

"What are you gawking at? There an accident or something?"

Springing away from the window, I face Sally. Before I can come up with a plausible excuse or distraction, she marches over and cranes her neck to look out the window.

"Oh look, it's Margie Swanson. She must be getting her groceries. She lives on one of the islands and comes to town once a month to pick up supplies. Now I see what's got your attention. Your young man is helping her carry her stuff to the boat."

She leans back and pats me on the shoulder. "You've got a keeper there."

My mouth opens so I can tell her he's not my anything, but then I snap it closed. I can't very well confess it's all a charade.

"I saw your friend, Mrs. Roberts, headed this way and thought you might like to know. I'll keep an eye on things back here for you."

"Oh." I cast my gaze around the kitchen. "There's nothing due to come out of the ovens for a while yet." I point to one of the rolling racks. "Those cookies should be cool by now if you want to bring them up front."

Sally nods and I walk out front as the bell over the front door jingles.

Mrs. Roberts steps in leaning heavily on her cane and looks around before smiling at me. "Hello, Franny."

"Good morning, Mrs. Roberts. What can I get for you? You're not out of meringues already, are you?"

She stops in front of the display case and rests both hands on top of the cane while she peers inside. "No, no, I have plenty of meringues left. I need something sweet for my bridge game tonight."

"Okay, do you have anything in mind? A cake? Pie? Tartlets?"

"I'm not sure, everything looks so tempting. I would prefer individual servings so we don't have to worry about making slices or plates and silverware. What would you recommend?"

"The fruit tartlets don't require more than a napkin. I could box up an assortment of cookies for you. There are also cupcakes, doughnuts, muffins, or these mini cheesecakes and mousse cakes."

"Oh my, I'm partial to cookies, but those little cakes look delicious."

"Would you like a sample or two to decide?" It's not something I frequently offer, but for Mrs. Roberts, I will bend the rules. "Why don't you have a seat and I'll bring a couple over?"

A rest before she heads back home couldn't hurt.

"Thank you, dear."

While she shuffles over to the chair, I pour her a cup of tea and grab a few items for her to sample.

"You know, you could call me anytime and tell me what you'd like. I'll deliver them to you."

"Oh, that's so kind of you, but I enjoy getting out for a stroll. It's good for me."

"Okay, but the offer is always open."

"Are you working alone today?"

"No, Sally is in back. She saw you coming and told me so I could visit with you." I glance over my shoulder towards the kitchen. Sally should've brought the cookies up front by now.

"Humph—I doubt her reasons are so altruistic."

"What do you mean?" Did Mrs. Roberts not like Sally?

They have both lived in town for as long as I can remember and are in the same generation, but they don't socialize together as far as I know.

She stirs her tea and then raises her chin. "You recall I told you about my late husband's penchant for charming other women?"

I nod once and freeze in place. *Sally?*

Her gaze meets mine and she nods. "Just so."

My mouth grows slack. *Sally?*

I clamp my lips together and gaze over my shoulder to the kitchen. *Holy crap!*

Had Sally been avoiding her since she started working here? How had I never noticed? Actually, Mrs. Roberts usually came in during the afternoons when Olivia worked. Intentionally?

I slide onto the chair across from her. She takes a bite of each confection, sips her tea, and looks up.

"They are all wonderful. I'll take two of each, please. Also, would you mind wrapping the rest of these up for me? I can't finish them and I would like to save them for later."

"Of course." I carry them over to the counter and box them up.

It doesn't look like she's going to elaborate.

What am I going to say to Sally? Should I even say anything? If she wanted to talk about it, she would have mentioned something.

Although, I can't imagine how that conversation will go. It's not like she is likely to say she didn't want to wait on Mrs. Roberts because she had an affair with Mr. Roberts.

I package the rest of her order and put both boxes in a bag.

Mrs. Roberts uses her cane to rise from the chair and walk over to the register.

Do I know any of the other women her husband had affairs with? Images of all the women around her age flash through my mind.

"The ladies will love your sweets, thank you." She hands me her money.

I smile and finish ringing up the sale.

"Enjoy, Mrs. Roberts. Have a good game." I can't think of anything else to say. I don't know the first thing about bridge and my brain is still stuck on the multitude of possibilities and ramifications of who Mr. Roberts was fooling around with.

The bell over the door announces her departure.

I huff out a breath and turn facing the kitchen. I'm going to follow Sally's lead. If she doesn't say anything, then neither will I.

Sally is drying her hands at the sink. I glance at the cookies all still sitting on the rack.

"The cookies were still a little warm, so I cleaned the counters instead."

I had checked them before she came into the kitchen to announce Mrs. Roberts' impending arrival. They weren't warm.

"Okay."

"They might be cool now. I'll bring them out now, if you want."

"No, that's okay. I'll bring him out in a little bit. You go ahead."

She nods and walks out of the kitchen with her head down.

Had she heard Mrs. Roberts tell me?

If she had stood by the archway and listened, she could have heard what was said.

The counter is clean and there are dishes drying in the rack. She might have been cleaning the entire time and heard nothing.

I shrug and walk over to lean on the counter. I have no desire to broach the topic with her anyway. It's really none of my business.

There's a knock on the back door. Mitch opens it and walks inside. "Hi."

"Hi."

"I wanted to tell you I'll be out of town for a few days. I've got a few things to tie up back in California."

"When will you be back?"

"I'm not sure. I'm going to stop and see my folks once I'm done, but no longer than a week."

A week?

No Mitch for an entire week?

I've gotten used to seeing him every day. Well, almost every day.

I guess that means no drives or accomplishing anything else on our list.

"You must miss them, being so far away."

"Yeah, I always try to make sure I see them at least once every couple of months. Sometimes it's hard if I'm on location but they've visited me a few times when I couldn't get away."

It must be nice to have a close relationship with your family, to want to spend time with them and not feel like a perpetual disappointment to them.

But then, how could any parent not be proud of Mitch?

"What are your plans for the week?"

"Nothing special."

Same as any other week, I'll be here at the bakery.

"When I get back, we'll have to plan to tackle one of the things on our list."

I smile.

"I looked it up, there's a train if driving up Mt. Washington scares you too much."

"The Cog. I'm not sure that would be any less scary, have you seen the track it climbs on? It's steep."

Mitch chuckles, leans against the counter next to the sink and folds his arms across his chest.

"We could try both and see which is worse. An experiment."

"You're going to enjoy torturing me, aren't you?"

"If you're really too scared, you don't have to do it. We can do something else."

"No, I want to."

"You don't look very convincing."

I stand straighter and lift my chin. "Better?"

"Okay, if you're sure, we'll plan it when I get back."

Let's hope my courage lasts that long.

"Be good while I'm gone. No running off with Blake."

Blake? Oh, Bobby.

Mitch heads for the door.

"I make no promises. Bring me back a souvenir."

He looks over his shoulder. "Promise and I'll bring you back anything you want."

Anything?

Smiling, I cross my arms around my waist. "Okay."

"Deal?"

"Deal."

He opens the door. "You going to tell me what you want?"

"Surprise me."

Mitch winks and walks out the door.

"Be safe." I call out before the door closes.

"Who was that?"

Olivia stands in the archway smiling at me.

Was it time for her shift already? A glance at the clock confirms it is.

"Hi Olivia."

She is still staring at the door.

"It was the new tenant upstairs."

Sally poked her head in the kitchen. "I'm heading out now."

"Thanks Sally, I'll see you tomorrow."

"Are you still coming over tonight after work? I'm planning on throwing shish kebabs on the grill. The boys insisted I buy a watermelon at the grocery store so outside dining is a must for the sticky faces and fingers."

No more hiding.

"I'm looking forward to it."

CHAPTER 13

"Ignore the mess."

Olivia picks up discarded backpacks and jackets when we walk in the door of her blue cape. She hangs them up on pegs next to the door and calls out, "I'm home."

Two blond dynamos race down the stairs and collide with her, giving her hugs before dashing back in the direction they came.

A petite woman with short blonde hair streaked with gray rises from a couch in the living area on the right and tucks a paperback book into a tote sized purse.

"Hi Mom. How were they today?"

"They were fine." She waves a hand and then smiles at me while slipping the shoulder straps of her purse over her shoulder. "Hello."

"Oh, I'm sorry. Franny this is my mother, Laura."

Laura shakes my hand and pats the top. "I've been in your bakery a few times. You make so many tempting treats I have to stop myself from stopping in too often."

"Thanks. It's nice to meet you."

"I've got to get dinner ready for your father so I will say hello and goodbye."

"Timmy. Tommy. Come say goodbye to your grandmother."

The boys rush down the stairs once again and wrap their arms around Laura's waist, almost knocking her over.

"Bye Grandma," they chorus.

She kisses them each on top of their heads.

"Now also say hello to our guest, Miss Dawson. You remember she owns the bakery I work for?"

"Hi Miss Dawson."

"Hi boys."

"Can we go back upstairs now?"

Olivia rolls her eyes. "Yes, but only for a few more minutes then it's homework time."

Laura leaves and the boys race back upstairs.

"Why don't we head to the kitchen?"

I follow her to the left, an open area split into the kitchen and dining room.

"Have a seat. I'll grab the ingredients for dinner."

"Can I help?"

"No, sit. You've been working all day and besides I've already made the shish kebabs. All I have left to prepare is a salad."

I sit down and put the small bag of cookies I brought for the boys on top of the oval oak table along with my purse.

"I didn't want to say anything in front of the boys in case it's a rule or something, but they can call me Franny." My mother has chastised me over breaking so many proper etiquettes over the years. The dictates jumble in my brain. I don't understand the reasoning behind half of them.

Olivia smiles as she pulls things from the fridge. "I try to teach them manners, but if you're comfortable, they can call you Franny."

A lawnmower buzzes from outside and Olivia frowns. "That would be my new neighbor. I swear he mows his lawn almost every day. Who does that?"

"No idea. I've never mowed a lawn in my life."

"Never?"

I shake my head and she laughs. "Feel free to learn by mowing mine anytime."

"Thanks, I'll keep that in mind if I ever get the urge." It's something I will have to tackle if I find a place of my own with a lawn. The task shouldn't be too difficult to accomplish. You turn it on and push it back and forth across the lawn.

Of course, there are sharp blades involved to cut the grass. Visions of bloody feet and missing toes and fingers pop into my head.

I could hire someone to mow the lawn.

"He's single and lives alone. Not what you'd call sociable either. I did the neighborly thing when he moved in and went over to introduce myself, even brought him cookies, and he sort of grunted at me and looked at me like I was an alien or something."

"He's not going to win any conversation awards?" Someone worse than me at talking to people. He might be rude instead of anxious.

"Definitely not."

"When did he move in?"

"A month ago."

She puts down the knife she is cutting the tomatoes with and glances upstairs and then over to me. "I did a search online for him and checked the sex offender list."

"Wow, you don't trust this guy, do you? I never heard of such a list. Did you find anything?"

"Wait until you're a parent, you'll take paranoia to a whole new level. The weird thing is I found nothing, not on the list or by searching his name. No social media accounts, nothing. Do you know how weird that is?"

"Not really." I shift in the chair. What would come up if I typed in my name? I'm not on any social media outlets. I have one for the bakery and a website, but nothing personal.

"Try it some time. There's always something, but not with this guy."

"Maybe he's just a private person?"

"There's private and then there's *private* for a reason, if you know what I mean. Like, witness protection, criminal, a serial killer."

I chuckle, but Olivia's not smiling. She is serious.

"I know I probably sound a little nuts, but these are the things I worry about now that I've got kids."

"Understandable, I can only imagine the things you have to worry about as a parent. Speaking as a person who is shy and not all that great at dealing with people, do you think he might have a similar problem?"

Olivia pushes the salad bowl to the side, leans against the counter with her hip and folds her arms. "Crap, now I feel like a bitch. What if he has a mental disability and here I've been thinking the worst?"

"No, I mean I have no idea, I've never met the guy. Don't feel bad for looking out for your kids."

"I should bring him more cookies and try again. Or maybe he doesn't like cookies. Brownies, I'll bring him brownies."

"Wait a minute, slow down, I'm only saying there could be another explanation. That doesn't mean you should rush over there, at least not alone. What if he is a criminal or something? I don't want to be responsible for you ending up chopped into little pieces."

Olivia stares at me and then we both burst out laughing.

"It's contagious. I've got you worrying now too. Little pieces?"

"Well you did say serial killer."

"True."

"Seriously, next time you get the urge to visit your neighbor call me. We'll go together."

"Good idea, then you can tell me if I'm crazy or just a bitch."

"You're not a bitch."

She grabs plates from a cabinet and sets them on the counter. "We all can be a bitch from time to time."

"Very true, some more than others." A few might just be born that way.

I might have fantasized occasionally about having the audacity to say whatever I want. Like telling Vanessa what an evil ogre she is.

Of course, I never act on it.

Which could very well be why she continues to torment me. Aren't you supposed to confront bullies to get them to back down?

Food for thought.

Olivia tilts her head up to the ceiling. "Boys, homework time!"

Their feet stomp down the stairs.

Olivia walks towards me. "I'm going to turn on the grill. Be right back." I crane my neck to watch her disappear down a short hallway separating the kitchen and living room.

The boys grab binders from their backpacks and sit at the table. One of them stares at the bag I placed on the table. "What's in there?"

The other one glances up from digging through his pencil case. He looks at the bag and then at me. "Is that for us?"

"Maybe. Finish your homework and you'll find out."

Olivia walks back into the kitchen. "After dinner."

"Right, what your mom said, after dinner. But I can still tell you what is in the bag after you do your homework." I peek at Olivia to make sure and she nods.

"I bet it's those cookies."

"Not the ones with the raisins. I hate raisins." The one on the left scrunches his nose and sticks out his tongue.

"There are no raisins, I promise."

He smiles. There's a slight gap between his two front teeth.

I look at his brother on the right. "What about you? Do you hate raisins too?"

"I like them in bread or cookies." There isn't a gap between his teeth.

"Okay, so which one of you is Timmy and which one is Tommy?"

The boys look at each other and smile.

The one on the right shrugs. "No one ever gets it right except family."

"They don't help either pretending to be one another to confuse people." Olivia walks over to the table and stands behind them. She puts a hand on each of their shoulders. "This one here is Tommy." He's the boy with no gap. "And this one is Timmy."

"Okay, I'll see if I can remember."

"You won't." Tommy assures me.

Olivia rolls her eyes and ruffles his hair. "Do your homework."

They both concentrate on their papers and what looks like fractions. Olivia walks over to the counter. I stand and follow.

"What can I do to help?"

"You can grab the plates and utensils there and bring them out to the deck."

I pick up the items she points to and carry them into the living room where I spot the back door. Stacking the utensils onto the plates, I open the door and step onto the wooden deck which spans the length of the house.

There's a patio table and chairs with a yellow striped umbrella so I walk over to set everything down. Olivia walks outside juggling a salad, shish kebabs, and a tray of sliced watermelon. She uses her hip and elbow to shut the door before I can reach her to help.

"Anything else I can bring out?"

"There are glasses and a pitcher of lemonade on the counter."

She carries the shish kebabs over to the grill while I go back inside.

The boys smile at me when I walk into the kitchen.

They've switched seats.

Smiling I walk over to the table and look down at the boy on the right's paper. "Timmy how is the homework going?"

"I'm Timmy." The boy on the left pipes up. I know he's Tommy because there's no gap in his teeth.

"Nope, I've got the two of you figured out so no trying to trick me or there'll be no cookies."

Tommy scowls. "How'd you know? Did Mom see us and tell you?"

"No, and I'm not telling you my secret detection system."

Timmy grins.

Tommy taps the pencil against his chin. "I'll figure it out."

"Maybe." I carry out the glasses and pitcher and tell Olivia about their switch.

She laughs. "How did you tell?"

"All I'm saying is once their baby teeth fall out, I might not be able to tell anymore."

"You should be safe for a few years. They seem to be taking after me and I didn't lose all of mine until I was almost a teenager."

Dinner was delicious and Olivia was correct. The boys had sticky watermelon juice on their hands and face when they finished. She cleaned them up with a container of wet wipes she had brought outside and they ran off to play on the playscape after helping us carry in the dishes.

We sit on the deck watching them after we clean everything up. Olivia has a glass of wine and I a diet soda.

"Their energy is astonishing."

Laughing, she leans back in her chair and crosses her legs. "They'll crash after story time and be out all night until the morning. Then they start again."

"No wonder you're so fit. You're chasing after them all the time."

"I don't know about fit, but they keep me busy."

Olivia sips her white wine. "Did you hear about that poor elderly woman they found?"

"No, what woman?"

"It was on the news. The story had me practically bawling. The mailman noticed her mailbox hadn't been emptied in days so he knocked on the door. No one answered. He knew she was older and lived alone, so he went around back to try that door too. Again, no answer. He started peeking in windows until he spotted her in the bathroom, dead. He called the police. It turned out she had been there for over a week. She had no family or friends so nobody missed her absence and checked on her."

"That is awful." A chill brushes the back of my neck.

Dying alone with no one caring, it's a horrible end to someone's life. What kind of life had she led that brought her to such circumstances? She could've outlived any family or friends. Or, had she not had any?

"I know, right? I called my grandparents to check on them and put reminders in my phone to do it more often."

My grandparents are all long gone.

"It's sad, but at least stories like that one remind people to cherish their loved ones while they still can."

Not all of us have loved ones.

Would anyone miss me if I were gone? People would notice the bakery wasn't open, I suppose.

My parents would eventually question my whereabouts since I live with them. If I get my own place though, who will check?

"I've totally brought down the mood now, haven't I?"

I rest my head on the back of the chair and stare up at the sky. "No, you're right, it makes you think. I've been contemplating making changes in my life."

"Like what?"

I shrug and roll my eyes. "I was in the doctor's office reading a magazine article about vision boards and life maps. So I made one of my own. However, nothing seems to be working out the way I envisioned."

"Life never does, does it? I could probably stand to make one for myself. I tend to describe my life as controlled chaos. What sort of things were on yours?"

"Well, my whole plan hinges on moving out of my parents' place. So far I have had little luck finding anything in my budget."

"What's supposed to happen if you move out?"

My cheeks heat and I hope the increasing shadows of dusk are enough to cover the blush. "Get a life basically. A social life."

She props her chin on the heel of her hand and stares at me. "I get that living with your parents can stifle a dating life somewhat, but there are work arounds. Inviting a guy back to your parents' place could be a mind field of issues, but there's always his place. Unless he lives with his parents too."

Laughter bubbles up my throat and I choke on the swallow of soda.

She grins and takes a drink of her wine.

"That would definitely happen to me."

"Don't feel bad. It's been ages since I've been on a date. We should help each other out with making our life plans work."

I tilt my head and stare at her. Here I thought Olivia was living a happy fulfilled life. I never would've guessed there was something missing for her too.

"I'm all for that. I could use any help I can get. In fact, you've already helped me by inviting me to dinner. I made a vow to get out more and stop hiding. Except for the bakery, I've been in danger of becoming a hermit."

She raises her glass. "Well then, here's to us expanding our horizons and maybe one of us will get laid too."

I clink my glass against hers. "We can hope."

Splats of water land on my hands and wet circles appear on my pants. I look up at the dark clouds overhead.

"It might be only a passing sprinkle." Olivia scoots her chair under the umbrella and I follow suit.

The drops increase.

"Or not. Boys come inside."

Olivia and I both stand, leaning as much of our bodies under the umbrella as we can. The boys laugh and run around the playscape trying to catch the rain drops in their mouths.

It rains in a steady stream.

"Boys!"

Either they don't hear her or are having too much fun, but they continue to run around the playscape having a blast.

I can't help the laugh bubbling up at the sight of them playing in the rain.

Olivia and I share a look and then dash out in the rain to dance around the playscape with her sons.

CHAPTER 14

The sea of clothes spread out before me is nirvana for a lot of people. Racks upon racks of tops, bottoms, dresses, and everything in between fills the store. Varying colors and patterns bleed together and give me a headache. How do people choose among so many options? Basic black works just fine for most situations.

Last night, as I was leaving, Olivia talked me into going shopping with her at the mall. Her sons are at school and the bakery is closed today, so she has the morning free.

It is my day off and I am at the mall.

"Oh look at this! It will look gorgeous on you!" She holds up a frothy blouse to my face. "The pale peach color against your ivory skin looks amazing."

Really? I peer closer at the top.

"It's silk, so it needs extra care but feel this texture. It's so worth it."

I finger the sleeve and I must admit the soft delicate material is nice. My idea of buying clothes is to wait until I am down to basically nothing to wear then go online and order something that looks good on the woman modeling the clothes and pray it will look half way decent on me when it arrives. Let's face it, they have models wearing the clothes and everything looks great on them because they are, well, models.

"Try it on." She holds the blouse out. Taking it, I glance around hoping there won't be a dressing room in sight, but no such luck, there is one right behind me.

Olivia gives me a slight tap on the shoulder. "Make sure you show me how it looks."

Do people really do this? Try on clothes and show each other how they look? A woman waltzes out of the dressing room to show two women waiting for her how she looks in the outfit she put on and I realize that yes, they do indeed.

Okay then, it can't be too hard. I just have to go in there, strip down to my bra in a tiny room with a half door where everyone can see not only from my calves to my toes but my shoulders up. Oh yes, and then I prance out for Olivia to critique how I look.

I sigh and shut the white door with vent slots filling the middle. Was that a decorating style? Because it sure wasn't for air circulation, there is plenty enough of that in the open space.

The blouse looks good hanging up on the hook. Hopefully it will look at least half as good on me. Glancing around to make sure I am hidden as much as possible, I yank my navy-blue T-shirt over my head and fold it before putting it on the tiny corner shelf. The blouse is smooth and cool as I draw it up my arms. The tiny pearlescent buttons reflect in the lights as I button the blouse. I tuck it into my white jeans not knowing if I should or not, but it seems like a top you tuck in.

"How are you doing Franny?"

I peek over the door. Olivia is standing outside my little compartment.

"Um, okay, I think." It is hard to tell in the narrow mirror, but it doesn't look bad.

"Let me see."

Opening the door, I step back as far as I can in the confined space. Modeling it in here is better than going out into the store.

"I knew it would look great!" Olivia looks me up and down. "Spin around. Let me see the back."

I present my back and she smooths the material against my lower back and sides.

"There, perfect. Your waist is so tiny. You need to wear more fitted clothes and show it off."

It is? I do? I look down and peruse my waist. It looks the same as it always does.

"Here, I found these for you to try on too." The pile of clothes she hangs on the hook momentarily boggles my mind. "This is so much fun."

The door swings shut, and her blonde ponytail bounces away. An assortment of colors and articles of clothing hang in front of me. She wants me to try all of these on?

THE ICE-COLD WATER trickles down my throat and soothes the nagging thirst that has grown over the last couple of hours. I tried on all the clothes Olivia fetched me and a few more as well. Several of them now rest in various bags sitting at my feet. Olivia has a few bags herself. We decided to end our shopping excursion at a restaurant in the mall. I must admit the shopping hasn't been as bad as I expected. I actually had fun and might not be entirely opposed to doing it again. In a few months' time.

We each order a sandwich and as the waitress strides away, Olivia rests her elbows on the round table and stares at me. "So, tell me what's going on with you and Mitch Atwater."

Choking on the swallow of water I just took, I set the glass on the table and wipe the drips of water from my chin.

She smiles and hands me a napkin. "I drove the boys to school this morning because I had to drop off cookies for their end of the year party and one of the other moms sidles up to me and starts pumping me for information about you and the local celebrity. I guess she assumed since I work at the bakery, I would know all about it."

Licking my lips, I gaze around the restaurant filled with booths and chattering people. What am I supposed to tell her? The sham we're dating? Certainly not the whole truth. I don't want to lie to her either. I mean friends aren't supposed to lie to each other, right? That doesn't mean they have to spill all their secrets either though does it? Crap, is friendship supposed to be hard?

"Franny?"

"I don't know what to say. We're friends." There that's the truth.

"Friends, huh? I heard the two of you were strolling along main street hand in hand the other day."

"Any chance you and Ryan will reconcile?"

Olivia sits back in her chair and smirks. "Okay, I get it. You're not ready to talk about it yet, but when you are, I want to hear about it, deal?"

"Deal."

"Ryan and I met my freshman year of college. I got pregnant, dropped out of school, got married, and we tried to make it work, but we were both miserable."

"I'm sorry. I shouldn't have pried. It's just that you two seem to be so close."

"Don't apologize. I was prying too. It's what friends do." She winks. "Ryan and I are close. We're much better friends than husband and wife. Which is great because of the boys, but we would still be friends even if we didn't have the boys keeping us together."

"You do an admirable job. I'd like to think I could be on good terms with an ex, but I'm not as nice as you."

Olivia laughs and drinks her iced tea. "You'd be amazed at how much bullshit you can swallow and accept when there are kids involved, but Ryan and I have to work at it. If he ever gets serious about a woman and wants to introduce the boys to her, I will have to learn to bite my tongue a lot."

"Girlfriends and boyfriends haven't been introduced yet?"

"No one serious. We've both dated a bit. Him, much more than me, but there has been no one serious enough where we've had the introducing the boys to them conversation. Ryan and I both agreed before the divorce not to allow anyone into the boys' lives without letting each other know first and agreeing it was time."

Our sandwiches arrive and I take a bite of my portobello mushroom sandwich while Olivia starts on her chicken panini. The combination of balsamic vinaigrette, mushroom, and ciabatta roll is tasty. I chose it because I thought it the healthier option, but the taste will make me order it again. Wiping my mouth with a napkin, I wait for Olivia to finish chewing before asking her another question.

"Do you ever think about going back to school? What did you plan on studying?"

"I had no idea what I wanted to do." She shrugs her shoulders and tilts her head while looking around the restaurant. "Sure, the thought crossed my mind a time or two, but honestly, I love being home for my boys. They drive me crazy at times, but I couldn't imagine doing it any other way. When they get older, I might consider going back, but it's not something I miss."

Scooting my chair forward, I fiddle with the corner of the placemat. "College wasn't for me, much to my mother's dismay."

"But she must be so proud of you owning a successful bakery."

I manage not to choke again as I take a sip of water. Proud? Uh no, not the word I would use.

"My mother has certain standards and expectations I don't measure up to. We are very different people."

"I'm sorry, Franny."

One corner of the paper placement is curled into a roll, so I shift over to the other side and start again. "It is what it is."

"It still hurts though doesn't it? What is it about a parent's disapproval that haunts us even into adulthood?"

"I don't know, but if you find the answer, let me know."

"Hey, that can be my life's work once the kids are grown. Of course by then it will be *my* disappointment *my* kids are dreading. Although I hope I won't be too demanding."

"You won't. Your love and approval for your sons shines through even when your exasperation over their latest mischief is apparent."

"Thank you. that's one of the nicest things someone has ever said to me. My boys are my life."

We finish our sandwiches while chatting of our mutual anticipation of the summer's arrival. Olivia's mother babysits the boys so she can still work at the bakery when they aren't in school. I never realized how much Olivia loves working at the bakery. She expressed interest in learning more about the baking side and I discovered she is an accomplished home baker.

It will be fun to train Olivia. I had planned to hire help in the kitchen farther down the road so I can build the catering side of my business.

Those plans are on hold until I decide about whether or not I should move the bakery.

Bill sent me an email a couple of days ago with potential commercial properties. All were out of town. There was nothing glaringly wrong with any of them.

I should get back to him and have him set up a viewing, but I keep putting it off.

I don't want to relocate the bakery.

The waitress brings the check and I pull out my wallet to pay.

Olivia pulls her purse off the back of her chair.

I hold up my hand. "It's my treat. You had me over for dinner, remember?"

She shrugs. "Okay, thanks. We can take turns. Next time it will be my treat."

After placing the money in the bill folder for the waitress, I rub my thumb up and down in the condensation on the outside of my glass.

If I don't relocate, then that means I go on renting.

I can do that.

What I can't do is continue living with my parents.

But if I buy a house, then I'll have that much less to make Mitch an offer to buy the building when the time comes. That is still my ultimate goal.

I can rent an apartment and still save towards making an offer he can't refuse.

"You look deep in thought."

I glance up at Olivia. The waitress picks up the bill folder and I tell her to keep the change. Once she leaves, I grab my purse and stand.

"You know that life plan we were talking about?"

Olivia nods as she rises and pushes in her chair. "Of course."

"I just came to a few decisions to help it along again."

"Like what?"

While we walk out of the mall, I tell her about my plans to buy the building and move into the apartment falling through and about hiring a realtor to show me other bakery options and houses.

Olivia stops. "You're thinking of moving the bakery?"

"I considered it, but I hate the idea. I'm going to find an apartment to rent so I can still move out, but keep the bakery where it is and go on renting until I can afford to offer enough money to prompt Mitch to sell it to me."

She starts walking again. "Have you talked to Mitch about it? Does he know you planned to buy the building?"

"No, I hadn't wrapped my head around everything yet. Now that I know moving the bakery isn't an option I want to explore, I'm going to ask him how much he'll accept for the building. He's only staying in the apartment while he renovates the house he bought anyway, so once that's ready he might be open to selling to me."

"That makes sense. You should talk to him soon though, then you will know one way or another and how much money you'll need if he will sell."

"You're right." I should have talked to him sooner, but I had still been in the shocked stage of him showing up and buying my building. Then I moved into the avoidance stage. That didn't last very long. We moved into the hesitantly open to friendship again stage. Now, where are we? Pretending to be dating for all the wrong reasons.

We reach her car and pile our loot into the backseat. Granite Cove is an hour away from the mall. Olivia insisted on driving, saying she enjoyed it. I could take it or leave it, so I didn't put up an argument. Olivia sings along with the radio and makes us both laugh. Her voice might not sell many records, but it is nice to listen to in the car. Much better than mine.

I lean back against the seat and gaze out the window. I'm moving forward with my life plan even if it's not in the way I originally thought. My social life is evolving. Olivia and I have hung out on two occasions and I believe we are friends.

On Sunday, Monica stopped in the bakery and I broached the subject of attending her next book club meeting. She smiled and told me she postponed the last one because a pipe burst under her sink and made a mess, so they rescheduled it for tonight. She asked me to come and I said yes. Sally smiled and gave me her nod of approval.

Monica retrieved her copy of the book they were reading from her car so I could at least glance through it and not feel left out when they discussed it. Thumbing through the pages, I got so engrossed with the steamy scenes I ignored the oven buzzer and burned two trays of cookies. I set the book aside after that and waited until I got home last night to read it. Unable to put it down, I read it cover to cover and then ordered more books from the author online this morning before Olivia picked me up.

As we drive through town, I spot a familiar truck and can't prevent the smile that blooms on my lips.

Mitch is back.

CHAPTER 15

I'm late. It's full on dark with only a sliver of moon to shine any light in the nighttime sky. Clouds hide the stars.

The steering wheel remains gripped in my damp palms despite the fact the engine is now cold. My foot taps against the rubber floor mat in a steady staccato.

It took me a good hour to work up the nerve to get in the car and drive over here. I almost canceled a half a dozen times.

Getting a social life and a hobby outside of baking be damned. The occupants of my stomach are threatening a mutiny.

I'm late, and yet here I still sit staring at the small ranch house with solar lights lighting the pathway from the driveway to the house and a floodlight shining on the driveway. I parked on the street since cars fill the driveway and a few are parked along the road.

Monica lives in a rural part of town where neighbors aren't in waving distance.

What made me think I am ready for this? Yes, I went over Olivia's house and went shopping with her today and I had fun on both occasions. Except for her twins though, it was one-on-one fun, not a bunch of people I don't know. A group I am expected to converse with and make intelligent comments. If I knew someone else I am comfortable with was in there, it wouldn't be so bad.

Yanking my phone from my purse, I dial Olivia's number.

"Hi Franny."

"Hi."

"Aren't you supposed to be at the book club tonight?"

"Yes, that's why I'm calling. How would you like to go with me?"

"I'd love to but, I've got the boys tonight."

"I'll watch them for you. You can go in my place."

Her chuckle echoes over the phone. "You'd rather babysit my demons than go to a get together serving wine and cake? What's going on?"

In a heartbeat. Kids are much easier. They don't expect witty conversation. They just want to play and have fun.

"I'm not a party person."

"Where are you?"

"In my car." Full confession time? "Sitting outside Monica's house."

"Okay, here's what I want you to do: Breathe in for three seconds, hold it for a count of four, exhale for three seconds, and then repeat. It will help you relax."

Nothing will help me relax.

"I don't hear you breathing Franny. Try it. It helps, I promise. I do it when my kids make me want to scream like a crazy person."

Fine, it can't hurt, I guess. In one, two, three. Hold one, two, three, four. Out one, two, three. Repeat.

"Better?"

Dropping my hands into my lap, I take stock. My heart is no longer pounding, and my nerves don't feel like over stretched guitar strings ready to snap. "Actually yes."

"Good. Now go enjoy yourself. This isn't supposed to be a chore."

"What am I supposed to talk to people about?"

"It's a book club. Talk about the book. Tell them how you burned the cookies, they'll get a kick out of that story." Olivia certainly had when I told her.

Frowning, I stare at the house once again.

"Franny, no one will judge you in there, and if one of them does, then that's on them, not you."

She's right, I know she is, but it's easier to understand that than to put it into practice.

"Open the door and get out of the car."

"Okay. Thanks, I will. I'll see you tomorrow."

"Oh no, don't hang up. I want to hear you getting out of the car and going to the door."

"Really?" Laughing, I climb out of the car and lock it. "There, I'm out."

"Start walking. I want to hear the doorbell and everything, then you can hang up."

"Olivia, this is ridiculous."

"It's helping isn't it?"

Looking down at the walkway I am now standing on, I must admit she is right. "Yup, I'm walking up to the door. Thanks for talking me through it. Sorry for dragging you into my piece of crazy town."

"Not a problem. We all have our own bits of crazy. That's what friends are for, either to talk you out of them or join in."

Laughter bubbles out as I push the button for the doorbell. Monica opens the door with a smile before my finger leaves the button.

"You made it. I'm so glad. Come in."

"Got to go Olivia."

"Have fun and I'm taking a raincheck on your offer to babysit."

"I'll be happy to babysit any time."

"Hah, you say that now, just wait. See you."

"Bye."

Stepping into the house, I glance around the living room and spot several familiar faces, including Sally sitting on the green couch. She grins and pats the cushion next to her. Shaking my head, I skirt around the chairs set up and plop down on the couch.

"Why didn't you tell me you belonged to the book club?"

"You didn't ask."

Monica stands on one side of the loosely formed circle and taps the side of her glass. "Ladies, most of you know our new arrival, but for those who don't this is Franny Dawson. She owns The Sweet Spot."

"Oh, I love that bakery." An older woman sitting in a mint green club chair across from me throws both her hands in the air making her triceps jiggle.

"Thank you."

"Introduce yourselves to her everyone. Franny what can I get you to drink?"

"Water would be great, thank you."

"I'm Tina Swanson. I'm a teacher at the elementary school with Monica." Tina's hunter green sundress complements her blonde hair and green eyes.

I smile.

The brunette sitting on the chair next to her waves. "I'm Kerry Barton. I'm also a teacher, but at the high school."

I've seen them in town and in my bakery, but we've never talked.

The older woman who said she liked my bakery stretches across the space between us and holds out her hand. "I'm Aggie, by the way."

I shake her hand. "It's nice to meet you."

A woman sits down next to me. Light brown hair brushes the edge of her jawline. Dark brown eyes, almost black, stare at me. "I'm Rebecca Terrance. I own the florist shop."

"Oh, you bought that last year, didn't you? My mother is much happier with your selection and service."

"That's good to hear. Wait, Dawson? Is Elaine Dawson your mother?"

"The one and only."

Rebecca smiles and sits back, crossing her legs. She swings her foot letting the sole of her three-inch heel tap against the heel of her foot. "Your mother is a discerning woman and one of my best customers."

My mother insists on fresh flowers throughout the house. As soon as one flower wilts, she tosses and replaces the whole bouquet.

"I haven't seen you at the Small Business Association meetings. You should attend."

It's on my to do list.

"I've been meaning to."

"We're trying to organize a marketing campaign for local businesses to participate in. You would be a terrific addition. The fare at the meetings would improve if you felt obliged to bring along confections from your bakery. Usually one of us brings store-bought packaged donuts."

"I can definitely do better than that."

"We are meeting next week at the library. Tuesday, seven o'clock."

"I'll be there." I swallow hard. Now I'm committed to go.

"Great!" She grins and I return her smile.

Okay, I'm stepping out of my comfort zone all over the place. No disasters yet.

Monica hands me a glass of ice water.

"Thank you."

She sits in a chair with a glass of wine in her hand. Jeans and a peach cable-knit sweater replace her normal school attire. "Okay ladies, what did you all think of the book?"

Aggie fans herself and we all chuckle. "It packed a lot of heat."

"I'll say, that scene in the shower? My pint of ice cream was soup by the time I remembered it was sitting on my nightstand." Tina patted her pink tinged cheeks.

"I burned two trays of cookies at the bakery because of that scene."

Laughter rings out in the room from everyone.

Sally swats my leg. "No more reading in the kitchen for you."

Conversation circles around the book for several more minutes before drifting off onto tangents and small talk. Monica serves the cake she purchased at my bakery and there are a couple moans of ecstasy as they sample the chocolate nirvana cake. It's three layers of chocolate cake with a one layer of chocolate mousse and one of white chocolate mousse, all covered in a chocolate ganache.

Monica sets her plate on the table. Her bracelets jangle together, tinkling a melodic sound.

"Franny, we rotate our meetings at each of our houses. The hostess supplies food and beverages and picks the book we all will read and discuss."

I can't envision inviting them over to my parents' house. I guess I could host at the bakery. There should be just enough room to fit all of us in front if I add a few chairs.

"Next up is Rebecca."

Monica sits down and all eyes gaze at Rebecca who smiles and reaches over to her tote bag leaning against the couch and pulls out a book. She holds it up for us all to see.

"It's a thriller. I thought we could all use a slight change of pace after the hot and heavy romance this month. We don't want to overload our hormones after all."

Aggie dons a pair of glasses and peers at the book Rebecca is holding up. Sally writes the title and author down on a napkin while the rest of the group snaps a photo on their phones. I grab my phone to do the same.

"It comes highly recommended. My cousin said she reread it twice, so if it's terrible we can all complain to her. She's coming for a visit and will join us next month."

Chuckling, I put my phone down on my leg and take a sip of water.

Rebecca leans towards me. "Let's exchange phone numbers. I can text you the details of the business meeting and my address for next month's book club."

"Oh, of course." I pick up my phone and enter her information and then give her mine.

"That's a clever idea. Franny do you mind exchanging information with all of us?" Monica smiles at me.

After a few mistypes trying to enter everyone's information, Rebecca laughs and takes my phone. "Here, I've got a cheat." She snaps a picture of each member and enters their phone numbers. "I'm always forgetting names, but I remember faces. So, I take everyone's picture and add it to their profile. You can add more of their information later."

"Thanks."

Everyone snaps pictures of one another. Aggie peers into her flip phone. "I don't think mine has that option."

Sally cackles after taking a picture of Tina and then shows the group her picture. Tina has one eye closed and looks a bit like a pirate because she was talking at the time and with the one eye closed it looks like she is saying, “Aargh.”

Tina rolls her eyes and shakes her head. “That always happens. I have to be the most unphotogenic person on the planet.”

“Oh I beg to differ.” Monica scrolls through her phone and shows us a photo of herself a family member posted on social media. Her eyes are closed, she has fish lips, and her hair is wrapped around half her face.

“My dear brother took that while we were on the ferry last year.”

Sally wipes the moisture from the corner of her eye. “Ah, brotherly love is a beautiful thing.”

Monica laughs. “It’s become a bit of a competition between us now. Who can take and post the worst picture of each other?” She shows us the photo she took of him with beer spitting from his mouth. “I took this one after waiting for him to take a drink of beer and then telling him I stuck the tip of the bottle under my armpit.”

We all laugh. Monica isn’t the prim and proper schoolteacher I pictured her as all this time.

Aggie hauls herself up from the chair. “It’s past my bedtime. I need to get going.”

Kerry stands and stretches. “I have papers to grade.”

“Me too.” Tina stands and starts giving out hugs.

I thank Monica for inviting me and promise to see everyone next month for the meeting and then I walk Sally out to her sedan.

“Goodnight, Sally.”

She pauses with her fingers on the handle of her car door. “I am proud of you, Franny. You’re finally coming out of your cocoon.”

“It feels a bit like that.”

She opens the door and turns back to me. “I overheard what Caroline Roberts told you about me.”

Oh boy!

“You haven’t treated me any different and I appreciate it.”

I step forward and lay my hand on her shoulder. “Sally, I admit what she said threw me, but that's really between you and her. I'm here any time you want to talk, but if you don't...well, that's okay too."

She squeezes my hand and stares off into the woods surrounding Monica's house. "I'm not trying to make excuses, but I had just lost my Herbert to cancer. I had retired the previous year and we were planning to buy an RV and tour each of the states. But then he got sick and it spread so quick. It was over before I could catch a breath. I was devastated and in a bad place. In walked Charlie Roberts with his bigger than life personality and I..."

Sally shakes her head and sniffles. "I was stupid."

"You were grieving and from what Mrs. Roberts has told me, he was good at manipulating people to get what he wanted."

"Yes, he was, but I still should have known better and I should have asked questions." She turns to look at me. "I swear I had no idea he was married. In hindsight, I should have. Perhaps I didn't want to know."

I give her a quick hug. "We all make mistakes and it's usually only when we look back that we can see the signs."

She nods. "I'm glad we had this talk, Franny. It's been bothering me something fierce."

"I'm glad too. I'm learning it's not a good practice to keep everything bottled up. Sometimes we have to take the first step and have the uncomfortable conversation."

She climbs into her car. "That's sound advice. I'll see you tomorrow." I close her door for her and wave.

It's good advice. Unfortunately, I haven't been following it myself. It's time Mitch and I talked about my building.

And about our past.

And maybe the future too.

CHAPTER 16

"You've been smiling for the past hour. Did you win the lottery or something?"

Laughing at Sally, I carry a tray of cookies to the front and put them in the case. "No, I'm just in a good mood I guess." I'm wearing one of my new outfits, a gray frilly skirt which ends just above my knees and a lavender wrap blouse. I keep twirling around the kitchen to make it swish against my legs. I have the beginnings of a social life and my life plan is back on track, albeit with some minor adjustments.

My head snaps up when the front door jingles, but it's not Mitch. Sally moves forward to help them and I return to the kitchen to continue baking.

A discreet knock at the back door spins me around. The familiar dark head sends a surge of pleasure through me.

One I'll have to analyze more closely. Later.

When I open the door, he leans on the doorjamb and smiles down at me.

"Any chance I can come in the kitchen to have coffee? I'm beat and not up to braving the front and the possible hordes."

His usual jogging clothes are absent. In their place are jeans and a black hoodie.

"Of course." I step back and he saunters in to lean against one of the counters.

"It always smells so incredible in here. It's like inhaling a piece of heaven."

I grin and head for the front to grab him a coffee. Sure enough the women are gathering and lingering hoping to catch his attention. They must have spotted his truck the same way I did. A few stand near the outside tables I have set up. There's only enough room to fit four black wrought-iron tables between the building and the sidewalk, but it provides a place for those who prefer to sit and enjoy a treat rather than dash in and out. I added a couple of potted plants to brighten up the space.

I spot Vanessa striding down the sidewalk so I grab a danish for him, cram the top on his cup of coffee, and hightail it back to the kitchen.

"You are a goddess." He takes the coffee and inhales deeply before taking a bite out of the danish. "Truly a goddess."

Chuckling, I shake my head while inside I'm beaming.

"So, tell me about your meeting. Was it successful?"

He blows on the coffee before attempting a sip.

"Yeah, they offered me the job. Although I haven't decided if I will do it or not. It's a great script and I find it interesting, but I don't know if I want to take on a new project right now."

"That's terrific! That you got the job."

He shrugs and takes another bite of danish.

"It's given me something to think about."

"What's it about? Would you have to go back to L.A. right away?"

"Actually, they will probably shoot most of it on location in New York. It's about a New York City cop and his descent into corruption."

New York is a hell of a lot closer than Los Angeles, but still not exactly a commutable distance.

"Sounds a bit dark."

"A large part of it is, but there are his relationships with his family and other members of the police force that intrigue me."

"Then you should do it. If they want you to direct it then they'll accommodate your schedule, won't they?"

His mouth lifts in a half smile. "They hinted as much, but I'm not completely sold yet."

He finishes the pastry and sips at his coffee while I roll out the crust for a pie.

"What about your parents? Did you have time to visit?"

"Briefly. Turns out they are taking a cruise down the coast to Mexico. It was poor timing on my part, which is why I'm back sooner than I thought."

"At least you saw them for a little while though, right?"

"Yeah, they were very excited about their trip. I'm glad, they deserve it."

Mitch wanders around the kitchen sipping his coffee.

"What's been going on here while I was away? Anything interesting? Your friend Brian been around?"

I am beginning to wonder if he keeps getting Bobby's name wrong on purpose or if he truly can't remember. Either way I'm not going to remind him in case he ever runs into him.

"No. I went shopping with Olivia and had a good time, much to my surprise."

"Why surprise?"

"Because I hate shopping, normally, but going with a friend made it kind of fun."

He moves behind me and my skin tingles.

"What are you making?"

His voice rumbles over my shoulder. His breath caresses the nape of my neck.

I swallow hard and clear my throat. "Pie. I'm making blueberry pies."

"Yum, I'll have to buy one when they're done. Speaking of which, I owe you for the coffee and danish."

"No, you don't. You've bought me dinner twice. Not to mention my clientele has multiplied because of your fan club."

"Well then, I'll make a point to go in the front more often to drive up sales."

Glancing up to find him peering over my shoulder, the smile freezes on my face and my hands stop rolling the crust.

He smiles and kisses me on the cheek.

I freeze in place. The warmth of his kiss brands my cheek.

"What do you say about me picking you up after work today and we head out to the house so I can show you those kitchen plans?"

I blink several times trying to gather my frazzled thoughts. "That sounds great."

The privacy of his house would provide a good backdrop for the conversation I need to have with him.

"Good, I need to finalize them with the architect so the contractors can be scheduled and the cabinets made. We need to start checking things off our summer list too. We can come up with a plan tonight."

Right, the list.

"All right let's start with one of the easier ones first and we can do it after I get off work one day this week."

"We do have a few hours of daylight left. Then we'll save the longer trips for when you're off on a Monday or Tuesday."

"I don't want to interfere with your schedule. It's just if the bakery is open, I need to be here."

"My schedule is fairly open so we can easily accommodate yours. I'm concentrating on the house right now. If I decide to take that job, then things might change, but that won't start for a while any way. There's plenty of time to finish our list."

I peek up at him watching me make the pies. I place the last shell in the dish and trim the edges.

"You ready for your reward?"

"My reward?"

"I promised you a souvenir if you didn't run off with Butch."

He reaches into his front pocket and pulls out a small silver wrapped box with a tiny bow on top and holds it out.

I raise my hand and then drop it. "Wait, I need to wash my hands." Jogging over to the sink I scrub my hands and dry them.

Mitch is leaning against the counter holding the gift in the palm of his hand smiling.

"You didn't tell me what you like, so I had to guess. When I saw this, I thought of you. I hope you like it."

"I will."

"You haven't seen it yet."

I only get gifts at Christmas and on my birthday from family. No one has ever surprised me with something like this.

I gingerly lift the box from his hand. It's light. The box is jewelry size. Could he have bought me jewelry? I don't wear much only because I don't have many pieces, or the money to buy them.

Flicking a fingernail under the fold of paper, I lift it.

"You're one of those, huh?"

I glance up from the package.

"There are two types of people when it comes to unwrapping gifts, those that rip right in and those who carefully save the paper."

Peeling the paper free, the box rocks in my hand. I set the paper down and lift the lid. Cushioned between sections of padding is a crystal cake on a stand.

"I thought you could put it in the window to catch the sunlight while you were working."

I'm cupping the delicate creation in both hands terrified I'll drop it.

"It's beautiful." Meeting his gaze, I smile. "Thank you so much. I love it."

Carrying it to the window over the counter, I place it in the center on the windowsill and step back.

"What do you think? Will it be safe there?"

Mitch follows me over. "I'm sure it will be fine. I was going to get you a bigger one, but I didn't think it would fit on the sill and I didn't know if you would want to display it somewhere else."

"Oh no, this one is perfect."

The sunlight makes it sparkle reflecting the light.

"I'm glad you like it."

Before I can lose my nerve, I kiss him softly on his cheek. He hasn't shaved this morning and there is rough stubble against my bottom lip.

He gazes down at me for a moment then he smiles and walks to the door. "I'll see you this afternoon."

I hum when the door closes. My hips sway a little to the rhythm dancing around in my head.

After I finish shaping the crusts into the pie plates, I set them in the fridge to chill while I make the filling. Mentally, I have already put one aside for him.

I freeze with my hand on the refrigerator door.

What the hell am I doing?

I'm falling for Mitch. Again.

Closing my eyes, I drop my forehead against the cold door and groan.

No! No! No!

I'm smarter than this.

I glance down at my heart. *Hear me heart, we are not going down this road again.*

CHAPTER 17

My sister, Lucinda, walks into the bakery minutes before closing. Her long blonde hair cascades over one sleeveless shoulder. A form fitting pink sheath dress encases her statuesque form. She is perfect from her symmetrical face to her matching pink polished toes playing peekaboo out of her three-inch heels.

Now, I love my sister. I really do. She has never done a single nasty thing to me. But I love her in Connecticut with her perfect husband in their perfect house with their perfect jobs. Not here where everyone compares the two of us and finds me sadly lacking.

My throat thickens and I swallow hard. I hate myself for feeling this way.

"Surprise!" Lucinda throws up her arms and strikes a pose.

"What are you doing here? Do Mom and Dad know? Have you been to the house yet? Is Mark with you?"

I rattle out the slew of questions while walking over to kiss her cheek and give her a hug. As her perfume settles around me, I remember how much I love my sister and I've missed her. I haven't seen her since Christmas.

"No to all of those." She laughs as she rubs my shoulders. "It's so good to see you."

"You too."

"How late are you open?" She glances behind her to the sign posted on the door. "You're almost done, right? I thought we could surprise Mom and Dad together."

"Oh, I have cleaning up to do and preparations for tomorrow. Besides Mom and Dad will want you all to themselves for a bit." I wave a hand in dismissal. "They see me every day."

Her frown escalates my guilt.

"Okay. You'll be home for dinner?"

I march back behind the counter. "Actually, I have plans, but we can talk after. How long are you staying, anyway?"

"A while."

Looking up from the display case I am straightening, I study her face. She's smiling, but it appears a little strained.

What does a while mean? There's an expression on her face I should explore, but the clock is ticking. Olivia finishes up with the last customer of the day and flips the sign to closed after escorting them out. I introduce them, but Lucinda reminds me they've met before. Of course they have, it's not like this is the first time my sister has come home for a visit and stopped in my bakery.

"I guess I'll see you at home then?"

I nod as I guide her to the door. "We'll have a nice long chat after Mom and Dad fawn over you a bit."

Her disappointment is clear, and I try not to cringe as I'm sure I'm in the running for the worst sister ever award. I lock the door behind her and rest my hand on the knob. Sighing, I turn around.

Shame tinges my heated cheeks as I meet Olivia's questioning gaze. "You can head on home to your boys. I'm all set here."

"Everything all right?"

A nod is all I can manage as I head into the back. The guilt settles over me like a bag of cement on my shoulders weighing me down. The right thing to do is cancel my night with Mitch and go home to participate in my sister's visit. Who knows how long she's here for?

She is obviously here for a reason. It's not like her to pop up out of the blue with no notice.

Oh Lord! Is she pregnant? Is that the news? Her and Mark have been married for a few years. They met in college, at Yale. Yes, she's smart too. In fact, both she and Mark are lawyers. Has she been promoted or something? Would that warrant a trip home?

She would look happier, though, if any of those things happened, wouldn't she?

There's nothing for me to do in the kitchen. I've already cleaned up and prepared for tomorrow, but because I told Lucinda I had more to do as an excuse not to have her waiting around, I wipe down the already clean sink and counters. I make a grocery list for supplies I'm running low on. Basically, I kill time while debating whether my guilty conscious will overpower my need to have a candid conversation with Mitch.

The knock on the back door ends the debate. I have to cancel.

Opening the door, Mitch's blue eyes are shining as he smiles down at me. His periwinkle blue shirt looks soft enough to touch.

A few hours won't make a difference, will they?

"Ready?"

Nibbling on my bottom lip, I nod, and then grab my purse and slip the strap over my head. It's only big enough to hold my phone, keys, identification, and debit card. When I walk to and from work, I can just slip the long strap across my chest and not worry.

I lock the door and pause once again. I'll make it up to her somehow, I swear.

I follow him to his truck in silence. He pulls away from the curb and makes a U-turn to head towards his house on the opposite side of town from my parents' house.

"You're very quiet. Everything okay?"

Tearing my gaze from the scene outside the window I've barely seen, I glance at his handsome profile. If I confess I'm feeling guilty about disappointing my sister, he might insist I go and take me to my parents' house. The guilt is ruining the evening anyway, perhaps I should go.

Ugh! No, damn it! A few hours aren't too much to ask. I doubt I'll be missed. Seriously, I would be just sitting on the couch while my parents fawn over her, anyway.

"Sorry, my mind was having an internal battle, but it's all done now. I'm excited to see the plans for the house and kitchen." I inhale sharply, then sigh. "I forgot the pie I put aside for you."

Mitch smiles. "That's okay, I picked up a few things earlier so we can have dinner at the house. We can save the pie for another time."

My heart latches onto the "another time" and melts a little over the prediction we will spend more time together.

Oh Lord! I need to rein in my emotions.

The wall surrounding this side of the estate is tall enough to keep prying eyes out but allow glimpses of the grounds contained within as we meander its length to the metal gate marking the driveway. Giant evergreens dominate the grounds sprinkled with clumps of white birch trees. The drive circles around to the house. The sight of the majestic house never fails to leave me enchanted.

As I step over the threshold into the house, Mitch speaks from behind me, "I set up a place in the dining room for us to eat. It's nothing fancy, but the walls haven't been torn down in there yet so there's no construction dust or anything to worry about."

When he opens the doors to the dining room, my mouth drops open. A table is in the middle of the room with a blue tablecloth and place settings. I'm not sure what I expected, but not for him to go to any trouble for me. He slips past me to set the box he carried in from the truck on a small folding table by the window and opens a cooler next to it. I recognize the logo on the boxes, they are from the Rosewood Bed & Breakfast. The owner is known for the picnic baskets she supplies to her guests and other patrons.

Mitch places the food on the table and holds out a bottle of wine. "I wasn't sure what you prefer, but this one is a favorite of mine."

I'm not telling him I don't like the taste of wine or any alcohol.

If ever there was a time to partake in a glass of wine, tonight is it. Perhaps it will lighten me up and help me relax.

Please don't let it make me sick.

"It looks fantastic! I can't believe you went to all this trouble."

"It wasn't any trouble." He pours us each a glass and then holds out a chair for me to sit.

Crap!

I tend to panic at this moment when a waiter holds the chair for me in a restaurant. How do you not rest all your weight on the chair so the chair can still be pushed in and not be left sitting there several feet away from the table as the waiter shoves with all his might to get the chair to the table or you're not hovering over it so that your legs get knocked out from beneath you?

My belly quivers and I haltingly walk over to the chair and perch on the edge clutching the sides. I rest most of my weight on my thighs and toes wishing I had started an exercise routine centered around squats and plies. Partly lifting the chair, I manage to scoot forward when he pushes the back of the chair.

Calamity averted.

He starts us off with a salad. I take a hesitant sip of the wine and to my delight I don't hate it. It's cool and smooth with a hint of citrus.

As we progress to the main meal, manicotti, I try to think of a way to broach the subject of buying the building from him.

My glass is half empty and a pleasant warmth tingles through me. Perhaps I should have started drinking wine years ago.

"Have you thought about the director's job you were offered?"

He frowns slightly and shrugs. "Not really, and I guess that's my answer. I want to be passionate over a project before I agree to take it on."

"Is that how you decide?"

"It is now. Back when I was acting, I was just happy to get the offers, so I agreed to most of them."

"Do you miss it? The acting?"

"Not one bit."

"Really?"

"Don't get me wrong, I'm thankful for the acting. It gave me opportunities I never would have had, but I was never that great at it. It was just a job they paid me an exorbitant amount of money for."

"How can you say you weren't great at it? You were so successful."

"I was successful because I lucked out and had people looking out for me. I was decent enough, but as a director, I wouldn't hire me."

He laughs when he looks at me. "The look on your face. Why is that so shocking?"

"I don't know. I guess you really surprised me with your answer. Maybe it's because I assumed acting was what you wanted to do."

"I enjoyed making movies. I didn't like everything that goes along with that. The public attention and scrutiny were not things I coveted or enjoyed. Acting opened the doors for me to do what I really enjoy doing, directing."

"I think you're selling yourself a little short on the acting, but I can understand not wanting to be in the spotlight."

The plastic folding chair is surprisingly comfortable, so I cross my legs and lean against the back taking another sip of wine.

Mitch glances over at the box he carried the food in. "I bought a dessert from the B&B too, but I doubt it compares to any of yours."

"Oh, what is it?"

"Some kind of chocolate cake."

"It never hurts to sample the competition."

He gets up to retrieve the cake and I can't help ogling the view he presents. He certainly has a way of filling out his trousers. My fingers itch to squeeze his cheeks. And I don't mean the ones on his handsome face.

The cake is nice enough, chocolate cake with chocolate frosting, but I'm not all that worried that my business will suffer from the competition. The meal was great though.

I nibble on my lip as he clears the table. Dinner is over and I still haven't garnered enough courage to talk about buying the building from him.

After helping Mitch pack everything up, we stroll into the kitchen where he spreads the plans out on the counter and shows me his and the architect's vision.

It will be a magnificent kitchen.

"Do you cook? I mean this kitchen will be amazing. It would be a shame if you didn't cook. Not that it means you shouldn't have a great kitchen whether you do or don't. I mean you might have a wife someday who cooks."

Or bakes.

"I cook a bit."

"Oh, good, that's good."

I study the plans and wait for the blush on my cheeks to go away.

"I love how this entire wall will be windows to take in the view. One of my favorite spots in the bakery is the counter under the back window in the kitchen so I can watch the sunrise while I'm baking."

I wander over towards the windows. "If you lengthened the island and deepened it a bit, you could have stools on the backside for informal eating. And that area over here would make a perfect little nook to have a circular bench breakfast area. If windows were added it would be spectacular. And you might consider adding another oven and a warming drawer if you plan on entertaining. Adding a counter area with a prep sink over here could be helpful when preparing multiple courses or having more than one person in the kitchen."

I spin around to stride over to the area planned for the refrigerator but bump smack into Mitch. "Oh."

He grasps my upper arms to steady me.

"Too much?"

"No, I like your ideas and your enthusiasm. It's cute how your face gets so animated and you whirl and flitter around like a butterfly."

"Oh, well, um, thanks, I think." I have no idea where to put my hands. They are sort of hanging there in mid-air between us, so I rest them against his chest with a slight pat. Geez, like I'm patting the head of a dog or something.

I take several steps back and grasp my hands behind my back. "There's something I'd like to discuss with you."

"Okay, what's so dire? You've got the same look on your face as you did when we were kids and you confessed you lost that swiss army knife I found on the bank of the stream."

Wincing, I tug on my earlobe. I didn't lose it. I hid it. I was afraid he would cut himself or something.

Maybe now wasn't the time for that confession.

I inhale deeply and let the air out in a rush.

"I had planned on buying my bakery building. I had been talking to Mr. Brick about it, but then he sold it to you instead."

He jerks his head back and then slowly shakes it side to side. "I didn't know. I'm sorry, Franny. No wonder you were so surprised that day on the bench."

Shrugging, I fold my arms around my waist. "Plans change. Although I had really been looking to getting out of my parent's house."

"You were going to live in the apartment?"

"Yup."

"I screwed up your plans, didn't I?"

Meeting his gaze, I smile. "Changed them for sure, but I'm not holding it against you. Anymore anyway."

Mitch takes my hands from my waist and holds them in his. "I'll make it up to you somehow. I promise."

"There's nothing to make up, you didn't know."

"Still, I feel awful about it." His thumbs rub the backs of my hands.

How awful? Awful enough to sell it to me?

Here goes nothing.

Gulping a breath of air, I gaze into his eyes.

"Any chance you'll consider selling the building to me? I'll give you a fair price."

Mitch squeezes my hands. "Of course, I will."

I throw my arms around his neck. "Thank you! Thank you!"

He wraps his arms around my back and laughs.

"You have no idea how much this means. I've been looking at other properties and hating every single one. I was growing resigned to continue renting and trying to find a cheap enough place to buy for me to live in, but that fell through too."

Mitch pulls back to look at me. "Why didn't you tell me any of this?"

I drop my arms and step back from him.

"Fear. Procrastination. Mostly fear."

"Fear of what? Me?"

"Not exactly. Fear of the situation as a whole. I had pinned all my plans on buying the building and when they fell through I kind of spiraled for a bit."

"I don't understand why you didn't say anything right off the bat. Why not tell me that day on the bench?"

"Shock. And it's not like we've kept in touch over the years."

"What does that mean? Did you think I bought the building knowing you had an arrangement to buy it?"

I open my mouth to refuse, but the truth of my suspicions nags at me and I snap it closed.

"Shit! Really, Franny?"

"I admit the thought crossed my mind briefly, but I discarded the idea."

Mitch shakes his head and leans against the counter, folding his arms across his chest.

"I can't believe you thought I would do that to you on purpose."

"I'm sorry."

He frowns. "No, I get it. I don't like it, but I understand."

Twisting my hands in front of me, I scrunch my nose. "So, we're good?"

Mitch gives me a half smile. "Yeah, we're good."

Phew.

"Um, Mitch?"

He looks at me with one eyebrow raised.

"Please don't be offended, but could we have a sales agreement put in writing? See, I didn't do that with Mr. Brick, and well, you see how that worked out."

"I'll have my lawyer draw papers up tomorrow, okay?"

"Thank you."

"Any other terms I should have him include? Does the end of summer work for you?"

Two more months living with my parents? Not ideal but finding another place could easily have taken longer.

"Yes, I really appreciate this. I can't thank you enough."

"Bake me something and we'll call it even."

Laughter tickles my throat. "I had no idea you were so easy."

Mitch winks.

"Any other ideas for designing the kitchen?"

"Can I think about it for a few days?"

"Yeah, I have a meeting with the architect at the end of the week."

I give him a quick salute. "Got it."

"Do you want another glass of wine?"

"I better get home. I have to get up early to be at the bakery." And I hadn't forgotten my sister's arrival.

CHAPTER 18

"They look beautiful together, don't they?" My mother hovers over my right shoulder while I stand at the kitchen sink looking out the window.

An ache radiates across my chest and I press the heel of my hand against it to relieve the pressure.

Mitch and Lucinda stand together on the back patio of my parents' house. The sun makes a halo of light around their bent heads.

Yes, they're two extraordinarily good-looking people.

What is he doing here?

"Like a painting. They would make such gorgeous children together." She plucks a drooping leaf from the plant on the windowsill and stuffs it down the garbage disposal.

I give her a sideways glance. "I'm not sure Mark would agree with you, Mother."

"If you had been home last night for your sister's arrival you would have heard that she left him."

Inhaling sharply, I grip the edge of the granite counter. Her bedroom door had been closed when I got home last night so I had retreated into my room.

I should have knocked on her door.

Instead, I jumped on the excuse to revel privately that the building would soon be mine and my original plan was back on track.

Selfishly, I was making plans for moving out while Lucinda is having her life turned upside down.

Mother taps her manicured nails on the counter. "For the best really. I never cared for him."

Really? Since when? You couldn't have been more thrilled to show him off to all your friends when they started dating and you threw them a lavish engagement party and wedding to which you invited hundreds of your closest friends. I can remember many conversations on Mark and his wonderful background and prospects. Now she claims she never cared for him?

I wince when their shared laughter reaches my ears. I'm transfixed by the sight of the two of them together even as the pain lashes my insides. It's like people who stare at a car accident and can't look away. I've never understood it before. Now I do.

"I can imagine the headlines now: Celebrity Finds Hidden Gem in Small Town and Falls in Love."

"You don't think you're getting ahead of yourself a little? If she just separated from Mark, I doubt she's ready to dive into a new relationship."

"Nonsense. That's exactly what she needs. Besides, the chemistry between the two of them is electric. When Lucinda opened the front door this morning and Mitch was standing there, I instantly knew her pending divorce was perfect timing. You'll see, it's undeniable."

Mitch must have stopped by to see me, not Lucinda. They didn't know each other. I always made sure of that.

The one time Mitch and I ran into Lucinda and her friends during one of our many teenage escapades was when we were getting ice cream at Billings creamery. I had been rambling on to Mitch about my latest epic dream to buy a sailboat and sail around the world. While describing all the exotic countries I intended to visit, I looked down to see Mitch's ice cream was becoming a melted puddle on the ground. About to tease him for wasting his ice cream, I finally noticed what had captured his rapt attention.

My sister reclined on one of the picnic benches surrounded by a group of boys coveting her attention. Itty bitty white shorts topped her long, tan legs. A baby blue halter top allowed her flat, tanned midriff to show. I was sure she chose it to accentuate her blue eyes and of course, her generous cup size. I flounced away without a word, tossing my unfinished cone in the garbage can. Mitch caught up a block away as I morosely meandered along the sidewalk. I brushed him off with a tale of a stomachache and avoided any chance encounters with my sister during my precious time with Mitch.

Maybe it was fate.

I interrupted the start of their fairy tale love story by keeping them apart all those years ago and now whatever cosmic entity which rules our destinies has thrown them back together.

I play with the tiny gold cross on my necklace.

Should I go out on the patio?

"I spoke to your friend Vanessa. She's looking to hire a new realtor because her business is doing so well."

"She's not my friend Mother, nor has she ever been."

"Don't be melodramatic Francine. The two of you grew up together, went to the same school." She waves her hand, the light reflecting from the diamonds in her rings bounces around the room. "Regardless, I did a little research and you can take classes at the community college and take a test to get your realtor's license."

"You want to be a real estate agent? That's great Mother."

"Don't be obtuse! Not me, you."

There is no doubt how little she thinks of my chosen career path.

Swallowing, my gaze bounces off the pair on the patio and out to the lake. I should have gone straight to my kayak once I got home, but instead I lingered to visit with my sister since I bailed last night. A white sail unfurls and fills from the wind and the sailboat skims across the top of the water in front of the house.

"I have a job."

"You need a career. Something that will provide for your future. Something you can build upon. You don't seriously intend to live with your father and I the rest of your days, do you?"

Bitterness fills my mouth.

I wrap my arms around my waist and grip the bony knot of my elbows in my hands. I shift to walk away but stop.

How can she not understand how important my bakery is to me? How can she carelessly discard the hours I devote to making it succeed?

"My bakery is my career. I work very hard to ensure I will have a future there. Why can't you see that? Why do you act like me owning a bakery is an embarrassment to you? Do you not care how that hurts me?"

Huffing out a harsh breath, she stands impossibly straighter. "Always the dramatics! I try to help you and instead of being thankful I'm looking out for you, you whine and attack me with accusations. You're ungrateful and selfish. You expect your father and I to support your whims. When are you going to grow up and be like your sister?"

"I'm not Lucinda and I never will be."

Shaking her head, she whirls away and leaves the kitchen to join Mitch and Lucinda on the patio.

I shove through the door and head for the stairs. If I were wearing shoes, I would have run out the front door.

After working at the bakery all day one of the first things I like to do is take my shoes off and wiggle my toes in the thick carpet by my bed. Of course, Mother has trained me well, so my shoes are in my closet upstairs not left by the front door.

Tears are pressing at my eyes and I'm shaking. Why did I think confronting her would solve anything?

Before I touch the banister, my father walks in the front door.

"Hi sweetheart." He moves forward to kiss me on the cheek. "What's this emergency your mother left me a message about? She told me I needed to come home right away. I'm never sure if I'll find the house on fire or simply a change in dinner plans."

"The later I think."

"Ah, so what's new with you? You've been scarce lately."

"Just work."

My mother's voice trails out of the living room. I fervently hope she's alone, but the soft murmur of Mitch's voice follows before the trio appears in my line of vision.

"Oh good, Grant, you're home. Look who has decided to join us for dinner. I've already made arrangements at the Country Club for the four of us."

My father glances at me.

"Francine has plans."

I stare at my mother for a moment. I don't have plans but it's clear she doesn't want me messing up the dinner dynamic or her matchmaking efforts between Mitch and Lucinda. That's fine, I certainly don't care to witness it.

"Enjoy." I kiss my father on the cheek and smile towards the group without meeting anyone's gaze and then I jog up the stairs to my room.

Plopping down on my bed, I'm not sure whether to scream or cry. Both, maybe.

I listen while the front door opens and closes, and the car starts and drives away. A plop of moisture splashes on my hand.

I guess crying wins.

A SLEEPLESS NIGHT spent tossing and turning resulted in a nightmare about being a bridesmaid at Mitch and Lucinda's wedding. I hit the snooze button on my alarm four times this morning.

Luckily, I can bake in my sleep.

I heard and ignored Lucinda's tentative knock on my bedroom door late last night. I'm mired in guilt once again, but I couldn't face her. My emotions were too raw. Hearing her marvel over Mitch would have sent me over the edge.

Sally taps the bell that signals she needs help, so I grab the layered cake I decorated this morning from the cooler and carry it to the front.

Customers pack the bakery. Why did Sally wait to call me for help? Had I missed an earlier appeal ruminating over my sister and Mitch?

Vanessa stands next to one of the glass cases drumming her purple rhinestone polished fingernails on the top of the glass. Bobby Calvert stands behind her. That, combined with the satisfied expression on Vanessa's face, stops me in my tracks.

Unfortunately, it doesn't stop the cake's momentum.

My hands wobble in an attempt to balance it.

I lose the battle and it somersaults toward the floor.

Lurching forward in a last-ditch effort to grab the cake, I watch with widened eyes and my mouth hanging open as it smashes into the floor and explodes over the tile.

I might have mourned the loss of the three-layer cake decorated with roses and the time to make it if it wasn't for the fact that I was following it down.

Grabbing for the counter, I step in frosting.

I miss the counter when my foot slides sideways and down I go.

Hitting the floor with a jarring thud, I land on my hands and knees.

Cold, sticky frosting smooshes against my chest. The sugary smell overwhelms my nose and throat and I choke.

Or it could be humiliation.

There's a snicker of laughter among the gasps of shock. I can easily identify its owner as my nemesis. She is always there to witness and broadcast my most embarrassing moments. Why should this one be any different?

Wanting to crawl into the back of the bakery, I debate my options.

Slink off in defeat and humiliation leaving behind pity and satisfied glee?

Or, accept I'm a born klutz and laugh it off. Thereby laughing at myself and allowing everyone to join in with me instead of laughing at me.

"Well, I guess cake juggling isn't a thing for a reason."

The chuckles spread and the tension lifts. I shove off the floor and stand, dusting my hands together. A glop of cake and frosting slide off my chest and plummet to the floor. A perfect rose remains stuck on the top edge of my apron. I scoop it onto my finger and peer at it. "You're all that's left of your brethren little guy."

I curtsy to the crowd and laughter ensues once again followed by a smattering of applause.

After grabbing paper towels I clean up the mess quickly before any more accidents can occur. Then I wash my hands and tug on a pair of plastic gloves to help Sally clear out the customers.

There is additional ribbing from a few of the customers which I respond to with a smile. I make sure Sally is the one to wait on Vanessa. I don't want to endure any nasty comments she may have ready for me.

Once most of the customers are taken care of, I disappear into the back to clean up and change into a different apron and shirt.

My lips twitch and a smile blooms on my face.

Normally, I might have slunk off to hide in humiliation spending hours if not full days lamenting over the incident and worrying if people were talking about it. Now, in a few moments time I brushed it off and laughed. Sure, a couple people might gossip over it, but who cares? Most likely, it will evolve into an amusing tale to share. I took control of the situation and made a choice to have fun with it.

Score one for me.

An hour or so later, Sally pops her head in the kitchen. "There's someone here to see you about ordering a special cake."

"I'll be right there."

After grabbing a pad of paper and pencil from my desk, I walk through the archway. A man with dark blond hair is waiting by the counter. He stands eye to eye with me, so approximately five foot ten. His polo shirt and shorts are carefully pressed, not a wrinkle in sight. I don't recognize him, but I can guess he's one of the summer people.

I stride forward with a smile and an outstretched hand. "Hello, I'm Franny. What can I do for you today?"

He flashes me a megawatt smile and grasps my hand covering it with his other hand and holding onto it. "Hi Franny. My name is Tom Keys."

I glance down at my hand still held in both of his and back up to his smiling face. "It's nice to meet you." Is he planning on letting it go any time soon?

"The pleasure is definitely mine. If I had known such a pretty baker was the proprietor, I would have been in much earlier."

The flattery is nice. I'm only human, but I'm not naïve enough to believe he is overtaken by my ordinary looks. This guy has an agenda.

"My parents have a special anniversary coming up and my siblings and I are planning a surprise party for them. I got tasked with handling the cake, but I'm in a bit of a bind. See, the party is this weekend. Is there any chance you could save me from my own ruin?"

Ah, and there it is. He waited until the last minute and now he's hoping charm will get him what he wants.

Is this what Charlie Roberts had been like?

Tugging my hand from his, I put my pencil and pad of paper on top of the counter. "Tell me what you need, and I'll let you know if I can deliver."

"Something special."

I look up from the paper waiting for him to elaborate, but he only smiles at me in return. *Okay then.* Some people come in knowing exactly what they want, or believe they do, others want me to do it all for them with minimal input from them. Tom here is obviously one of the later. Good in some ways, but not necessarily easy. I need guidance to make sure the cake I design fits the occasion and who I'm designing it for. It's my reputation which will suffer if it isn't.

"What anniversary is it?"

"Thirtieth."

"How many people will attend the party?"

"Not too many. Fifty or so, I imagine."

So a full-blown event, not a casual get together, and I bet it's over fifty. "How about favorite flavors of your parents and is there any allergies I need to be aware of?"

"Chocolate is always good, and no allergies. Make it pretty. My mother loves her gardens. Flowers might be nice."

"Does she have a favorite flower?"

"Uh, roses?"

His answers to the remaining questions are just as vague. I can do the cake, but it will cost him. He doesn't flinch at the number. I'm probably undercharging for such a last-minute order. Either that, or money isn't a concern to him.

That must be a nice feeling.

"I will have it ready for pickup at twelve o'clock." I had already told him the time, but I wanted to make sure he understood I was not delivering it. It requires more time to arrange delivery and coverage for the bakery.

"I promise to be prompt." He writes a check for the full amount and lays it on the counter. "There, now that business is complete, why don't you allow me to take you out to dinner?"

So his flirting wasn't just to get me to make the cake at the last minute? He really is interested in me?

"Sorry, she's spoken for."

I spin towards the archway. Mitch is standing in the opening. He must've come in the back.

Tom glances up and then back. "My loss." He takes my hand resting on the counter and kisses the back of it. I stare at it hoping I eliminated all traces of the earlier cake mishap. "You've saved me from disaster. My siblings would have murdered me if I didn't show up with a cake. Perhaps my timing will be better in the future."

Mitch steps to the side to let me pass into the kitchen.

My mind is spinning. Spoken for? He isn't perpetuating the dating myth, is he? I thought that was finished. He hasn't mentioned it lately and after he went out with my sister and parents last night everyone in town will believe they are an item.

Wait a minute, how did he know that wasn't Bobby that I had my supposed crush on?

"You're welcome." He wanders over and pops one of the cookies on the counter into his mouth.

"Exactly what am I supposed to be thanking you for?"

"Saving you from the prepster." He jerks a thumb in the direction Tom had disappeared and stares at my face. "Please tell me that wasn't Barney. You have to have better taste than that."

"No, that wasn't him."

"Damn, these are addictive." He puts another cookie into his mouth.

I couldn't blame him, could I? As far as he knew I am interested in Bobby, and that's who he was trying to help me with. It's not like he could know that Tom is the first guy to ask me out in more than a year, other than Mitch that is for our fake date.

And how is he going to explain our fake relationship to my sister? Had he done so already? Please, no.

If he is continuing the charade, did that mean he isn't planning on dating Lucinda?

"How did dinner go last night?"

He peers at me over another cookie. "Fine, I like your family. Your father has a lot of funny stories."

"Yes, he does."

"What were your plans you couldn't join us? You didn't snag a date with Benji without telling me, did you?"

"No." What am I supposed to say I had no plans and my mother lied because she didn't want me along? "It was a long day. I had a headache." Both true. After my crying jag, my head had pulsed with agony.

Mitch leans on the counter next to me and crosses his arms over his chest. "So, I figure it's time to discuss the art of flirting and letting the guy know you're interested, and he has a chance with you."

CHAPTER 19

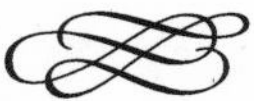

"A common theme my acting coach preached is our facial expressions not only convey our emotions, but they can prompt people to mimic or share the emotion. For instance, you know how if someone smiles it makes you smile in return?"

Not exactly how I envisioned this conversation going.

"Yes, I guess."

"The point is if you project an inviting demeanor, you're likely to receive one in return."

"Okay, so you're saying smile a lot at him?"

Mitch's chuckle sends a warmth surging through me. I love the way his eyes wrinkle at the corners and his eyes brighten.

"Not exactly, but it's a start."

"Margeaux used to practice in front of the mirror making expressions. She is famous for her flirtation with the camera during a photo shoot."

Margeaux, as in his super model ex. "You don't talk about her much."

He shrugs and looks away. "She had a lot of demons. I tried my best to help her, but it was never enough."

"You can't save someone if they aren't ready to be saved."

"Very true. She's doing better now, getting the help she needs."

"That's good." I sketch the cake I plan to make for Tom's parents. "Do you think once she's healthy you'll get back together?"

Holding my breath waiting for his answer, I continue planning the cake. He doesn't respond right away and my lungs demand air. I inhale and peek up at him to catch his expression. He's staring at the piece of paper I am drawing on. Is he contemplating an answer? Did it mean he is considering getting back with her?

His gaze raises to meet mine. "I didn't realize you could draw."

I look back down at my paper. "I can't. It's just a cake plan."

"That's a detailed cake. I have trouble drawing anything beyond a stick figure."

Shrugging, I tap the pencil against the paper. Is he avoiding my question?

"And the answer is no, I'll always care for Margeaux, but we're just friends." Mitch rubs his hands together. "So, back to the flirting. The eyes play a big part too."

Dropping the pencil, I lean my hip against the counter next to him. He faces me and taps the corner of my eye with his index finger.

"Make eye contact and keep it a little longer than a glance. Don't just drop your gaze, hold his."

I swallow hard and stare into his blue eyes. My heartbeat speeds up the longer we gaze into each other's eyes.

"A touch can convey a dozen words in an instant." He covers my hand with his own and raises his other hand to trail a curved finger along the side of my face.

Goosebumps multiply down my arms.

"And of course, the kiss can say it all." He lifts my chin and drops his gaze to my lips.

Mitch's head bends slowly toward mine. When our lips meet, my whole body sighs in relief.

His hand slides along my jaw to cradle my head and his other hand slips along my side to flatten against my back. My hands raise, seemingly of their own accord, and loop over his shoulders so my fingers can delve into the thick, soft hair on the nape of his neck.

The kiss deepens and our tongues begin a hesitant dance.

The pressure of his hand at my back increases, tugging me flush against his body. A soft moan whispers between us, and I realize it was mine.

Our mouths devour one another's as he maneuvers me so my back is against the counter, pressing our bodies even closer together.

A loud clearing of someone's throat echoes through the kitchen.

Mitch drops his hands and steps away from me.

I spot Sally standing in the archway between the front and back of the bakery and my cheeks burn. "My shift is over, and Olivia has arrived."

I open my mouth to respond, but no words come so I nod instead and wrap my arms around my waist.

"I guess lessons will have to continue later. How about scratching off hiking from our list today? You free after closing?"

Hiking?

"Yeah sure."

Mitch snags a cookie on his way out the back door. My gaze tracks him until he disappears out of view. How could he kiss me like that and then waltz away? It had to mean something to him, didn't it? He was an actor once and had kissed more than one female lead. Was that all it was, another act?

His hardened body pressed against mine indicated he had certainly been feeling something. I managed to turn him on.

Arousal meant attraction, at least on some level. Didn't it?

The floor above creaks from Mitch walking across it. The water turns on in the shower upstairs. It's the middle of the day, and Mitch showered after his run this morning.

Perhaps he found himself in need of a cold shower after his kissing lesson.

Smiling, I remove the rest of the cookies from the cooling racks. I wasn't the only one affected by that kiss.

~

During the lull after lunch, I ran home to get sneakers, shorts, and a T-shirt to change into after work for the hike. Okay, it was more like a speed walk than a run.

"Got a hot date with the town's sexy new resident again?"

Olivia leans against the trim in the archway to the kitchen. I've got the kitchen work completed early and I am about to go change.

How could I possibly explain the fake girlfriend and crush plan to her without sounding like a complete idiot? Answer… I can't.

"We're going hiking and it's not a date, we're friends."

Her gaze swerves from me to the back door as it opens and Mitch walks in.

My shoulders tense.

Will he find Olivia attractive?

Duh, of course he will. She's a beautiful blonde.

Swallowing my insecurities and shoving them into a corner of my brain in a trunk with a giant padlock, I smile.

"Mitch this is Olivia, my friend and invaluable helper here at the bakery."

They both stride towards one another and shake hands.

"Nice to meet you."

"Same, I'm a fan of your movies. Especially *The Last Redemption,* you totally deserved the Oscar for that film. I cried bucket loads watching it—both times."

"Thanks, I appreciate it. The script was brilliant and the actors brought it to life along with an extensive crew."

Not an arrogant bone in his gorgeous body. He could easily take credit for choreographing the masterpiece, but instead he praises others' efforts.

My heart soars.

"Enjoy your hike you two." Olivia waves as she leaves.

"Thanks Olivia, see you tomorrow. Tell Timmy and Tommy hello for me. I still owe you a babysitting stint."

"Oh, don't worry, I won't forget. I'm holding it in reserve."

Laughing, I glance over to Mitch when the door closes behind her.

"Her kids, I presume?"

"Yes, twins, they're adorable."

"You ready to go?"

"I just need a quick minute to change." Yanking off my apron, I grab the bag of clothes and sneakers from my desk chair and go into the bathroom. "Why don't you grab two waters from the cooler out front?"

"I've got everything we need in the truck."

"Okay, I'll be quick." I close the door and slip off my shoes while tugging my blouse over my head instead of unbuttoning it. A button pops off and pings against the mirror before dropping into the sink.

"No rush."

With my arms still held hostage over my head by the top since I didn't unbutton the sleeves either, I glance at the closed door and cringe. I can just imagine the look on his face if I have to ask for his help to extricate me from my clothes.

I'll rip the shirt to shreds first.

It's already lost a button, anyway. The chances of me sewing it back on? Slim to none. It will sit in a pile on the floor of my closet with other damaged garments needing repair until I purge the closet and chuck them all.

Stuffing my head back into the blouse and shimmying until it falls enough for me to unbutton the sleeves and remove it properly, I strip and don the jean shorts and a yellow T-shirt. I hop around on one foot trying to put my sneakers on in the confined space and bang into the wall.

"Everything okay?"

Cringing, I finish tying the sneaker. "All good." I need thicker walls in here.

I cast a last glance in the mirror, smooth stray hairs back into my ponytail and open the door.

"Sorry, my clothes and I had a slight disagreement."

His chuckle dies as his gaze rakes me from head to toe.

Did I forget to button my shorts or something?

Peering down, I inspect my clothes. Everything is in place.

Mitch clears his throat and opens the back door. "Ready?"

"I think so, but to be clear when you say hike you mean a stroll up a hill, right? Not a mountain climb, or an intense scrabble over trails only a mountain goat would traverse."

"Don't worry, I picked something simple. There's a beginner's level trail right here in town. It goes to the top of a hill for a nice panoramic view of one of the smaller lakes and it's only a few miles round trip."

Crossing behind the sporting goods store into the parking lot where Mitch parked his truck, I wonder if I should ask for a more specific number other than a few. Are we talking three or four, or anywhere up to ten?

There's a large brown backpack on the passenger seat when he opens the door for me. Mitch stuffs it behind the seat.

What's in the backpack? What do we need besides a couple of bottles of water? His definition of a hike and mine probably vary greatly. Peeking at his shoes before he disappears around the front of the truck, I silently groan.

He's wearing hiking boots, not sneakers.

Settling into the seat and shutting the door, I pull the seatbelt across me and hope I'm not going to need physical therapy after this jaunt up a hill. Or a rescue team.

"I thought we could have a picnic dinner when we reach the top so I have a couple sandwiches and stuff."

"Oh, do you want me to grab dessert from the bakery?"

I didn't realize we were having dinner, but it is already five o'clock.

"Nope, got it covered."

Mitch takes a couple of side roads I didn't even know existed and drives into a small empty dirt parking lot. There's a brown sign pointing to a dirt trail into the woods.

Here we go.

I stand next to the truck wiping my damp palms on my shorts while he puts the backpack on.

"Oh, one second." I leap forward and grab my phone out of my purse before he shuts and locks the truck door.

Stuffing it into my back pocket, I follow him over to the path.

Tall trees with thick trunks line the trail for the first stretch. Once the path veers up, the trees become more spread apart. Small gray rocks jut up from the ground turning the hike into an obstacle course for someone like me.

"Look on the branch to the right."

I gaze in the direction he's pointing. A bright red cardinal perches on the branch amidst the green leaves.

"Pretty."

"It's a male. The females are mostly brown with reddish accents."

I can relate.

The bird puffs up, emits a metallic chirp, and then flies away.

The sun beats down on us as we climb ever up in a winding pattern. I wipe my brow with the back of my hand. I should have thought to bring a hat.

Mitch is in the lead. There isn't a speck of perspiration on him or any labored breaths drifting back. Of course, they might be hard to hear over my own huffs and puffs.

"How are you doing?"

I smile at him glancing over his shoulder.

"I'm fine."

"It's not much farther."

Oh good, so less than an hour each way, and the way back is downhill so if I make it to the top it should be smooth sailing from there.

A thick tree root winding underneath the path negates that theory and I stumble over it, smacking my hand against the papery bark of a cedar tree.

"You okay?"

Mitch grasps my arm and inspects me.

"Yup, I need to pay attention to where I'm stepping is all."

"Do you need a water break or can you wait until we get to the top?" He checks the app on his phone he's using to monitor our progress. "It's about five more minutes."

I wave an arm towards the path. "Lead on."

Other than a stubbed toe and a slightly dinged ego, I'm fine.

The path ends on a wide granite ledge. Baby blue sky dotted with puffy cotton balls of white are overhead. Beyond the ledge, treetops drop off like a ski jump ending in the distant blue gray waters of a lake which appears no greater than a pond even though I know it's several miles long and wide.

Mitch walks close to the edge and I squeak in alarm.

He looks back at me. "It's something isn't it? Come on over here."

"Uh, no, I can see just fine from over here. Could you please move away from the edge?"

Chuckling, he takes a step closer and peers down.

"Mitch!"

"Relax, there's another ledge a couple feet below and another a few feet beyond that. At worst, I'd have a couple of scrapes if I slipped."

"I'll take your word for it."

He smiles and walks toward me.

"How about water and a sandwich?" Sliding off the backpack, he looks around the rocky plateau and wanders over to a flat spot underneath the canopy of branches and leaves from a large tree.

I gingerly step over the rough surface to join him searching for any creepy crawlies along the way. I may have been a bit of a tomboy growing up but that didn't extend to playing with bugs or snakes.

Mitch spreads a green plaid blanket over the rocky surface and stacks water bottles, wrapped sandwiches, chip bags, containers of cut up fruit, and napkins onto the blanket.

"Your feast awaits, fair lady."

Smiling I plop down on the blanket and fold my legs together in front of me, facing him.

A breeze rustles the leaves overhead and cools the nape of my neck.

I guzzle half the bottle of water while Mitch unwraps his sandwich and takes a bite.

"What do you think of the hike so far? Is the view worth the walk up?"

"Yes, I could and would do this again."

The air is crisp and clean. Not a single motor or any other evidence of modern technology can be heard.

"Good, then we'll have to plan another one. Soon you'll be hiking the advanced trails. We'll have to get you proper footgear first though."

"Let's stick to the beginner trails for a while before tackling anything harder. I'm more of a wader than a diver. I like to get my feet wet, then cautiously submerge while the rest of me acclimates."

"I seem to remember a different scenario."

The kayak incident will haunt me for years. I scrunch my nose. "There's choice and there's involuntary participation."

Turkey, ham, roast beef, and swiss cheese on a ciabatta roll with lettuce, tomato, and honey mustard are all layered together in a rainbow of colors and delicious crunch. My stomach thanks me with a low rumble.

I peek at Mitch to see if he noticed, but he is opening a bag of chips.

"Are you a sweet or salty person?"

One eyebrow raises and he glances at the chip in his hand. "I can't be both?"

"Most people crave one or the other. I, obviously, am a sweets person."

"You'd be in the wrong business if you weren't. I like chips with a sandwich, but if I had to choose one or another, I'd have to pick sweets. In case you haven't noticed, I have a thing for cookies and chocolate of any kind."

"I may have noticed."

He winks and bites another chip.

"What's your favorite meal? If you could have anything what would it be?"

After taking another bite of his sandwich and a sip of water, he shrugs. "I don't have a favorite. I like pretty much everything. What about you?"

"That's easy, all desserts."

"A meal with only desserts?"

"Yes, any regular meal is only what I have to get through to get to the important part."

"Then I hope you won't be too disappointed with what I have for dessert. It's not an assortment, but it is phenomenal."

"Oh?"

Where and from whom did he get dessert?

Mitch pulls a familiar box out of his backpack.

"I snuck into the bakery earlier and bought this after I saw you walking along the docks."

Laughing, I look inside The Sweet Spot box. Two pieces of apple crumb cake are nestled inside with forks and napkins rolled up beside them.

"Sneaky, and it's one of my favorites."

"I know. Sally told me."

After we finish eating, we recline on the blanket resting on our elbows. I tilt my head back towards the sky.

I close my eyes and listen to the birds chirping and the wind blowing. A peaceful lassitude pervades my body all the way to my fingers and toes. I could lie all the way down and take a nap.

"We should start back. We don't want to be traversing the trail in the dark, not for your first hike, anyway."

I don't want to navigate any path in the dark. It would be like holding a neon sign over my head saying danger danger, accident imminent.

We pack everything back into the backpack and I walk as close to the edge as I am willing to get and snap a few pictures of the view with my phone and a half dozen of Mitch hefting the backpack onto his shoulders.

Mitch walks over and puts his arm around my shoulders and holds up his own phone to take a selfie of us with the view in the background.

I quickly raise my phone and do the same.

The trip down is less grueling and we descend quicker than the climb up.

The path evens out and I recognize the tree dense area near the parking lot. A spot of black fur under a bush stops me in my tracks.

I bend down to peer under the bushes. Has a cat gotten lost?

There are not many houses around. What if it's hurt?

I step off the path and gingerly step over broken twigs and rocks. "Here kitty, kitty."

"Franny?"

Mitch is walking back up the path toward me.

"There's a cat."

"It might be wild and scratch you. Hold on, wait for me."

He jogs up the path and I glance back down to where I saw the cat.

An acrid stench burns my eyes and nose.

Gagging, I stumble back onto the path.

It isn't a cat, it's a skunk.

Through watering eyes, I see Mitch staring at me in horror before he covers his mouth with his hand and bends over at the waist laughing uproariously.

He sobers quickly when I take a few steps closer and the stench hits him.

"A cat?" A few more snickers escape him before he claps his hand over his mouth and nose.

I don't know if his eyes are watering from laughter or the smell of me wearing *eau du* skunk.

My stomach rolls and I clench my lips together in an effort not to smell myself.

To his credit, he doesn't ditch me. He walks a few steps to the side of me as we reach the open parking area. His truck is still the only vehicle and I'm thankful no one else is here to witness my humiliation.

What am I going to do? I can't get into his truck. His brand-new truck will smell of skunk. Not to mention the pungent smell will nauseatingly drench the enclosed space.

Who can I call? What could I possibly say? No one will want me in their vehicle.

I gaze at the back of his truck.

"I'll ride in the back."

"You're not riding in the bed of the truck. Come on, the sooner we get out of here, the sooner we can get you cleaned up."

Mitch holds open the passenger door but I veer towards the back.

"No. Thank you for offering, but I'm not ruining your new truck and besides even I can't stand the smell of me in the open air, inside the truck it will be intolerable. At least in the back, the wind might wash a portion of it away."

He follows me to the back. "Franny, it's not safe. Don't worry about the smell."

"People do it all the time and it's not like it's a long trip. There's no way I'm getting in the cab. Please don't argue with me."

I climb over the tailgate and plop down on the black rigid plastic lining the bed of the truck.

Mitch stares at me with his arms hanging over the side clearly undecided if he should press the issue.

"Please."

The misery etched on my face must have convinced him. He takes off the backpack and fishes around inside for the blanket and holds it out.

"Here, this should make it slightly more comfortable."

I shake my head. "It'll be ruined."

"I don't care. Take it, it's the only way I'm not going to continue arguing to get you inside the cab."

I grab the blanket and stuff it under my butt.

He glances around the bed and frowns. "I'll go slow."

"The faster you go, the more wind." I unfold the blanket and lie down on top of it. "There, safe and sound. Please just take me home."

The driver's door slams shut and the engine rumbles to life. The bed vibrates and I bounce a little while he drives out of the parking lot.

At least no one will see me down here, unless they have a higher truck.

The road is smooth and the wind whips around me carrying a substantial portion of the stench away from my nose.

My mother will kill me for stepping foot in her house like this.

I close my eyes and take shallow breaths through my mouth hoping I don't swallow a bug.

The truck slows to a crawl and I open my eyes. There are buildings looming on either side of the truck.

Lifting my head, I peer over the tailgate.

Mitch is driving down the alleyway between my bakery and the sporting goods store. I could reach out and touch the buildings if I scoot to the sides.

What is he doing? The alleyway isn't meant for vehicles and why isn't he taking me home?

He parks by the back stairs and hops out.

"What are we doing here?"

"It's closer to the grocery store. You can take a shower while I go buy the ingredients to get rid of the odor. I did a quick search on the internet on the way here, hydrogen peroxide, baking soda, and liquid detergent should get it out."

"What about tomato juice?" Didn't that get out the smell of skunk?

"Old wives' tale. Come on." He opens the tailgate and holds up a hand to help me down but I ignore it and jump. I don't want to make him stink too.

Following him up the stairs with my arms wrapped tightly around my waist, I stop halfway up.

"Are you sure about this? What if I stink up your apartment?"

"Yes, I'm sure."

The door swings open and Mitch moves aside. "The bathroom is straight back attached to the bedroom. Get in the shower and I'll be right back. There's soap and shampoo to start with in there."

He jogs down the stairs and I step into the apartment. The truck starts as I close the door.

Careful not to touch anything unnecessary, I go into the bathroom and turn on the water. I strip everything off me while the water heats and grab a washcloth from the shelf.

I'll replace whatever I contaminate.

The shower drenches my hair and body. I open the cap of the shower gel. A woodsy scent wafts from the bottle. I've caught a whiff of the aroma before on Mitch.

Breathing deep, I stick my nose practically in the gel then squirt a generous puddle onto the washcloth and scrub everywhere. I subject my hair to the same treatment with the shampoo.

Once I'm done washing several times, I sit on the bottom of the shower and let the water pour over my bent head and rain down on my body. I wrap my arms around my folded knees.

The skunk odor still permeates my skin. The scent of the soap and the deluge of water have dampened it somewhat, or perhaps I'm becoming accustomed to the smell.

God, I hope not.

There's a knock at the door.

"Franny? I've got the stuff and I mixed it. It says to use it right away. I'm going to open the door, okay?"

Oh my God!

Mitch is coming in here?

"Wait a minute!"

I pull my knees tighter to my chest and glance around to make sure I'm covered. What a nightmare. It's like dreaming you went to school naked, only this is real and Mitch will see me like a drowned stinky rat.

The door opens a crack.

"Franny?"

"Just put it on the floor please."

Mitch opens the door and steps in.

I gape and curl tighter into a ball.

He places a pitcher next to the shower and leaves the room all without looking at me.

"I'll bring more."

When the door closes behind him, I open the door and grab the pitcher. A bubbly concoction swirls inside.

I stand up and dump it over my head.

Mitch brings me two more mixtures. Each time I huddle on the bottom of the shower while he places it on the floor and leaves keeping his gaze averted.

The water grows cold, so I shut it off and grab a towel.

My clothes are gone. He must have taken my discarded clothes during one of his deliveries. Not that I would have put any of them near me again, but I don't exactly relish him handling my undergarments either.

I would have worn something sexier if I had known this would happen.

With my track record, I shouldn't have left the house wearing anything but my best.

The thick towel is large enough to cover me from my chest to the tops of my thighs, but what do I do now?

There's a soft knock on the door.

"I put clothes on the bed for you."

"Thank you."

I open the bathroom door and peek out. A pair of blue sweatpants and a pullover sweatshirt are folded on the bed.

Checking to see the bedroom door is closed, I drop the towel and pull on the clothes.

They are soft and warm and I snuggle a bit before picking up the towel from the floor. Not sure what to do with it, I end up putting it back in the bathroom.

Mitch is standing in the living room when I open the bedroom door.

"So, ready for another hike?"

CHAPTER 20

Mitch and Lucinda sit together on a bench in the park. On *our* bench. Their heads are angled towards one another. The wind carries away their words, but I can tell they're deep in conversation.

The song I hummed walking home from the bakery dies. Yesterday's hike hadn't gone precisely as planned, but Mitch was able to make me laugh about it by the time he brought me home. I had knocked on Lucinda's door, but she hadn't answered. Either she was out or it was her turn to ignore me. Who could blame her?

Instead, I find the two of them together.

Our kiss really had meant nothing to him.

It was only an acting exercise. A lesson to help his buddy, the woman who constantly gets into one mess after another. The kitchen door, the kayak, the skunk, he witnessed them all, and I can't even claim they were isolated events not likely to happen again.

It's the story of my life. A never-ending string of clumsiness or plain stupidity. I mean who sees black and white fur in the woods and thinks it's a lost or injured cat? No, a sensible person would know it was likely a skunk.

Why did I let my heart get involved? I should've kept avoiding him instead of believing I would be content being just friends. And this pretend dating game was a monumentally stupid idea. The warning signs were flashing but I blissfully continued on my way ignoring them.

He doesn't see me as someone he could become romantically involved with. How could he? I can't compete with Lucinda.

She's blonde perfection and I'm orange disaster.

The urge to run surges through me, but my feet aren't cooperating. My chest shudders and I clasp a hand over my mouth as tears course down my face. Sobs shake my frame and finally my feet heed my distress and I spin away.

I can't go home. The last thing I need is to run into my parents and have them witness my despair. I can't go back to the bakery because then I will have to go back through town, and I don't want anyone to see my meltdown.

Scrubbing my cheeks and sniffling, I skirt the edges of the park avoiding the pathways. My mother mentioned one of the neighbors, the Youngs, are away on vacation. I head in that direction, fervently hoping I got the week right and I'm not going to show up in their backyard and find them entertaining on the back deck or something.

Finally, the park is behind me. I pause in the small stretch of woods between the park and the neighbor's yard. Everything looks quiet, so I step over a branch and work my way towards the lake. They have a small, rocky shoreline with a short wooden dock. I plop down on the end of the dock with my legs dangling above the water and stare out at the lake.

There's a weight in my chest that wasn't there before, and a gnawing pain in my stomach. The thought of Lucinda and Mitch becoming a couple and having to endure family gatherings and making polite chitchat while my mind is screaming in pain is more than I can bear.

I'll have to leave Granite Cove if it comes to pass. Start somewhere fresh, where no one knows me as Fatty Fanny, the family disappointment, the sister hiding in Lucinda's shadow, or the woman who fell for Mitch Atwater again.

Ugh!

I close my eyes and fling myself back to lie prone on the dock.

Get it together. I don't even know for sure if they're dating. Just because they're two beautiful people who look like a match made in heaven doesn't mean they are one.

Fate may be throwing them together, with a great deal of help from my mother, but I shouldn't let my negativity and low self-esteem prompt me to jump to conclusions. It's not allowed in my new life plan.

There could be a perfectly logical, platonic reason for them to be together again, with their heads tilted towards one another like they're whispering endearments to each other.

Sniffling, I rub the tears from my cheeks and angle my face towards the cool breeze blowing off the lake. A loon floats a few yards out in the water.

Solitary like me.

"Franny?"

Sucking in a harsh breath, I glance over my shoulder. A man is standing a few feet behind me. The sun paints him black so I can't identify him. I use my hand to shield my eyes.

"Everything all right?"

It's Bobby Calvert.

I scramble to a sitting position, smoothing down my clothes.

"Um...yeah. Hi Bobby. I was on my way home from the bakery and thought I would just take a moment to enjoy the lake. The Youngs are away, aren't they? I didn't think they would mind." Surreptitiously wiping the rest of the tears from my cheeks, I tuck strands of hair behind my ear.

"Yeah, they're on vacation. They're one of my customers. I was clipping a hedge in the front yard."

Oh. Was it too much to hope he hadn't witnessed my breakdown?

"Cute, aren't they?"

I follow his gaze to the lake. The loon isn't alone after all. Another loon and two babies have appeared.

"Adorable."

"Some find their call sad, but to me, it's peaceful."

He steps closer to my perch on the dock. His blond hair and tanned skin from working long hours in the sun are clear now. He's wearing faded jeans and a plaid shirt with the sleeves rolled up past his elbows and unbuttoned to reveal a white T-shirt underneath. Bobby Calvert is a handsome man.

"I agree with you. I enjoy sitting on my parents' screened porch in the evenings listening to the loons call to each other."

"When dusk arrives, and the lake smooths to a shimmering reflection of the sky, the setting sun is surrounded by waves of color, and then you hear the wail of a loon and the answering call of its mate."

"You paint a pretty picture."

Bobby shrugs and steps from the grass onto the rocky shore. "Mind if I join you?" He points to the jumble of large rocks next to the dock.

I smile and wave a hand. "Be my guest."

He sits on the largest rock a few feet away from me. "Still have awhile to go until the sun sets."

"It's one of my favorite times of day."

"I've seen you kayaking around that time before."

I angle my head to look at his face. "You have?"

"Yeah, I like to fish and it's one of my favorite times too."

Imagine that, I hadn't noticed. I draw my legs up and turn so I face him. "I can be oblivious when I'm focused on something else, or my mind is off dreaming up new recipes to try."

"It's a trait creative types share."

"You think I'm a creative type?"

"You make delicious concoctions in that bakery of yours. It's certainly creative in my opinion."

Smiling, I look back at the lake. "Thank you."

"Especially when you make those raspberry things. I can't remember what they're called, but it's got a flaky crust and then a mouthful of heaven when you take a bite."

"Raspberry turnovers? I'll make a batch for you tomorrow."

"Really? I'll be there when you open."

Laughing, I glance over to catch him smiling while he draws in the dirt with a stick. A rough shape of the loon emerges.

"Looks like you've got a touch of the creative type too."

Bobby laughs. "Not really."

"You have to be creative to shape the hedges and create manicured yards and gardens. I couldn't do that."

We sit in silence enjoying the lake, and I am thankful for his timely interruption of my self-pity party.

"Would you like to get dinner some time?"

I swing my head around to stare at him, still staring out at the lake. He had said the words. I hadn't imagined them. Was fate trying to tell me something? Had I randomly chosen Bobby for my imaginary crush or had destiny been sending me a signal to open my eyes and see what is right in front of me?

He is more in my orbit, a local, quiet like me.

I jump to my feet. "Yes, I would."

He jerks his head back and stares at me.

Okay, I might have been a little over enthusiastic with my response. Did I scare him off already?

A smile stretches across his mouth. "How's tomorrow night sound?"

Sunday night. Nothing on my schedule except to agonize over Mitch and Lucinda.

"It sounds great."

Bobby nods and stands. "Come on, I'll give you a lift home."

"Okay, thanks."

I follow him to his truck parked in front of the house. I can't help but compare it to Mitch's truck. A trailer is attached to the truck with a fancy riding lawnmower and various other landscaping tools. He opens the passenger door for me and moves papers and a hat off the seat for me to sit.

My parents' house is only down the street, so the drive is short. He enters their driveway and parks. "I'll pick you up here around six? Or do you prefer I meet you at the bakery after closing?"

"Here's good." It would give me a chance to freshen up after work.

"I'll see you then."

"Goodnight, and thanks." I climb out of the truck and stroll to the front door with a wave. He waits until I open the front door before reversing and driving away.

What a thought-provoking turn of events.

"Who was that?"

Lucinda is peering through the glass on the side panels of the door. I glance around behind her. Please tell me Mitch isn't here with her. Had he walked her home the same way he walked me home that day on the bench?

"Bobby Calvert."

"Oh, I went to school with him." She turns away from the glass and I can't help but peer at her lips to see if there are any telltale signs of kissing remaining. They look normal. There is a trace of lip balm still evident. Did that mean Mitch hadn't kissed her? If she had reapplied the balm, then it would be clearer on her lips.

"I know." So did I, but Bobby had been in her graduating class.

My mother waltzes into the foyer, her high heels tapping against the floor. "Lucinda, there you are, I want to discuss my plans for a little get together."

I take the opportunity to sail up the stairs. Damning my cowardice with every step along the hallway, I hesitate, but I cannot make myself turn around and go back down the stairs or even wait to see if she comes upstairs. She's left her husband and I've said nothing to her.

I'm a horrible sister.

Tapping my head against the wall, I stare at the stairs behind me. Will she follow me up the stairs or has my mother absconded with her for the night?

Shouldn't she take longer to get over a marriage instead of moving on to someone new? My someone?

Would I care if she was spending time with anyone except Mitch?

No, I wouldn't.

Pushing away from the wall, I continue to my room. I still can't talk to her. If she talks about Mitch, I might burst into tears in front of her or worse, say something I can never take back.

Shutting my bedroom door, I stride to the bathroom and shut that door too. Just in case she follows me into my room if she escapes my mother and her plans. Turning the shower on, I lean against the vanity and close my eyes. My mother is probably planning a get together to throw Mitch and Lucinda together again. Not that they appear to need her matchmaking efforts.

A knock sounds on my bedroom door and I stiffen. Tiptoeing to the closed bathroom door, I lean my head against it and listen.

The bedroom door opens, and Lucinda calls my name. Why didn't I lock it?

I cringe at my silence and hold my breath, waiting for her to leave.

A moment later the door shuts, and I sag against the bathroom door.

This must stop. I can't avoid her forever.

CHAPTER 21

Light dances in his eyes, reflecting from the flames crackling in the fireplace. The antique wall sconces dotted around the room provide a soft golden glow. White tablecloths and short bud vases filled with a single flower decorate each table in the room. When Bobby drove into the parking lot of the White Birch Inn for our date, I had to smile. I've wanted to eat here for a while, but not alone. The inn perches on a small rise at the corner of the cove, providing a sweeping view of the village and lake.

I never go to restaurants by myself, which means I don't eat out much unless it's with family. It's not like anyone will shine a spotlight on me if I do, and point and jeer, but that's the image that pops into my head. One more way I let worrying what other people might think of me to stop me from doing something I might enjoy.

Our conversation flows effortlessly, like between old friends, and neither one of us appears to feel the need to fill the silences with empty chatter. His blond hair has a slight curl to it. I've only seen him wearing a hat before, so I've never noticed. He's wearing tan pants and a white dress shirt instead of the standard jeans. He's put in a little effort. For me?

The waitress takes our orders and Bobby gazes at me. "So, if the date goes well will you make more of those raspberry turnovers you made this morning?"

"You bought half a dozen. You're not sick of them yet?" He showed up right after opening this morning to ensure he got his treat.

"Not by a long shot. I told you they're a weakness of mine."

"I guess so. It surprised me you were there so early on Sunday morning. I prefer to sleep in on my days off."

"My internal alarm goes off at the same time every day whether or not it's a scheduled workday. Besides, a lot of the best fishing is at the crack of dawn. It pays to get out before everyone else does and disturbs the fish."

"You must have seen the beautiful sunrise this morning then. I was watching it from the back window of the bakery."

"I sure did. I trolled along the shore of the cove, watching it rise over the water."

"Did you catch anything?"

"A couple small mouth bass, nothing to tell fish stories about." He smiles and wiggles his eyebrows.

"Nothing about the one that got away?"

"Got away from what?"

I freeze, reaching for my glass of water. Blinking several times, hoping the sight before me is an illusion, I stare stupidly at Mitch standing next to the table with Lucinda a step behind him. My stomach drops into the black hole yawning under my chair and I want to dive in after it, anything to avoid facing them.

Slinking under the table is out. So is forming a fake smile to act like I am happy to see the two of them together.

Bobby stands and shakes Mitch's hand. "Bobby Calvert, nice to meet you. Franny and I were talking about fishing."

"Ah, fish, not my area of expertise. You must know my date, Lucinda." Mitch puts his hand at the small of her back and I look away.

Lucinda smiles warmly. "Of course, we went to school together. Hello Bobby. It's nice to see you."

Bobby gives a single nod and places a hand on the back of his chair, glancing at me.

"You don't mind if we join you, do you?" Mitch doesn't wait for an answer but holds out a chair for my sister to slide into wearing a black skirt and blue shell. He then strides around the table to take the chair on my right.

Just kill me now!

A double date with Mitch and Lucinda is something straight out of my nightmares. I twist the napkin in my lap and pray for divine intervention.

Bobby settles back into his chair. He gazes at me, perhaps looking for a clue on how to proceed or what is transpiring, but I am at a complete loss and offer no help. What should I say? No, you can't join us. No, you cannot date each other at all.

My fingers are digging into the sides of my chair, I could excuse myself to use the bathroom and sneak out a back door. The restrooms are in the back of the building. I bet I can make it through the kitchen to a back door from there.

It would only prolong the inevitable. I have to face all these people on a regular basis. Which is worse enduring the meal, or living with the shame of abandoning my date and running and hiding?

"I haven't been to the inn in years. It's lovely, isn't it? And the fire in the fireplace is a nice touch." Lucinda smiles as she glances around the table.

Bobby and I both murmur, "Mhmm," and then share a smile.

The waitress arrives with two additional place settings and hands Mitch and Lucinda menus.

"What did you order, Franny?" Mitch stares at me over the menu opened in his hands.

"Um, Pasta Bolognese."

"Sounds good. I'll have the same. Lucinda?"

We all glance toward her as she smiles up at the waitress. "I'll have the Chicken Caesar Salad, please."

After the waitress leaves to put in their orders, Mitch looks at Bobby. "So, Bobby is it? Tell me about yourself. What do you do? Ever been married? Kids? Skeletons in the closet?"

Eyes bugging out of my head, I slide my cross back and forth on my necklace and glare at Mitch, but he ignores me.

Lucinda coughs into her napkin and then takes a sip of water.

Bobby rotates his glass. "I own a landscaping business. No. No. And none of your business."

A flat smile on his face, Mitch returns Bobby's stare. "Fair enough."

Lucinda sets her glass down, rests her elbows on the table, and leans toward Bobby. "Do you remember the state championship game senior year?" She looks at Mitch. "He threw a touchdown pass that broke the school record. Bobby was the quarterback."

"It was a long time ago." Bobby sips at his beer.

I forgot that he had played on the football team.

Mitch scoots his chair closer to mine, angling it toward the fireplace. He hooks his arm over the back of the chair and crosses his ankle over his knee. "I never played any sports myself, at least not school sports. I didn't regularly attend high school so there wasn't the opportunity."

He'd been busy making movies as a teenager. I never really thought about what it must have been like for him. "Were you tutored on the set?"

"Yeah, there are all sorts of regulations for child actors. One of them is to ensure I could get my studies done. I got my G.E.D."

"I can't imagine missing out on high school. It was such a fun time." Lucinda shakes her head and frowns.

Yeah, for you, maybe. Personally, having a tutor and skipping the drama and angst of high school would've been heaven for me.

Lucinda brushes a lock of hair out of her eyes. "So you didn't go to prom, school trips, senior night, graduation?"

Mitch glances at her and smiles. "Nope, but don't get me wrong, I'm thankful for the experiences I did have instead."

The only one of those that I attended was graduation. It was mandatory if I wanted my diploma.

Lucinda leans towards Bobby. "Bobby, can you imagine missing out on all those wonderful experiences?"

"Sure can since I didn't go to any of them either." He takes a long drink of his beer and watches the fire.

Really? Why not? He'd been popular in school, the quarterback. I want to ask him, but he doesn't look happy with the topic of conversation. Or perhaps he's upset with our uninvited guests.

"Oh, I hadn't realized." Lucinda grabs a piece of bread from the dish in the middle of the table, but then stares at it like she doesn't know what to do with it. She drops it on her bread plate and puts her hands in her lap.

Thick silence permeates the table. I lean forward in my chair. "Personally, the only one I attended was graduation, so it looks like you might be in the minority on this one Lucinda. It's nice that you have such fond memories to cherish though." Lucinda smiles at me and I spot the waitress carrying a platter towards our table. "Oh look, our food is ready."

The waitress arrives and distributes our meals. Lucinda picks up her fork and pushes the lettuce around on her plate. Bobby cuts into his steak. Mitch winks at me before twirling his fork in the pasta and taking a bite.

I nibble at my pasta and calculate how long until the dinner will be over and how I can signal Bobby it is time to leave.

Lucinda dabs at the corner of her mouth with a napkin. "Mother is planning a Fourth of July party. Mitch and Bobby, you must come."

"I'd love to."

I glance at Mitch. Mother will be thrilled. Of course, she is probably only throwing it to matchmake between Mitch and Lucinda, so if he doesn't go, she is likely to drag him there herself.

Bobby gives a faint smile but doesn't respond, he keeps eating his steak.

Is he upset they interrupted our date? He had gotten rather taciturn after their arrival. Is it Mitch? Bobby doesn't seem the type to be awestruck by celebrities. Perhaps he hadn't cared for Mitch's questions, but then he hadn't seemed to care for Lucinda's either. I can't imagine someone not taken with my sister, especially someone she went to school with. I thought all the boys were in love with her back then.

Lucinda describes our mother's plans for the party. "Everything will be decorated in red, white, and blue, of course, and we'll have a wonderful view of the town fireworks on the lake. The invitation list keeps growing. She'll end up inviting half the town before she finishes."

"The important question is what are you making for dessert?" Mitch grins at me.

"Mother prefers her parties catered."

His grin fades and is replaced with a frown. He reaches under the table and squeezes my hand resting in my lap.

I jump, knocking the leg of the table with my knee.

The table rattles and water splashes out of the glasses.

"I'm sorry!"

Mitch chuckles, releases my hand, and picks up his napkin and dabs at the water pooling on the edge of his plate. "Don't worry about it."

"Franny, I'm sure Mother would love to have you make a dessert if you want to, but she probably wants you to relax and enjoy the party rather than have to work."

I smile at her. I don't bother saying that our mother has refused each time I have offered to bake something for one of her get togethers. She's never stepped foot in my bakery either. My father has, he'll swing by after a round of golf for a treat and whisper, "Don't tell your mother," in a joking conspiratorial way. I'm never sure if he means don't mention the treats or that he visited my bakery.

I guess I don't want to hear the answer.

"Mitch, describe a few of the fabulous Hollywood parties you've been to." Lucinda nibbles on her salad.

"I'm afraid I'm not much of a party person. My life is tame."

"Oh now, don't be so modest, surely you must have several juicy stories to tell us about living in Hollywood and working with celebrities."

Mitch sets down his fork. "I've never lived in Hollywood. I have a place up the coast." He shrugs. "Celebrities are just people. They all have their quirks, the same as everyone else. The only difference is they are on display for the public to see. I don't have any exciting stories to share."

Pushing my food around on my plate, I break off a tiny piece of the freshly made egg noodles and scoop a bite full of the sauce onto my fork. My appetite fled around the time Mitch and Lucinda arrived. But I don't want to call attention to myself or my predicament by not eating anything. The savory sauce is flavorful and I'm sure on another occasion I would enjoy it, but it sticks in my throat and I have to guzzle half my water glass to get it to go down.

Lucinda glances around the table. She is trying to engage everyone in conversation, but we aren't cooperating. Bobby's limited responses dissuade her from continuing the nostalgia route. Mitch isn't giving her much either. I cast around for a safe subject to broach, but I am coming up empty.

The waitress refills my water glass and I run my fingers through the cool condensation gathering on the glass. "Has anyone heard the weather report for the next couple of days?"

Ugh, there it is, my old standby.

"I think it's supposed to be sunny." Lucinda chimes in and I smile and glance at Bobby.

"Bobby, that must be good for business. It must make things difficult for you when it rains."

He looks up to meet my gaze.

I drop my hand, hoping this will start a conversation to alleviate the awkward silence that has descended over the table.

Instead of my hand landing on my leg as I intended, my palm hits the edge of my plate, toppling it off the table into my lap.

The pasta covered in thick sauce lands on my thigh and then slides to the floor with a loud splat to join the wobbling plate before it settles. A long noodle trails down my leg like a snake.

I stare at the mess in horror.

How am I going to joke this one away?

Mitch jumps up and squats next to me with a napkin and starts wiping my leg. The dress I'm wearing is black, but there is no way even the dark color can hide this disaster.

"I…I got it, thank you." I grab my own napkin and attempt to clean up the mess I made, but my hands are slow and unsteady. My leg is hot from the sauce, but my face and neck are on fire.

Lucinda calls over the waitress who takes over my fruitless efforts. She arrives with a handful of napkins and a busboy who disappears with the plate and a pile of napkins after efficiently cleaning up the mess.

I stare at the shiny spot on the floor.

Mitch tosses a handful of folded money on the table and grabs my hand. "Come on Franny, my apartment is right down the street. You can get cleaned up there." He glances at Bobby when he stands. "You can make sure Lucinda gets home, can't you?"

He doesn't wait for an answer but tugs me to a stand and starts walking.

I glance at Bobby and mumble, "I'm so sorry!"

Trailing after Mitch with my face on fire, I stare at the floor in front of my feet. I had asked for divine intervention to end the dinner but hadn't counted on my own clumsiness rearing its ugly head.

But then again, here I am heading for Mitch's apartment with him rather than enduring a painful dinner with him and my sister.

Perhaps my clumsiness is a godsend.

CHAPTER 22

Mitch holds my hand in a tight grip and strides through the restaurant. Luckily, my legs are long, and I can keep up. He gives a short nod or wave to the few people in the restaurant and waiting area who are brave enough to approach him, perhaps for an autograph or picture. Mitch is usually courteous and accommodating to fans, but tonight he appears on a mission to get me out of the restaurant.

Once we leave the inn, he turns toward the sidewalk rather than the parking lot. I spot his truck out of the corner of my eye.

"What about your truck?"

"I'll get it later."

Okay, what is the all-fired hurry? Yes, my leg is wet from the heap of pasta and sauce and my dress has a wet spot that resembles medusa and her head of snakes, but I've done worse to myself with my clumsiness.

"Where's the fire?"

He glances over his shoulder at me, tiny lines appear between his dark eyebrows. "What?"

"You're not planning on breaking into a jog or anything, are you? Because I tried it once, and only once. Unsurprisingly, it was a disaster. My feet somehow tripped over themselves and I fell, twisting my ankle and leaving a nasty scrape down the length of my arm where I hit the pavement."

Mitch slows his pace and shakes his head. "Better?"

"Yes, thank you."

His thumb rubs the palm of my hand in a lazy circle while we stride down the sidewalk.

The outside lights of The Sweet Spot shine ahead. Only a few buildings separate my bakery from the inn.

Climbing the stairs to the apartment, nerves build in my system. What will happen behind that door? Will he hand me another pair of sweatpants and hoodie and then drive me home? In the truck he left back at the inn?

Miserable and reeking of skunk the last time I was here, I hadn't looked around much.

The interior of the apartment isn't much different from what I remember. Considering I had planned on living here, I have imagined the space many times. I want to paint the worn oak cabinets in the kitchen white. It is a small kitchen, approximately the size of my mother's walk-in closet, but it's enough space for one, maybe two. The counters are a brown and tan Formica and the sink is a basic stainless-steel model on the small side, but again enough to accommodate a single person living here. I will change out both though when I move in.

He hasn't painted or changed anything in the living room except to add a couch and television. The brown rug and cream-colored walls are the same. It's rather spartan, and much cleaner than I envisioned a bachelor's apartment to be. There are no dirty dishes lying in the sink or on the counter even.

He hasn't let go of my hand and continues through the living room towards the bedroom and bathroom. The same cream walls and brown rug decorate the bedroom. A king-size dark wooden bed and dresser dominate the room.

My gaze is riveted on the bed. It's made. Was it made last time? I can't remember.

Who makes their bed unless they're expecting company? My mother does, of course, and expects me to. I've been chastised more than once for not completing the task. Does a single guy make his bed and clean up the apartment if he's not expecting company? He had been on a date with Lucinda. Had he planned to bring her back here?

A sick knot forms in my stomach.

"Here's a T-shirt. It'll be long, but..." He shrugs and opens another drawer and snags a pair of shorts and hands them both to me. "I'm fresh out of sweatpants and sweatshirts."

Of course he is, I still have both sets from my previous disasters. I should have washed and returned them. Instead, I sleep in them.

"I'll wait out in the living room." He jerks his thumb in its direction, then smiles. "Unless you need any help?"

I slow blink. Is he flirting with me?

What would he do if I said yes? Swap plans with one sister for another?

A chill passes over me.

"I think I've got it."

He points towards the bathroom. "You can wash up in there."

I stare at the door he closed behind him. Had he planned to seduce my sister, but now is flirting with me? Am I crazy and reading more into everything than what is really there?

I start to sit on the bed but halt halfway. I don't want to get sauce on his bed.

Carrying the clothes into the bathroom, I set them on the vanity and shut the bathroom door. There aren't any bottles of aftershave, lotion, or even toothpaste on the beige countertop. I am tempted to peek in the drawers of the oak vanity but I restrain myself.

There's the same shampoo and shower gel from my last visit on the shelf in the shower.

Jerking the dress over my head, I roll it into a ball and set it aside. The poor dress is past saving at this point. I slip off my sandals and nudge them aside.

The scent of garlic and Italian seasonings fill the small space. Hopefully it's the dress and not me. Plucking a cream-colored washcloth from a shelf over the toilet, I run the water until it is warm and then wet the washcloth adding a bit of soap to clean my leg. I might as well rinse the area on my dress while I'm at it, in case there's a possibility it can be cleaned.

Rolling it like a long tube, I place it on the other side of the vanity and inspect the clothes he's given me to wear. At this rate, I'll have my very own Mitch drawer of clothes.

The white T-shirt ends at the top of my thighs. I momentarily wish I was a confident woman who could sashay out in just the T-shirt. What would he do or say? Would he ignore it, being used to women dressed in so little? Would he find me attractive? Or would he act uncomfortable and ask me where the shorts are?

I tug on the navy blue shorts. He gave them to me to wear after all, and I'm not brave enough to test his response. When it comes to my baking, there is no self-doubt, but everywhere else in life I am a churning miasma of uncertainty.

My reflection stares back at me from the mirror. My wild hair is tamed into a French braid and the makeup I sparingly applied for my date with Bobby is still miraculously in place. I tend to forget when I wear makeup and by the time I do remember to look in a mirror, my mascara is smudged under my eyes and my lipstick is half chewed off.

I open the bathroom door and shuffle into the bedroom with my dress in my hands. The bed creaks when I perch on the edge to put on my sandals. Cringing, I glance at the door. A cabinet opens and closes in the kitchen, so he hasn't gone to get his truck. What is he planning?

Open the door and find out!

I swing it open as he walks out of the kitchen with a mug in his hand. "I thought you could use a cup of tea to warm you up. It's decaffeinated so it won't keep you up late."

"Thanks." I'm not much of a tea drinker, but it is thoughtful of him.

"Do you want to sit?" He signals towards the couch with the mug.

Taking the mug from him, I nod and amble over to the gray couch and sit. The cushion is deep and soft, so I scoot back and rest my back against the corner, cradling the warm mug in both hands.

Mitch goes back into the kitchen and returns with a mug of his own and sits next to me.

"Do you always keep your apartment this clean?"

He glances around and shrugs. "I guess. My parents were strict about cleaning up after myself, and then once I got well known I learned to put away anything remotely personal or it might get stolen or show up in a tabloid picture or something."

So, not a planned seduction of my sister? The night is looking up and up.

"People have really stolen your stuff from your home?"

"Yup, from my hotel room, trailer on the set, some people have no boundaries."

"I'm sorry, that's terrible."

"I'm not in the public eye much anymore so I haven't thought about it in a while, it's just become a habit."

"What do your parents think of you buying a place here?"

"They didn't get it at first, but they've always been supportive of me no matter what I did. They plan to visit at the end of the summer. I'm hoping the house will be far enough along by then for them to stay there."

"That's nice. I have to admit I only have a vague memory of them from the summers you spent here." The tea had cooled enough for me to sip at, so I blow lightly over the top and take a swallow. There is a hint of mint and lemon.

"Yeah, they were going through a rough patch at the time, they didn't socialize much when they were here."

"They obviously worked it out."

"I think that last summer saved their marriage. My mom had been struggling for years with infertility after she had me. She had had another miscarriage that year and it had sent her into a depression. My dad took us here hoping to change the downward spiral they were on."

"That must have been hard on you. I had no idea." Holding the mug with my right hand, I rub his shoulder with my left hand.

Mitch takes my hand from his shoulder, laces our fingers together, and rests them on his thigh. "I wasn't aware of all the details back then, but I knew something was wrong."

Our arms brush against one another. His skin is warm and too irresistible not to lean against. "Your mom had no more children after that?"

"No, they decided it was too painful and didn't want to put any of us through that again. Now she keeps waiting for me to settle down and provide her with grandkids to spoil."

"And how do you feel about that?"

"I'd like a few, eventually."

"A few?"

He chuckles. "Yeah, I bought that big house. It would be nice to have kids to enjoy it." He takes a sip of his tea and rests the mug on his opposite thigh and then looks at me. "What about you? Do you plan to have kids?"

I take a swallow of tea, and then another. How do I feel about kids? "I don't know. I mean I guess I always assumed I would have one or two someday, but I've never really thought about it too much."

"You haven't planned out your future with Bobby?"

"No, I haven't."

"Good."

"Good? What does that mean?"

"I don't see him in your future."

"Oh? You're a psychic now?" Although after the fiasco the date ended in, he is probably right. Bobby isn't likely to ask me out again even if I promise to make him raspberry turnovers.

"No, but you have to admit the date was not going well even before I rescued you."

"Rescued me? The date was going just fine until you and my sister showed up. It all went downhill from there."

"Oh, come on, admit it, the guy barely said two words throughout dinner despite Lucinda's valiant efforts. You needed us there to save you."

Wow, he really thinks I am so completely inept that I can't handle the date on my own. I tug my hand free and lean forward to set the tea on the coffee table.

"Bobby had plenty to say before you arrived. I actually thought it was going well." Yes, I'm a klutz and I made a mess, and I have a tough time thinking of things to say sometimes, but does he really believe I'm such a disaster?

"You need more lessons before you're ready to accept any dates." He sets his cup down next to mine.

He wants to give me more lessons? I don't know whether to smile or cry. On one hand, he thinks I am such a loser I could never get Bobby on my own. On the other hand, more lessons mean more time with him.

Scooping me up in his arms, he deposits me on his lap.

I gasp and latch onto his shoulders to balance myself. My legs dangle over the side of his thighs. "What are you doing?"

"Lessons, remember?"

What kind of lessons require me on his lap?

Not that I'm complaining.

One of his hands rests on my bare thigh under the edge of the borrowed shorts, and the other is wrapped around my back. His lids lower and he leans forward to touch his lips to mine.

There is no slow build up or teasing this time. His tongue immediately seeks an entry I eagerly grant. The taste of mint and lemon fill my mouth.

His hand raises the T-shirt at my back and slides against my bare skin. His palm scorches a path up my back under the shirt.

Mitch's lips leave mine to feather kisses along my jaw and neck. My hands cup the back of his head holding him to me.

He grasps my hip and back and lays me onto the couch and settles over me.

Our gazes lock for an instant. He places a series of drugging kisses on my lips. My eyes drift closed.

My heart pounds in my ears as my body melts beneath the hardness of his.

I'm enveloped by the warmth of his body stretching the length of my own. His knees dig into the couch against my legs enclosing me in his heat. I slip my arms underneath his and clutch his back, praying the pleasure won't end.

His tongue strokes and curls around mine. He caresses my neck and shoulder, weaving a path of fire every place he touches.

A vibration against my leg startles and confuses me until Mitch jerks out of my arms and grabs his phone from his pants' pocket. He glances at the face of the phone and stands, rubbing the back of his neck.

"It's your sister."

He answers the phone and paces over towards the cabinet holding the television.

I scramble to a sitting position and wrap my arms around my drawn knees. Lucinda calls and he drops everything, drops me, to answer.

CHAPTER 23

"You left your purse on the back of the chair at the restaurant. Your sister didn't want you to worry. She has it." Mitch paces in front of the television rubbing the back of his neck.

All I can manage is a nod, not really caring if he sees my response or not. What am I doing here? Spinning romantic fantasies around a man who is way out of my league and has me firmly planted in the friend zone despite the hot and heavy kissing of a moment ago? How could he be so unaffected? A man who is getting involved with my sister.

"Hang tight while I go grab my truck and give you a lift home."

He disappears out the door and jogs down the steps. I gaze at the door and briefly consider making a run for it, but that smacks of cowardice and goes against the new leaf I'm supposed to be turning over.

I will not be able to avoid Mitch or Lucinda, so I better get used to it. That doesn't mean I wish to watch them fall in love, but I don't want to lose his friendship either.

Standing on wobbly knees, I grab my dress from the table and clutch it to my chest. My lips tremble as I battle back the tears threatening to fall.

By the time Mitch arrives in front of the bakery, I am waiting in the alleyway between The Sweet Spot and Ski's and Things, the sporting goods store next door.

The ride home to my parents' house is done in silence. I sense his gaze on me several times, but I keep my head pointed away and look out the passenger window not really seeing a thing.

I don't know what to say.

The ride is blessedly short, and he enters the driveway and parks.

"We need to talk."

My hand freezes on the door handle and a ball of acid churns in my stomach. I can guess the topic of the conversation will be something along the lines of tonight went too far and he doesn't want me to get the wrong idea. Operation fake girlfriend is over.

I wholeheartedly agree, but I'm not ready for that discussion. I need a little distance first.

"Sure, mind if we postpone it until tomorrow? I've got a pounding headache." Opening the door, I jump to the ground before the automatic running board even has a chance to lower and shut the door.

A lie, but it sounds better than saying my insides feel like they're turning inside out.

The headlights are blinding as I trudge in front of his truck. There's a whirring sound as he lowers his window.

"Franny?"

Swallowing the persistent lump in my throat, I angle my head slightly in his direction as I pause at the beginning of the walk.

Please, please don't say you're sorry. Don't say it was a mistake. Don't say you don't want to hurt me, and you value our friendship. Don't say all the things I know you want to say.

"We'll talk tomorrow. Good night."

"Goodnight," I whisper.

I clutch my dress against my chest while I shove open the front door and peek around the entryway. The last thing I need right now is to run into one of my family members.

Thankfully, the house is quiet with no one in sight. I tiptoe up the stairs and along the hall to my room, breathing a sigh of relief as I slip into my room.

It gets stuck in my throat.

Lucinda is sitting on my bed.

"You've been avoiding me."

Judgment time. "Why would you think that?" Evade until I can come up with a reasonable explanation.

My purse is sitting on the bed next to her. I pick it up and find my phone tucked inside. "Thanks for bringing this home for me."

She nods and continues to watch me. "What's going on Franny? Every time I try to talk to you, you make an excuse and disappear."

I sit next to her on the bed and grip the edge of the mattress. "I'm sorry."

"I don't want your apology. I want to know why?"

"Because I'm a coward." My emotions are raw and my control dances on a razor's edge. Tears fill my eyes and I clamp down on my bottom lip.

"Bullshit."

Frowning, I glance at her. That wasn't exactly easy to admit, and I didn't expect her to dismiss it, or swear. My mother frowns on swearing and Lucinda being the perfect daughter, never swears. At least not to my knowledge.

"You're one of the bravest people I know."

My mouth drops open and I'm gaping at her like a fish, but what the hell is she talking about? No one has ever described me as brave.

"Don't look at me like that. You take chances. You rebel." She throws her hands up in the air. "You make your own choices despite what others think you should do. You didn't follow someone else's plan. You made your own."

Lucinda falls back on the bed and stares up at the ceiling blinking rapidly. I lay down next to her and stare up too. Never would I have imagined someone describing me that way, especially not my sister.

I suppose, where my bakery is concerned, I did do those things. It's in the rest of my life I'm a coward.

Resting my hands on my stomach, I gaze at her profile. "Did you follow someone else's plan?"

"That's all I ever do. Mom and Dad's plan. Mark's plan."

The perfection I viewed my sister's life as is crumbling faster than the cinnamon muffins I make. "What happened with Mark?"

"He's been cheating. He's done it before and sworn he'd never do it again, but now he wants it in the open. Stay married and have his affairs too."

Holy Crap! "What a dirtbag!"

A snort of laughter escapes her, and she rolls to her side facing me. The bed squeaks and the mattress dips. "Yeah, he is that."

"I'm sorry." I turn on my side and prop my head in my hand resting on my elbow. "What are you going to do?"

"With my life? Not a clue. With him? I filed for divorce before I left."

"Do Mom and Dad know?"

"Not all the details, just that he cheated, and the marriage is over." She rubs one of the decorative buttons on my comforter. "They don't know I quit my job either."

She peeks up at my face and I quickly try to pop my eyes back into their sockets and smooth my expression.

"Why did you quit? Didn't Mom say you were on the fast track to partner?"

She covers her face with her hands and drops onto her back. "I know. Mom and Dad will say I've lost my mind. Maybe I have."

"Listen Luce, stop worrying what they think, and perhaps if you explain to your boss you were in a bad place when you quit, they'll take you back."

She peeks at me through her fingers.

"What?" I ask.

"You've never called me Luce before."

"Oh sorry."

"No, I like it. No one has ever called me by a nickname before. I always envied you being called Franny instead of Francine all the time."

It's a day of discovery.

"Well Luce, if I had known, I would have called you that a long time ago."

Smiling, she looks back up at the ceiling after dropping her arms to her sides.

"Any other revelations you'd care to share? We seem to be on a roll."

"Just one. I don't want my job back. I hated every minute of it."

"Well, okay then, what do you want to do?"

"Not a clue."

I roll onto to my back and drum my fingers on my abdomen. "So, you don't want to be a lawyer anymore?"

"Mom and Dad are going to completely freak, aren't they?"

"Mom, yes. Dad, probably not. He'll go play a round of golf and wait for Mom to finish her tirade."

"Will you be there when I tell them?"

"Of course."

She takes one of my hands in hers and rests them between us on the bed. I give her hand a squeeze.

The comforter rustles when she twists her head toward mine. "So, what's going on between you and Mitch?"

CHAPTER 24

"If you get any more rigid, you could pass for a corpse."

Forcing my body to relax and take a deep breath, I scramble for a coherent sentence to answer her, but nothing comes to mind. Why is she asking? Does she have an interest in him and is worried about our relationship? I let go of her hand and rub my roiling stomach.

"Wow, I don't know if your silence or body is more telling." She props her head on her palm, digging her elbow into the bed, and stares at me. "Spill it, Franny."

I give her a sideways glare and continue to stare at the ceiling. "Why are you asking?"

"Because you're my sister and I care about you."

"Care, as in you think I will get hurt? Because he couldn't possibly be interested in me? Or because you're attracted to him?"

The silence lengthens and the twelve-inch gap between us feels more like a mile.

So much for the sisterly comradery of a few moments ago. Tears prick behind my eyes and I stare fixedly at a popped nail or screw pushing the sheetrock out in the ceiling forming a tiny circle.

Grasping my chin, she turns my head toward her. "Francine

Dawson you are a beautiful, courageous, smart, wonderful, woman and any guy would be lucky to have your interest."

Her scowl pinches her eyebrows together and wrinkles her forehead. "You keep making that face and you will get premature wrinkles."

She rolls her eyes and lets go of my chin. "You sound like Mother."

The cringe is followed by a shiver of dread. "Please don't say that."

"You know people say it's inevitable that daughters end up turning into their mothers, right?"

"That will not happen. Not to me at least. You, I'm not so sure about. You already resemble her and have the perfection aura that surrounds you."

"I'm not perfect by any means. I've told you the mess my life is in."

"It doesn't make you any less perfect, it probably makes you more so because you were married to such a scum bag and stayed at a job you hated. How did you do it? I wouldn't have had the strength."

"It wasn't strength, it was weakness. I was afraid to leave. You're the strong one because you would never have stuck around."

Rolling over onto my stomach I rest my cheek on my folded hands. "You're not weak, Luce."

"How about we make a pact? You'll tell me I'm strong when I'm feeling weak, and I'll remind you how wonderful you are when you're starting to doubt yourself, deal?"

She holds out her hand for me to shake and I grasp it with my own. "Deal."

"Good. So now will you tell me what's going on with you and Mitch?"

"What makes you think anything is going on? You were the one on a date with him."

"It wasn't a date and you were the one he left with."

"What do you mean it wasn't a date?"

"He showed up here looking for you after you had already left with Bobby. When I said as much, he asked me if I was hungry." She shrugged. "I was bored more than anything, so I went along with him.

I'm not sure how he knew you were at the inn, but I don't think it was a coincidence we ended up eating there."

Mitch was looking for me? Why? Because he was jealous, or because he was worried I'd screw up my date with Bobby and he wanted to be there as a friend to rescue me?

Studying her expression, I ask, "So you're not interested in him?"

"Of course not! I just filed for divorce. The last thing I'm thinking about is getting involved with anyone. Although he is quite handsome and charming. He had Mom and Dad completely dazzled the other night at the club. He did it all so effortlessly too. You should have been there."

"I wasn't invited. You must realize Mom has decided the two of you are perfect together. She's practically planning your wedding."

"Mom can be overzealous but I promise you there is nothing going on between Mitch and me. Nor will there be."

"Okay, so you're not interested in him. It doesn't mean he isn't interested in you."

"Trust me, I know when a guy is interested, and he has shown zero signs. I get the distinct friend vibe from him."

"What were you two doing in the park together?"

"We weren't together. At least not at first and not for long. I was feeling sorry for myself and went for a stroll in the park and ended up sitting on the bench sniffling. I heard giggling and I twisted around to see Mitch surrounded by a group of teenage girls. He posed for a dozen or so selfies with them before spotting me on the bench and excusing himself from the bunch to come over to me. He could tell I was upset and sweetly asked if there was anything he could do. When I said no, he told me he'd never been married, but he's been through breakups before and even if they're ending for all the right reasons, it's still an ending and it's okay to mourn the loss."

She sighs. "He was incredibly sweet and kind. Then he made me laugh telling me a story about the time an obsessed fan followed him into the men's room."

I just fell head over heels in love with Mitch.

It hurts, it's a real physical ache, but it's also a yearning and hope that burgeons inside me.

The fear and heartbreak that Mitch and Lucinda are falling in love is gone.

"Hello? I'm still waiting for the details. You two have obviously been spending time together and unless I'm wrong, you are interested in him, right?"

Grabbing my pillow and burying my face in it, I groan.

I roll over with a sigh and fluff the pillow under my head. "He was my first kiss and I've never gotten over him."

"Wait a minute, how was he your first kiss? I realize you haven't dated all that much, but you have dated."

"It happened when I was thirteen and he was fourteen."

"You've known Mitch that long? How come I didn't know that? Where did you two meet?"

"We met on the beach. His parents had rented a place on the lake for the summer. I was on the town beach shaping a lump of clay I had painstakingly scooped up from the bottom edges of the rock that protruded from the water approximately ten feet from shore. Gritty sand and gray clay covered my pink and white striped swimsuit. A shadow appeared over my shoulder asking me, 'Whatcha doing?' He squatted to inspect my creation and after stumbling over the first few words as I stared at the dark-haired boy, I hesitantly explained the process of digging out the clay, shaping it, letting it dry in the sun. We spent the rest of the summer together playing on the beach and exploring the town. Mitch and I were together almost every day. He came back the next two years. I lived for summer. Then he left, after giving me my first kiss, and I never heard from him again."

"How did I not know this? Do Mom and Dad? Does anyone in town? I would think they would have put up a sign: Vacation spot of Mitch Atwater, or something."

I chuckle. "Mrs. Roberts is the only one I'm aware of who does, I don't think anyone else in town knows or remembers."

"Wait a minute, he's the scrawny boy you were always disappearing with!" Frowning, she got the pinched look again. "You were just a kid, what was he doing kissing you?"

"Luce, I was thirteen. How old were you when you got your first kiss?"

"It depends. Exactly what kind of kiss are we talking about?"

We'd been sitting on the end of my dock dipping our toes in the water after spending the day together as usual. No one had been home. My father was still working then, and my mother was off doing whatever she did all day. Lucinda had gone away with a friend so I had felt safe bringing him home to have a snack. Afterwards, we'd wandered outside and ended up on the dock. I'd smiled at him after splashing his leg with water and he'd leaned over and kissed me. It lasted only a second.

"The kiss was entirely innocent, just a quick peck on the lips really, but it meant the world to me."

It was the only kiss he gave me that summer, but my heart had already fallen for him even before he gave me my first kiss.

He'd left the following week.

"Well, that's okay then."

A soft snort of laughter rattles in my chest. "And how old were you when you received your first kiss?"

"Never you mind. Tell me more about your relationship with Mitch."

"There's not much more to tell. He left at the end of the summer and I never saw him again until a few weeks ago. I wasn't even sure he would remember me."

"Obviously he did."

"Yes, but as his buddy, not someone he could be interested in romantically."

"Are you sure about that? He seemed inordinately concerned over you at dinner and he rushed you away from Bobby the first chance he got. What happened when you got to his apartment? I mean you are wearing what I assume are his T-shirt and shorts."

Heat steals over my face.

"That blush is certainly telling. What happened Franny?"

"Not what you think. I mean he gave me his clothes to change into because my dress was a mess. We didn't—you know."

"What? You didn't have sex?"

"No, we didn't."

Lucinda rolls onto her stomach and crosses her feet in the air behind her. "Franny, have you had sex before?"

My face burns. I close my eyes and count to ten hoping to cool my cheeks.

"No, but if you launch into a lecture about the birds and the bees, I will be justified in killing you."

"Duly noted, but if you ever need to talk—I'm here."

"Thanks."

"So, have you made any overtures towards Mitch to let him know how you feel?"

"Not exactly."

"Define not exactly."

Operation fake girlfriend and fake crush come spilling out in a torrent of words. Her eyes get wider and wider as the story unfolds.

When I am done, I cross my arms over my eyes and wait for the shock to wear off and my sister to respond.

"He's been teaching you how to kiss?"

I nod without dropping my arms.

"With tongue, hands and full body contact?"

"Yes, what's your point?"

"My point is unless he's a real son of a bitch and taking advantage of you, then I can't see any other plausible reason to take it so far unless he is interested in you. Back to the full body contact part, you are aware guys can't exactly hide when they're aroused?"

I drop my arms and stare at her.

"Yes, I mean he was not unaffected."

"Okay, and I haven't gotten the impression that Mitch is the type of guy to take advantage."

"No, of course not."

"Then the evidence speaks for itself."

CHAPTER 25

Operation Mitch's Seduction is underway. Now that I have Lucinda's assurance she isn't attracted to him and doesn't think he is in to her, my conscience is clear. I barely got any sleep last night after she had left to go to her own room. I couldn't stop thinking over what she said about him acting interested in me.

She urged me to be upfront and tell him how I felt. My confidence level has not risen quite that high. I envy people born with a natural self-confidence which flows from them in everything they say and do. Or maybe it's how they were raised? Were they praised constantly as a child? Where does it come from and more importantly where can I get my dose?

Instead, I've come up with a plan to seduce him and get him to see we can be more than friends.

Arriving at the bakery bright and early this morning despite it being Monday and the bakery is closed, I whipped up decadent chocolate truffles. I'm usually here on Mondays working anyway catching up on paperwork or planning the week, but this morning I'm taking the chocolates to Mitch on the pretense I need him as a tester and to thank him for his rescue last night.

I've poured myself into a pair of white short shorts and a snug green tank top. The new bra I bought while shopping with Olivia lifts and smooshes my breasts together giving the illusion I have decent cleavage. I applied a fair amount of makeup this morning after watching several online videos and battled my hair into submission with a ton of product. The results don't look half bad.

Sounds started filtering from his apartment over an hour ago. That should be enough time for him to wake up. I don't want to wait too long and have him disappear for the day. Picking up the plate of truffles, I take a deep breath, throw my shoulders back, and head for the door.

My steps slow while I traverse the steps wearing the three-inch heel sandals I squeezed my feet into. My ankles wobble, my heels throb, but damn they look good.

Holding the plate in one hand, I smooth my clothes with the other and wiggle to straighten my new cleavage and then knock on the door before I lose my courage.

Mitch opens the door and I get an inner thrill when his gaze wanders from my head to my toes and back up again. I watch his Adam's apple bounce as he swallows.

"Good morning. I hope I didn't catch you at a bad time, but I need a taste tester." I hold out the plate of chocolates. "And I wanted to thank you for rescuing me again last night."

He steps back and holds the door open. His white T-shirt stretches taut across his chest. "I'm always happy to taste anything you have to offer."

Smiling, I sashay past him putting an extra sway to my hips. So far so good.

I slide the plate onto the narrow counter in the kitchen and pick up a chocolate and hold it up to his mouth. He stares at me over my hand and obediently opens his mouth. I place the chocolate on his tongue trailing my thumb against his full lower lip.

He closes his lips and chews the chocolate while keeping his gaze on mine.

"Delicious."

Of course they are, I perfected the recipe years ago, but he doesn't need to know that.

"Then they're ready for me to sell in the bakery?"

"I should try another one to be sure."

I expect him to take another one from the plate, but he continues staring at me, so I pick up a truffle and hold it up to his mouth. He opens his lips and takes the chocolate from me dragging his lips over my fingers the entire way.

I swallow hard when my womb clenches.

A tingling starts in my core and radiates out.

That is beyond the friend zone, right?

The sound of birds singing suddenly fills the room. For a second, I think my imagination is overloading and dipping into cartoon mode like when the princess falls in love with the prince and animals sing to rejoice.

"That's my mom." Mitch strides across the room to answer his cell phone resting on the coffee table in front of the couch.

His ringtone for his mother sounds like something out of a fairy tale? How sweet is that? Mine is the theme to *Jaws*.

"Hi Mom."

While he talks to his mother, I maneuver around the peninsula of the counter to lean my hip against the edge in what I hope is a sexy pose. Briefly, I try to paste a come-hither look on my face, but thankfully his face is momentarily pointed away and doesn't see the expression I am certain comes across looking like a choking victim.

I shimmy to expose a little more cleavage and cock my hip out a little more planting my hand on my waist.

My ankle wobbles and then collapses.

Making a mad grab for the counter while my body careens towards the floor, my hands slap against the edge.

A rip of material echoes around me.

I'm frozen in place while gripping the edge of the counter as if I'm attempting to do a squatting pull up.

Hastily I leverage my arms up onto the counter and try to stand. A shot of pain seizes my ankle and I wince. Resting as much weight as possible on my opposite foot and holding on to the counter, I stand.

That isn't what concerns me the most, however.

The cool draft of air against my backside is priority number one.

I swivel my head in Mitch's direction and almost sob in relief when his back is still turned towards me. He is busy describing the renovations on the house to his mother.

Swatting at my ass with one hand while the other supports my weight against the counter, I find the split material and the cool skin of my lower cheeks exposed.

Why had I let Olivia talk me into buying a thong? She said panty lines would show with these shorts and a thong wouldn't. Yeah well, clearly, she hadn't anticipated this.

I inch my way around the counter using it as a crutch and keep my front towards Mitch in case he turns around. If I can just make it to the door and down the stairs, I have a sweatshirt in the bakery I can wrap around my waist.

Thank God I drove this morning instead of walking. I didn't want to perspire and smudge my makeup and my feet aren't prepared for a long hike in heels. Looks like my ankles and shorts weren't prepared either.

The cold metal of the door handle is in my grasp behind my back when he spots me at the door.

I smile and grip the handle tighter.

"I just remembered I left the oven on downstairs." Hopefully he will believe the blatant lie and not know that making truffles does not require an oven.

Mitch frowns and raises a finger signaling for me to wait a minute. I shake my head and shuffle backwards out the door.

Pain stabs at my ankle and I grab for the railing to gain my balance. I consider plopping on my butt and scooting down the stairs but then the image of splinters on my ass nixes the idea.

Bending over, I unstrap the sandals, tuck them against my side, and limp down the stairs into the bakery.

The door opens just as I finish tying the arms of my sweatshirt around my waist. Whirling around while holding onto the back of the stool I am using for balance, I expect Mitch to be standing in the doorway, but it's Bobby.

"Hey, I saw your car and wanted to stop in and check on you after last night."

"Oh, hi Bobby. Come in. I'm fine, just clumsy."

Straightening the sweatshirt to make sure my backside is adequately covered I smile in his direction.

"The way he rushed you out of there I was afraid you had gotten burned."

"No, no, I'm fine, really. I'm sorry about that. I ruined the dinner."

"We can have another go at it sometime."

He wanted another date? Why wasn't he running in the opposite direction? He really is a sweet guy. My pulse doesn't jump at the sight of him though. My breath doesn't hitch in my chest, and his smile doesn't make me melt. It would be so much easier if I felt that way about him.

"Um..."

He pushes his hair off his forehead and adjusts his baseball cap. "Yeah, I kind of thought that was the way the wind blew. It was obvious there's something going on between you two."

"It was? I mean, I'm sorry, I was having a nice time with you."

"Don't worry about it. Make sure he treats you right."

"I will. Thanks, Bobby."

Perhaps I should have said there is nothing definite between Mitch and I, but that might have sounded like there might be a chance for Bobby and I and there isn't. There's no spark. Certainly not the raging inferno I feel with Mitch.

Locking the back door, I limp my way to the front of the bakery using every counter and chair for support. I want to get to my car and get home before Mitch ends his call and comes looking for me.

Operation Mitch's Seduction will have to be put on hold until I put ice on this ankle and buy sturdier shorts.

CHAPTER 26

There's a soft knock on my door and then Lucinda pokes her head in. "You busy?"

I glance down at the mound I make in the middle of my bed with my foot propped up on a pillow and the new book I received in the mail open in my hands and shrug. I'm reading because I need to rest my ankle so I can work Wednesday, and I hope I can discern romance or seduction tips from the book. Tips I can actually implement and are plausible for an average woman to employ.

"Not particularly."

Lucinda scoots in the door and over to my bed holding a wooden cane.

"Is that Grandmother Laurel's?" She always had an umbrella stand full of various canes when you walked into her house. I never saw her use a single one. She broke her foot once and refused to leave the house until it healed enough for her to manage it without support. We took turns staying with her and helping her.

"Yes, I took it from the closet. I thought you could use it."

"Thanks, although I'm not planning on going anywhere until tomorrow. I have a small business meeting tomorrow night."

Sitting on the edge of my bed, she plucks at the bedspread. "I was hoping you would come downstairs and be there when I tell Mom and Dad about quitting my job."

"Oh, they're both home?"

"Yes, Dad came home a little while ago from the club and Mom is in the living room planning the Fourth of July party. She's in a good mood."

Mother in a good mood is crucial when delivering unwelcome news.

I scoot myself up more and place the book on the nightstand. "Okay, but I'm only there for moral support. A silent supporter."

"Understood." She grins and yanks back the comforter covering the rest of me to help me slide out of bed. "Thanks Franny."

"Mm hmm." Standing, I snatch the cane from where she leaned it against my nightstand and lean my weight on it while testing the strength of my ankle. It's sore, but better than yesterday.

Lucinda wraps an arm around my waist. "Here, you can lean on me."

We manage about four feet then our out of sync steps send me grasping for the wall and my sister hopping around on one foot when I squish her toes with the cane.

Wincing, I lean against the wall.

"Are you okay?"

She nods and rests her hands on her knees for a moment before straightening. "Okay, that isn't going to work. Can you manage all right with the cane?"

"I think so. Are you sure you don't need one too?"

Chuckling, she shakes her head. "No, I'm good."

We amble down the hall with me using the wall for additional support and Lucinda slowing her steps to walk beside me.

"Have you talked to Mark since you left?"

"He's called a few times and left messages. I'm letting my lawyer handle it all. I don't want to talk to him."

"Is he still trying to get you to come back?"

"Oh yes, he emailed me an article on the benefits of an open marriage."

"You're joking."

"Sadly, no I'm not."

"Sorry Luce."

She shrugs. "Do you remember that time we spent a couple of weeks on Cape Cod when we were kids?"

I grasp the railing and take one step at a time.

"Sure, I was ten or eleven."

"I've been thinking it would be nice to take a trip there again. Would you like to go with me?"

Pausing on the bottom step, I glance at her. "I could probably go for a Monday and Tuesday, but I can't close the bakery."

"Oh, I wasn't thinking. You have to be there every day to do all the baking, don't you? You haven't taken a vacation since you opened The Sweet Spot, have you?"

"No, I can't. Someday I can train someone enough so I'll be able to. Actually, Olivia has expressed interest."

"That would be helpful to you. You should be able to have time off."

It's never bothered me because I didn't have anywhere to go or someone to go with. A couple days with Luce might be fun.

"We could still try a couple days. I could come down and meet you there."

She nods. "It's something to think about. Let's get this over with."

We hobble into the living room. Mother looks over from the secretariat where she has a few stacks of paper on the open flip down desk. "What are you girls up to? Is that a cane? What have you done now Francine?"

I lower myself to the couch and send a meaningful look my sister's way. She'd better get this over with.

"I twisted my ankle."

Mother shakes her head and glances back to her papers.

"I will get Dad. He's in the kitchen."

Lucinda strides off to the kitchen and I glance at my mother's profile and then out to the lake. I lean the cane against the arm of the couch and clasp my hands in my lap.

Mother removes her reading glasses and stares at me. "Why is your sister getting your father?"

"That's for her to tell you."

Her eyes narrow and she drops her glasses on top of the papers and stands. I swivel my head around looking for Lucinda. Where is she? My mother lowers herself to the couch which sits in an L shape to mine and crosses her legs.

The weight of her stare is like a laser targeting system pointed straight at me.

"Francine."

I keep my gaze pinned to the closed kitchen door willing it to open. "Yes, Mother?"

"Are you in some kind of trouble?"

I swing my head around. She sits with her hands folded over her knee. Navy slacks and an ivory silk blouse flow over her body. How does she manage to look like she just stepped off the pages of a magazine? Her clothes are wrinkle free and perfectly in place.

Sighing, I gaze at the coffee table. How horrified would she be if I rested my ankle on it?

It's probably not worth the risk to find out.

"Francine."

Her voice rises a notch with a strident edge. Oh yes, she thinks the conversation is about me and I must be in trouble. When have I ever gotten in trouble? Other than accidents or mishaps that is.

"No, I'm not in any trouble and it's not about me."

A perplexed expression crosses her face. "Then what is this about? Is it about her divorce? Is Mark causing problems?"

I snort. Not the kind you're thinking of.

One manicured eyebrow raises.

Clearing my throat, I glance at the door again.

Finally, Lucinda and my father walk out of the kitchen. My sister glances from me to my mother.

Yes, you left me alone with her. The inquisition has started.

My father ambles over to kiss me on the cheek. "What's this?" He jerks his chin to the cane.

"I twisted my ankle and Luce thought it would help."

"Lucinda. Use her full name. Nicknames are common and cheapen the name."

My sister sits next to me. "I like it."

We share a small smile.

"What is this about, Lucinda?"

My father sits next to my mother and smiles at the two of us. Luce takes a deep breath.

"I quit my job and want to move back here, to Granite Cove."

The silence thickens and lengthens. I insisted on being a silent supporter, but as my gaze ping pongs between the pinched look on my mother's face and the concerned one on my father's, I grasp for something to say.

"Isn't that wonderful? She's moving home!"

Lucinda squeezes my hand resting between us. Her palm is a little damp and I marvel over the fact she is so nervous. I mean, of course, she is, but I thought I was the only one to suffer from anxiety and terror facing my mother.

Our father smiles. "You always have a home here with us. It'll be nice to have all my girls under my roof again."

"Have you contacted a law firm in New Hampshire? What about your license?" Mother's head swivels to pin her stare on my father. "What about contacting your old firm? You were a partner. Surely that carries weight enough to get your daughter a position?"

My father is more than a decade older than my mother. They met at a fundraiser and he likes to say he swept her off her feet, but I can't imagine that happening. I think my mother set her cap for the handsome distinguished lawyer and let him believe he did the pursuing.

"I'm not planning to practice law."

"What do you mean? What do you plan to do?" My mother glares at me like I have something to do with this.

"I don't know yet."

Mother's polished nails drum on her leg. Father clears his throat and glances at my mother.

"I want to take a little time to figure out what I want to do."

"Nonsense, you're not throwing away years of education and experience."

"Now, now, dear, that's not what she's saying." My father pats my mother's leg and smiles at my sister. "Take the summer to work through the divorce. I'm sure once that is handled everything will fall back into place."

Lucinda's hand is digging into mine. I peek at her. Her face is frozen with no emotion on it whatsoever.

I clear my throat. "Now is the perfect time for her to figure out what she wants to do. The divorce has upended her plans. She needs time to work through that and being single again."

The glacial stare aimed my way from my mother has me fingering my cross like I'm trying to ward off evil or something. My grandmother Emmy gave it to me when I was a little girl. She gave one to Luce too, but I'm the one who never takes it off.

"Frivolous behavior will not do her any favors. She needs to move on, not wallow."

"She's getting divorced. I think that warrants a little wallowing."

"How would you know? You've never even been engaged."

Does that mean I'm not allowed to have an opinion?

Of course it does.

I open my mouth to respond, but Lucinda leans forward. "I understand you're disappointed, but this is my life and my decision."

Hallelujah! You go sis!

Her voice trembles a little and cracks in places, but I'm beaming for her.

Mother tries staring her down, but Lucinda returns her gaze and doesn't falter. I squeeze her hand.

My father's gaze darts back and forth between them. "Your mother is only concerned for you. We don't want you to make any hasty decisions you might regret."

"You should have come to us before you resigned. You're being impulsive."

Again, she shoots a glare in my direction then her attention returns to Lucinda. I'm sure she believes somehow this is my fault.

"If I decide to return to practicing law, I'm sure I will have no trouble doing so, but right now I have no idea what I want except to be with my family."

My father taps his reading glasses against his leg. "Like I said, take the summer, and then decide. Everything will work out for the best."

My mother glares at my father this time and then she raises her chin and gazes at Lucinda.

"Fine, what's done is done. Take the summer to get your life back in order."

Lucinda's shoulder sags against mine.

"Thank you."

My mother suddenly brightens. "We'll call it a sabbatical. Your return home can be the theme of our Fourth of July party."

Isn't Independence Day the theme of the party?

"In fact, perhaps this is fortuitous. An extended stay at home will allow Lucinda's and Mitch's budding relationship to flourish."

I sink into the back cushion. Lucinda is looking at me. I glance at her and she is imploring me with her eyes.

What?

"I am not interested in Mitch." She looks at me again.

Oh no, don't you dare say I am. I give a quick shake to my head and squeeze her hand.

"Don't be ridiculous. Of course you are."

"No, I'm not. I just filed for divorce. I'm not interested in anyone."

"The best thing to do is move on to someone new. It will speed up your recovery."

As if she had a broken bone instead of a broken heart.

"Mother, it's not going to happen."

"With the right strategy anything can happen. I've been careful with the guest list and eliminated most of the attractive young women. We can't not invite them all because that would be too obvious, however I'm only inviting those that have fatal flaws that will overshadow their beauty. You will have no competition."

She should have been a politician or a crime boss.

Lucinda rubs her forehead. My father stands and kisses each of us on the cheek.

"I'll leave the party planning to you girls." He leaves the room and I wish I could follow.

"You'll wear blue, it will bring out your eyes. I'll make an appointment with my stylist for your hair."

What would my mother say if I enlisted her help with Mitch?

She'd laugh in my face most likely.

"No." Lucinda stands and strides out of the room.

She's left me alone in the room with my mother, again.

CHAPTER 27

The white pillars supporting the entrance to the library are as thick as my hips. I hobble to the steps as fast as my ankle allows before I can change my mind.

I committed myself to attending the small business meeting and I should for many reasons, the most important being for the benefit of my bakery.

It's also proof I'm done with hiding.

Right, so get your butt in there.

I'm not exactly dressed in business attire. Sneakers adorn my feet because of my ankle, so I put on a pair of navy Capris and a burgundy blouse. It's the best I could manage.

Balancing the box of assorted muffins, cookies, and pastries I brought from the bakery, I open the large wooden door and peek inside. I haven't set foot in here since high school.

The wooden tables and chairs on either side are the same—so are the row after row of bookshelves lining the perimeter of the room. There's a circular metal desk in the center of the space I don't recall.

The door opens behind me and I glance over my shoulder.

Rebecca waltzes in wearing a slim black skirt and a purple blouse with black heels. She grins when she spots me.

"You made it."

"I did, but I'm not sure where to go."

She loops her arm through one of mine. "Downstairs in the meeting room."

We walk to the back-left corner where a set of stairs leads up and down.

I follow her down the stairs to a wide hallway with doors on each side and an open area in the front which looks like a kid's reading area with bean bag chairs and half shelves. Rebecca opens the first door on the right. Five people are milling about near a coffee pot set up on a small table. A long table and chairs dominate the room.

"Hi everyone. This is Franny Dawson, for those of you who aren't aware. She owns The Sweet Spot."

Mr. Hanson, who owns the grocery store, waves. "Hi Franny."

A short woman with long brown hair walks over and introduces herself. "Hi, I'm Paula Moskvitch. I own the Rosewood Bed & Breakfast."

A tall thin man in jeans and a plaid button-down shirt leans over the table to shake my hand. "Miles Shaw. I own The Village Liquor Shop."

"Ian Flannigan, Flannigan's Pub." The man waves from the corner.

"Hi there. I'm Derek and I own Petopia."

"I've wondered about your place. Is it a pet store?"

"We sell pet toys and care products, but we also have a grooming salon and a daycare area too. Do you have a pet?"

"No, I'm afraid not."

Rebecca takes the box from me and peeks inside. "Will you marry me?"

I laugh. "Are you that easy?"

"Yes."

"What have you got there? Don't go hogging the goodies, Rebecca." Ian shoulders his way across to peer over her shoulder and grabs one side of the box.

Rebecca swats at his hand and glares at him. "Back off Flannigan. I get first dibs since she's my friend and I invited her."

He holds his palms up in the air. "Easy there, killer."

She brings the box to the table with the coffee maker and opens it up as everyone circles around her except me.

"What's all the excitement?"

A woman with light brown hair ending at her shoulders stops next to me.

"Bakery goods."

"Oh, you must be Franny. I'm Evie Brown. I own Pretty Bits, the souvenir shop."

"Yes, hi, it's nice to meet you."

People take their treats and coffee and sit at the table. Evie strolls over to peek in the box and Rebecca sets her items down on the table next to me and pulls out a chair.

"Sit. It looks like it will be a light meeting tonight. Usually there's around a dozen of us. Vanessa, our self-appointed leader, is usually here. She's a local realtor, you know her?"

I freeze pulling out the chair next to her.

It never occurred to me she might be here.

Plopping down in the chair, I sigh. "Yes, I know her."

"Problem?"

"We both grew up here in town. She was popular. I was not. We've never been friendly."

More like mortal enemies. At least that is how she has always treated me. I just try to avoid her whenever possible.

"Ah, you have a history. I get it. I have my own."

After everyone takes a seat, Rebecca clears her throat. "Okay everyone, if we hope to have the local business fair by the end of the summer, we need to make a bunch of decisions. Namely, when and where and who will organize what."

She leans towards me. "We want to set up booths so every business owner can not only advertise their products or service but introduce the community to what they offer and show why shopping local benefits everyone."

A nice idea.

"I nominate Rebecca to organize it." Ian gives her a wide grin.

"I'd be happy to."

"Good, that's decided." Mr. Hanson looks around the room. "Unless anyone has any objections?"

Everyone declines and Rebecca pulls out a tablet from her purse. "Okay then, date and venue. Anyone have any suggestions?"

"Sorry I'm late." Kelly, the dog owner from the park rushes into the room. She drops into a chair at the end of the table and scans the room.

Rebecca glances up from her tablet. "Hi Kelly, this is Franny."

Kelly smiles and nods at Rebecca. "We've met. Hi Franny. What business do you own?"

"The Sweet Spot."

"Ooh, I love that place." Her gaze lands on the box I brought and she pops to a stand. "Will you be my new best friend?"

Rebecca laughs. "I've already proposed to her so I guess you can take the friend spot."

Kelly grins and then peers into the box with her hands behind her back.

"She owns the new dress shop in town, Dress to Impress."

I noticed the sign driving through town before, but I've never been inside. I'll have to take a look.

Kelly licks the frosting from her thumb and waltzes back to her seat with a cupcake and napkin in one hand and a coffee in the other. An emerald green dress skims her figure and cinches at the waist. Does she design the dresses or buy them from someone who does? Is it one of her designs?

"Where were we? Oh yes, locations. Anyone have a suggestion?"

"The high school? We could have it in one sport fields or if it rains in the gym?" Miles says.

Paula raises her hand then lowers it. "The town park next to the lake would be close to the village and get more foot traffic but I'm not sure what we would do if it rains."

"Those are both good options. I can call the town hall and the school and find out who we need permission from and if it's even possible." She types on her tablet. "I guess when will depend on the answers to those questions but I think we have to shoot for the end of August. Anything else is too soon."

"I can send out mailers to the town once we have the details set." Evie fiddles with a pen on a pad of paper.

"I'll contact all the businesses and see who's interested in having a booth at the fair. The more we have the better the draw." Derek stands to refill his coffee cup and take another cookie.

Ian drums his fingers on the table. "We need to establish how much a booth will cost. We can't foot the bill for everyone."

Rebecca busily types on her tablet. "There will be a nominal fee to have a booth set up to cover the organizational costs."

Nibbling on my lip, I lean forward. "What about having entertainment and food? Besides those of us who sell food I mean. A bouncy house or something for the kids. Maybe some games with little prizes? I think we have to make it a family friendly event to entice people."

Rebecca nods at me. "Excellent suggestion."

"Those things cost money." Mr. Hanson folds his hands on his belly. "We'll have to charge more for the booths, but Franny is right about attracting families. The whole point is making the community aware of our businesses and what we offer."

As the meeting wears on, I gain more confidence and voice my opinion and suggestions. By the time it ends, I volunteer to organize the entertainment.

Ian walks over to fill his coffee cup and leans against the wall. "We need something big to draw in the crowds."

"How about Mitch Atwater?"

Holy crap! Please tell me I didn't say that out loud.

All eyes are on me.

Yup, I did. What the heck was I thinking?

"Would he be willing to make an appearance?" Kelly asks.

"I mean…he might be willing to sign autographs or something."

Rebecca stands. "Excellent Franny! Okay guys and gals, I will contact the other members who weren't here and make a volunteer list. We'll have to meet again, but for now we'll communicate by email. Any objections?"

A chorus of "no" fills the room.

"Good, then let's all get the hell out of here and get some rest. Tomorrow is another workday."

Rebecca strides to the front. "And if anyone wants any more treats, you better speak up now otherwise they are going home with me to feed my sugar addiction."

"Hand over the box, killer." Ian approaches her holding out his hand.

She opens the lid. "I'm not handing over anything to you."

I smile and wave to everyone as I walk to the door. Kelly stares at the couple and then shrugs. "I'm not getting involved in that. Toodles."

"Wait for me, Franny."

Rebecca hands out a couple more confections and then closes the lid and grabs her belongings off the table.

We walk out of the building together. "So, what did you think of your first meeting?"

"It was good. I'm glad you invited me. The fair is a promising idea."

"There's a lot to do in a brief time, but we've got a good group here and can get it done."

"Is Ian part of that history you mentioned?"

She gives me a sideways glance. "That conversation will require a great deal of alcohol and more sweets. We'll have to schedule a girl's night for that one."

CHAPTER 28

Feet dragging with only the occasional slight hitch in my gate, I unlock the back door of the bakery and trudge inside. My tender ankle had a full day of rest and so have I, hiding in my room for the past day and a half except for the small business meeting last night. Lucinda and I binge watched *The Gilmore Girls* and indulged in ice cream therapy.

Flicking on the light switches and hobbling around the room preheating the ovens and yanking out ingredients from the refrigerator and cabinets, I ruminate over my failed seduction attempt. I need a fail-safe plan or at least a *me* safe plan.

Hands covered in flour and bread dough, I freeze when someone comes down the outside stairs. Mitch rarely rises this early. Has someone been in his apartment all night? A woman now making the early morning slink of shame before the town wakes up and witnesses her sneaking out of Mitch's apartment?

Who am I kidding? Any woman lucky enough to have spent the night would skip around in broad daylight with a grin plastered on her face.

Peering out the window, I wait for a glimpse of the woman I will vow to hate for all eternity. The green-eyed monster perches on my shoulder and digs in its claws.

Punching rather than kneading the dough, I shove it aside before I do further damage.

A large silhouette crosses in front of the window and stops at my back door. Unless I have drastically miscalculated where Mitch's interests lay, the person outside didn't spend the night with him.

A knock rattles the door and I flip the switch to turn on the light. I'm not going to open the door without knowing who stands on the other side.

Mitch's handsome face shines through the glass.

After unlocking and opening the door, I step back to let him pass. The door shuts with a soft click and I face him with a smile.

He holds out his hand palm up. "Phone."

I blink. "What? I don't have your phone." He was on it the last time I saw him. Did he not remember? Why does he think I have it?

"Not mine, yours. Give me your phone."

I look over at my desk on the side of the room where I drop it every morning. He follows my gaze and strides over to the desk to snatch up my phone sitting in the center of the desk.

"Um, why do you want my phone?"

He walks back and grabs my flour and dough coated hand by the wrist. A smirk appears at the sight of my hands. "Which finger do you use for fingerprint identification?"

"I beg your pardon?"

"To open your phone."

"Oh, my index finger." I wiggle the finger and a puff of flour rises in the air.

He tugs my hand higher and opens his mouth. Blinking rapidly and staring at him with my mouth agape, he encloses the tip of my finger in the warmth of his mouth. I should warn him raw bread dough won't taste good.

His tongue swirls around my finger.

I guess he doesn't care.

A shiver dances down my spine.

My finger pops out of his mouth like a lollipop all shiny clean and wet. He blows softly to dry it and places it on my phone.

I assist him by turning my hand and the home screen opens on my phone. "What do you need my phone for?"

He turns the phone toward him and starts pushing buttons I can't see. "I'm programming in my number and sending yours to my phone so that the next time you disappear abruptly I have a way to contact you without driving all over town or knocking on your parents' front door. Your sister and I exchanged numbers days ago, yet I don't have yours."

"Oh." He wanted to contact me? A balloon of happiness fills me.

"We have yet to have that talk."

The balloon pops and fizzles away.

"Right—the talk. We should schedule a time for that. I'm busy with getting the bakery ready to open right now."

"Fine, I'll meet you at closing. We'll grab dinner."

"Sure, okay." Great, I have approximately twelve hours to come up with a new plan and divert him away from his talk. I can't very well seduce him if he suggests we stop spending time together.

Maybe I'm wrong and that's not the topic. He could say he's realized that he's fallen madly in love with me.

A girl can dream.

I DASH out after the midday rush to deliver meringues to Mrs. Roberts. She's sitting in her familiar spot on the porch.

"Hi Mrs. Roberts. I brought you a fresh supply of meringues."

"Hello Franny. Are you limping?"

"Oh." I wave my hand at my ankle. "I twisted my ankle. It's no big deal."

"Did you do that on your date the other night with young Calvert?"

I glance towards the inn. She must have seen me arrive with Bobby. Had she seen me leave with Mitch?

"Um—no. I did it after."

"Sit a spell."

"Just for a few minutes. I need to get back to the bakery."

"You work too hard."

Yeah, maybe I do.

"Tell me about your date."

"With Bobby?"

She nods and rocks her chair. "He's a nice boy. He turned out well despite the hardships life dealt him."

Frowning, I wait for her to elaborate. What hardships? I don't have a clue what she's talking about.

She continues to rock and stare towards the lake.

"What hardships?"

"I suppose if you're dating him you should be aware of events in his past."

I'm not dating him, but I want to hear what she's talking about.

"It's on account of him I kept my mouth shut." She grips the arms of her chair and frowns. "He was just a boy. I didn't want to see his life ruined any more than it already was."

"I don't understand. What did you keep silent about?"

"His mother was one of the women my Charlie was fooling around with."

Oh, her husband got around, didn't he?

Were Bobby's parents still alive?

If they are, I don't think they live in town. At least I've never come across them.

"It was his father's boat that Charlie was killed on."

I gasp. Killed?

"They ruled it accidental, but the police weren't aware he was messing around with the wife."

I drop back against my chair. *Wow!*

"I don't have any proof there was foul play, but it's quite a coincidence if there wasn't."

"What happened to Bobby's parents?"

She shrugs. "His father was hurt in the accident too. I don't think he ever recovered. The mother left town and never returned."

Poor Bobby!

"The guilt has festered inside me for so long. Not telling the truth is a sin, but that boy had been hurt enough."

She stares at me. "Do you think I did the right thing?"

Do I?

I reach over and hold her hand. "I don't know. If it wasn't an accident, then a murderer walks free."

"I know it. I pray every night I'm wrong."

She uses her cane to stand. "It's time for my afternoon nap. Thank you for the meringues and for listening to an old woman's troubles."

I stand and give her a hug. "If there's anything I can ever do for you, all you need to do is ask. You've been such a comfort to me since the first time you called me over when I was walking home from school." Back then, I would forgo the bus in favor of walking to avoid whatever ill intentions Vanessa and her friends had in store for me.

"It's you who's been a comfort to me. Now off with you. I know you've got work to do."

I wait until she disappears inside, then I return to the bakery.

My gait is slow, but my ankle has little to do with it.

The burden she's carried all these years…would I have made the same choice?

For Bobby's sake I hope Mrs. Roberts is wrong about her suspicions.

THE HECTIC DAY ends and I have barely given Mitch and his talk a thought. Until now.

My hair unraveled from the braid I manipulated it into this morning. Assorted batters and ingredients splatter my apron and dot my arms, white T-shirt, and lavender Capris. The minimal makeup I applied this morning is long gone and I hadn't thought to carry any with me to freshen up because I never wear the stuff.

Entering the bathroom, I hope to salvage something and make myself a tad bit more presentable since sexy is out of the question at this point.

I'm only able to remove the remnants from my arms and clothes before the back door opens and Mitch calls my name, I slink out of the bathroom doing my best to smooth the wrinkles out of my clothes.

"You shouldn't leave your back door unlocked. Especially when you're here alone."

He's right. It isn't the first time I have been given that advice and I'm sure it won't be the last. The crime rate in Granite Cove isn't exactly running rampant, but I can still stand to be better at security. I keep it locked in the mornings before opening when I'm alone, but during the day if I open it for any reason, I tend to leave it unlocked. Subconsciously, I must believe terrible things only happen in the dark, not broad daylight.

"I'll do better."

Did he expect an argument? Because he looks surprised at my ready compliance. "Good. Are you all set?"

I glance around the bakery and nod. The bakery is, anyway, I on the other hand feel like a mess coming unglued.

Instead of heading for his truck as I assumed he would, he goes up the stairs to his apartment. Did he need to grab something else before going out to dinner or were we having the talk in private and then getting something to eat?

He holds the door for me, and I step past him into the apartment wiping my damp palms on my thighs.

"I picked up Chinese takeout. I thought we could eat here if that's okay?"

"Of course, sounds great."

I turn toward the peninsula where he has already placed dishes and utensils and the white containers of food. So much for hoping to delay the conversation by going somewhere in public. I scoot onto the stool he holds out for me. Our shoulders brush as he sits on the stool next to mine and starts opening the containers.

"I wasn't sure what you liked, so I ordered a bunch of different choices."

"I pretty much love it all so you can't go wrong."

We fill our plates with an assortment of Sesame Chicken, Shrimp Fried Rice, Boneless Spareribs, and Egg rolls and start eating. The sauces are sweet and tangy.

I keep glancing at him out of the corner of my eye and shift the food around on my plate. I take the first few bites in rapid succession to avoid talking and now the food is sitting in my stomach like a lump of lead.

"Why did you leave in such a hurry the other day?"

My mouth opens to perpetuate the lie of the left on oven, but I can't do it. I don't want to confess my humiliating shorts incident either. "I twisted my ankle and besides you were busy on the phone with your Mom."

"I saw Bobby go in your back door and then you were both gone."

Glancing over at him, I catch him staring at me with his fork resting on the side of his plate. Is he wondering about the plan to make Bobby jealous? Another mess I can lay at Vanessa's door. If she hadn't threatened to reveal my crush on Mitch to him, I never would have had to come up with the fictitious crush on Bobby. Then again, I might not have gotten the kissing lessons from Mitch either, so maybe I can be grateful to her for once. I'm not about to go running over to thank her anytime soon, however.

"He stopped by to check on me."

"And?"

"And what?"

"Did he ask you out again? Is that where you disappeared to?"

"Yes and no." I wipe my mouth with the napkin and take a sip of water.

"Why are you being so evasive?"

Because my brain is still stuck on what Mrs. Roberts revealed about Bobby and his parents.

He twirls his fork between his thumb and forefinger. I shrug and meet his gaze.

"I'm not trying to be. Bobby asked me out, but I didn't go out with him then. I told you I twisted my ankle."

Mitch glances at my feet resting on the bar between the legs of the stool. "Your ankle okay now?"

"It's still a little tender, but it's much better after staying off it the rest of Monday and all day yesterday."

"So you haven't gone out with him again?"

"No."

He smiles and resumes eating.

Okay, what is that about? Did he not want me going out with Bobby? Could he possibly be jealous? Wasn't that one of the first strategies he mentioned when he proposed this fake dating plan?

Mitch puts his fork down and turns his stool to face me. "About that talk…"

"There's something I need to confess."

He gazes at me expectantly.

I rub my hands down my thighs. "I went to the small business meeting and they're planning an event later this summer to promote local businesses. I got a little overzealous and I volunteered you to make an appearance."

I close my eyes and scrunch my face.

"I'll do it."

I pop open my eyes. "You will?"

He nods. "For you."

I grin. "Thank you! I promise I'll never do it again. Well, not without talking to you first."

"You will owe me."

"Anything, name it."

"Careful what you promise, Franny."

I don't think it's in my power to deny him anything.

I take a bite of the food.

"How are the house renovations coming along?"

"Progress is being made, but they keep finding things that need to be fixed or updated every time they open a wall. The mechanicals like the furnace and central air are installed. The plumbing and electrical are on schedule to finish next week. There's a crew working on the bathrooms. The kitchen will wait until next month because the cabinets are being custom made and it was the last room I decided on."

"Still, that's a lot to get done. You must be excited seeing it unfold."

"I am. It's like the house is coming back to life after hibernating for a few decades."

"It will be beautiful when it's done."

"Would you like to see what they've done so far?"

Grinning, I nod enthusiastically. "I'd love to."

"Your parents' party is on Saturday, how about Friday after work?"

I forgot about their party. Mother hasn't given up on matchmaking between Lucinda and Mitch despite my sister's vehement protests.

"Friday is good. I'll meet you there. How about I bring dinner for us this time?"

"You sure? I can pick you up after closing and have something ready."

"I'm sure. I'd like to handle dinner."

He smiles. "Okay, I won't argue."

Great, I will plan something special. Something fool proof. A delicious dinner, with an aphrodisiac or two.

Operation Mitch's Seduction is back on track.

CHAPTER 29

Staring at the array of containers on the counter, I go down the checklist one more time. Oysters for the appetizer, Strawberry Spinach salad with Honey Balsamic Vinaigrette, Chicken Cordon bleu with Herbed Potato Fans, and the crowning touch, Chocolate Torte with pistachio and Maca. I researched foods used as aphrodisiacs and added them to every course at least once.

One of them has to work, right?

After I put all the carefully wrapped insulated containers in a box, I add his favorite bottle of wine. I heft the box and carry out the front of the bakery and place it on a table while I set the alarm and lock the door.

I am huffing and puffing by the time I reach my car and place the box on the back seat. Leaning against my driver's door I catch my breath and slide onto the seat and crank the air conditioning to cool me off.

My blue sundress is sleeveless at least so I won't have perspiration stains to worry about. I pull out onto the street and then slap off the air conditioning. I need to keep the food warm for my dinner with Mitch. It's not like he has an oven to heat anything in.

His house is less than ten minutes from the bakery so everything should be perfect.

If we eat quickly.

What if he wants to show me the work done on the house first? The oysters can't last that long.

Breathe.

I practice the breathing technique Olivia taught me and it helps.

Driving up to his house, I peek in my rearview mirror to check my hair and makeup are still in place. It takes a few glances and a quick swerve back onto the driveway to see that my hair is still tamed into a clip at the back of my neck and my sedate but sexy eye makeup is not smudged.

Mitch opens the front door as I put the car in park. He jogs down and kisses me on the cheek.

"You made it. I was about to call."

"Getting everything ready took a little longer than I anticipated." Okay, the black eyeliner and smudging technique took longer than I planned.

He grabs the box.

"Something sure smells amazing."

Smiling, I follow him up the path to the house. "I hope you are hungry because the appetizer has a time limit."

"Starving. I thought we could eat outside on the back patio. I bought a table and chairs the other day. We should be able to catch the sunset."

"That sounds lovely." I hadn't thought of where we would eat. I'm glad he is prepared. It would have been awkward standing at the kitchen counter eating my romantic dinner, if there even is still a kitchen counter.

I follow him through the house peeking at everything as we walk by. Fresh sheetrock covers the walls in most of the rooms. He's made a lot of progress.

A bronze colored metal table with a glass top and matching chairs is centered on the patio. A white candle flickers in a hurricane lamp.

Dishes and utensils sit on green placemats. A hunter green umbrella covers it all.

"I picked up a set of dishes and glasses the other day too. I got tired of eating on disposable plates with plastic utensils."

Wincing over the plastic plates and utensils in a bag at the bottom of the box, I hurry over and start unpacking the box he sets down on one of the chairs.

"It looks beautiful." Much more romantic than I had planned.

"What can I do?"

"Sit and enjoy."

Mitch takes a seat in front of one of the place settings. He set them up with one on the end and one next to it facing the lake. He takes the seat on the end and I set out the platter of oysters in front of him.

"Oysters, wow, they look great."

"They're the ones on a time limit, so please try one."

Scooting my chair in, I watch him take a bite.

His eyes widen. Oh no, am I too late? I should have prepared something that transported easier, not something which needed to be served immediately. Damn it, I've ruined the dinner with the first course.

"This is delicious. You didn't tell me you could cook too."

Relaxing into the cushion on the chair, I smile and reach for an oyster myself.

"I'm so glad. Of course, I can cook. I just don't get to do it all that often living with my parents."

Trying not to slurp, I bite into the oyster and am relieved. It tastes pretty good.

"That reminds me, my lawyer sent over the papers to transfer ownership of the building over to you. You and your lawyer can look them over and tell me if anything needs to be changed."

"Thank you. I can't tell you what it means to me that you're selling me the building."

"If I'd known you were planning to buy it, I never would have made an offer on it."

I smile and reach over to squeeze his hand.

He keeps my hand in his.

I wish I could bottle this moment. Etch it into my memory along with the love bubbling up inside me. I want this to work so badly. He has to see me as more than a friend, doesn't he?

"I'm dying to see what else you have hidden in that box."

"Oh!"

I let go of his hand and reach into the box, taking out the salad. The wine bottle is still there. I bite my lip and lift it out along with a wine opener and the wine glasses I tucked in the box.

"I forgot about the wine."

Mitch takes the bottle and the opener and reads the label. "One of my favorites."

"I made a Strawberry Salad with Honey Vinaigrette." While he fills our glasses with the wine, I set out the salads and pour the dressing over each.

When the sweet and tangy taste fills my mouth, I sigh inwardly. I sampled it at the bakery but worry still coursed through me.

His salad is half gone before I've taken three bites of mine.

He glances at me over his fork. "It's fantastic."

Smiling, I sip at the wine, and look over the lawn down to the lake.

"What do you plan to do with the grounds?"

Scanning the area, he takes another bite of his salad. "I want to repair the pathways and the formal gardens. There's even what's left of a small hedge maze on the other side of the house."

"Really? I'd love to see it."

"We can take a walk after dinner. This must have been the spot for grand entertaining at one time. It will take a lot of time and effort, but I want to recreate as much of the grounds as I can."

"I used to fantasize about ladies with parasols and long dresses waltzing along the garden paths on the arms of gentlemen dressed in suits with a harp playing in the background. They would dance on the patio with their skirts twirling around their ankles."

Mitch is smiling and my cheeks heat.

"I've imagined it similarly."

"Really?"

He nods and leans back in his chair. "The more I uncovered of the gardens and pathways, the more I thought about the parties they must have had. I want to put in a boathouse too, but farther along the cove, so it doesn't block the view of the lake."

"I can't wait to see it when you're finished."

"I plan to hire a landscape designer. You could help recreate your vision, tell him what you see."

"Oh, I know nothing about plants."

"Neither do I, but I know whether or not I like something when I see it. That's all I'm suggesting."

"I'd like to help." A little devil sitting on my shoulder tests my new theory on jealousy. "You should hire Bobby."

His eyes narrow and he takes a long drink of wine. "I'll think about it." Mitch clasps the utensils in his fists and taps the bottoms of his knife and fork on the table. "What's next?"

Laughing, I pull out the main course. "Chicken Cordon bleu with potatoes."

"How did you know that it's one of my favorites?"

"Is it really?"

He nods and cuts into the chicken and takes a bite.

I pause cutting into mine when he groans. A tingle in my core radiates out at the sound.

"You should add a restaurant on to the bakery. You're an incredible cook."

Pleasure infuses me, and I grin.

Three courses down and all a hit. All that's left is dessert and I'm sure that will be a slam dunk. What can go wrong with chocolate? I am confident when it comes to baking.

What if he's allergic to nuts?

Oh God!

He would have told me, wouldn't he?

"Mitch, you're not allergic to nuts, are you? I mean I should have asked beforehand, but it didn't occur to me until now."

He pauses with the fork halfway to his mouth. "Are there nuts in this?" His cheeks balloon, and his eyes widen.

My mouth drops open and I shove the chair back leaping to my feet. “Oh my God! Are you having a reaction?”

Mitch laughs and grabs my hand. “Relax, I’m joking. I have no allergies.”

Slumping back into the chair, I huff out a breath. “Not funny, you scared me.”

“I’m sorry, but you looked so worried. I couldn’t help it.”

“I should withhold your dessert for that.”

“You wouldn’t.”

“You sure about that?”

He grins and winks at me. “You’re too sweet to torture me that way.”

Am I too sweet?

Does he prefer women who aren’t sweet? His ex-girlfriend was rumored to be difficult to work with. I don’t know if it was gossip or truth. Regardless, the women he’s dated are exciting and flashy, and let’s not forget gorgeous.

The most thrilling thing I’ve ever done? Besides try to seduce Mitch and fail miserably? I can’t think of a single thing.

Maybe I should take up skydiving.

My fear of heights might get in the way.

Then there’s the whole opening a parachute on time or plummeting to your death aspect.

Nope, I can’t jump out of an airplane, even for Mitch.

If he were dying and it was the only way to save him, then I would do it, but not just so I could appear more electrifying.

Besides, the sheer terror I’m sure I would experience and the probable projectile vomiting upon landing would negate any points for exciting behavior I might get.

“You’re quiet. You’re not plotting to keep whatever dessert you made from me, are you? I promise no more bad jokes.”

Smiling, I shake my head. “No, you can have dessert.”

Standing, he holds out a hand. “I have an idea.”

“Um, okay, do you mind sharing what this idea is?” I place my hand in his and he tugs so I stand.

Mitch takes out his phone and plays music.

"Your vision of dancing inspired me."

He places his phone on the table and puts my other hand on his shoulder. Classical music flows from the phone full of strings and a soft melody.

"Mitch, I don't dance."

"Why not?" His hand rests on my waist and I desperately wish I was a woman who could step into his arms and waltz along the patio.

"Because I tried it when I was a kid. I took ballet lessons. I was so awful my mother made me quit."

He frowns and pulls me closer.

"Everyone can dance. We're not performing calculated steps. Move with me and listen to the music."

Biting my lip, I stare at our feet facing each other.

Mitch puts a hand underneath my chin and lifts. "Don't worry about your feet."

"Ha, you say that, but wait until I stomp on your toes or trip you."

Putting his hand behind my back, he tugs me closer and kisses me.

His lips whisper across mine.

His hand presses against my back and the other grasps my hand applying pressure there as well.

I move against him.

He steps and sways and I follow his movements as his lips trail across my cheek to my ear.

"See, anyone can dance. You just need to relax and feel the music."

My eyes flutter open and I stare over his shoulder.

Right, dancing.

My lips twitch because this is nice. I am dancing with Mitch, even though I would rather he continues the kissing.

He leads me across the patio in his arms.

Leaning my head against his shoulder, I close my eyes and breathe deep. His scent entwines with the lightest touch of gardenias from the lit candle. The warmth of his hand on my back seeps through my clothes and skin.

A crash echoes from the house.

We stumble apart.

"Wait here."

Mitch strides into the house and I shut off the music then pace the length of the patio. Should I follow him inside? He said to wait here, but what if he gets hurt? What if part of the old house collapsed? The renovations could have jarred something.

I step towards the door when a shuffle behind me causes me to swing around.

"Are you the housekeeper?"

A man in jeans and a ratty T-shirt stands on the edge of the patio with a camera in his hand.

"What?"

"This is Mitch Atwater's place isn't it? I heard in town he's been spotted with a blonde bombshell. I'll pay you if you give me any useful leads."

He's a reporter or the lesser version, anyway, paparazzi. The blonde bombshell must be my sister.

"This is private property. I'm calling the police." I stride over to the table and snatch my phone out of my purse.

"Chill out lady. I only want a shot of Mitch and his new ladylove. His ex, Margeaux, is posting all over social media that they're back together again and she's planning a wedding. Know anything about that? She been here?"

I freeze for a second.

Mitch would have told me, wouldn't he?

Was that the talk he wanted to have?

My stomach drops and tears fill my eyes.

I blink them back and grit my teeth. Getting rid of this trespasser is the priority.

I pretend to dial, hoping I'm not making a mistake. Should I call the police, or would Mitch want it kept quiet?

"Yes, I'd like to report a trespasser. This man is on my property and won't leave. Average height, brown hair, jeans."

The man turns and jogs around the side of the house.

I lower my phone and run for the house.

Locking the door behind me, I sprint down the hallway. Someone is coming down the stairs, and I pray it's Mitch.

He spots me when I reach the foyer and jogs down the remaining steps, grabbing me by the shoulders.

"What is it?"

"There was a man on the patio. He wanted confirmation this was your house."

"Are you all right? Did he hurt you?"

"No, I made believe I was calling the police reporting a trespasser and he took off."

"Damn it, I knew the information would get out eventually, but I thought I would have more time. I need to get the security system installed sooner than I had scheduled." He hugs me. "Are you sure you're okay?"

"Yes, I wasn't sure if you would want me to actually call the police or not."

"If a stranger comes near you again, you call the police. Why didn't you call for me?"

"I didn't want him to know he was right, and you lived here."

Mitch's sigh ruffles my hair. "Promise me you won't take any more chances. Most of these guys are harmless, but you never know what kind of crazy might appear. You wouldn't believe the stalkers Margeaux has had to deal with."

Margeaux. Was that guy telling the truth?

"He said she's saying you two are back together."

"What?"

"That guy. He said Margeaux is posting that you and she are a couple again and getting married."

"Those guys will say anything to get a reaction so they can take a picture and sell it. You can't listen to their crap."

I force a smile to my lips, but tension still rides my shoulders.

"You should get that security system installed right away."

"I will." He releases me and steps away. "I'm sorry he ruined our dance. I don't think we should continue our dinner on the patio."

"What was the crash? Did he try to break into the house?"

"Probably. There's scaffolding on the side of the house. It looks like he must have knocked part of it down. I walked through the rest of the house to check, but the scaffolding is the only explanation I found."

Rubbing my shoulders, I look around the foyer. "Are all the windows and doors locked? I locked the French doors when I came in."

"Yes. Why don't you go up to the master bedroom and I'll grab the stuff from the patio? We can still have our dessert and enjoy the sunset. There's no table or anything up there, but it shouldn't be too awkward holding the plates."

"Are you sure you should go out on the patio? What if he's still lurking around?"

"I'll be careful and quick. He's probably long gone."

"I'll come with you."

"No, I want you to go upstairs just in case."

"I should be there to help if he's still here."

"You can watch from the balcony and call the police if you spot him, okay?"

It is a better vantage point. I could see if he is anywhere around the house, or at least the back.

"Okay."

"Thank you."

Mitch disappears down the hallway and I run up the stairs to keep lookout for him.

I stride the length of the balcony and back while he grabs everything off the table and carries it inside. The man is out of sight or gone.

Could he be somewhere in the bushes snapping pictures?

Mitch's soft tread across the floorboards prompts me to turn away from scanning the tree line.

He's holding two plates with the chocolate torte on each.

I step into the room and shut the door. "We should eat inside in case he's still out there somewhere."

Mitch hands me a plate. "It's part of my life. He'll get his picture eventually, but if it scares you, we can stay inside."

"I'm not scared. I just didn't think you wanted him to get a photo."

He shrugs. "Like I said, he will eventually, or someone else will. That doesn't mean I'll tolerate the trespassing. It also doesn't mean I'm going to hide inside all the time."

"Well then, let's go out on the balcony and watch the sunset."

Mitch smiles and opens the door.

The colors aren't as vivid tonight, but the peach and grays are still beautiful. A man in a fishing boat casts his line outside the cove. He's not much more than a dark outline in front of the setting sun.

"What is in this? There's a flavor I can't identify. It's so good."

Smiling, I take a bite of my piece. "I can't divulge my recipes." I don't taste a difference but maybe the aphrodisiac is working.

That photographer didn't ruin the entire night. I refuse to let him. I'm considering this date a success.

Even if his words about Margeaux are stuck in my head. A quick internet search when I get home should get rid of that worry.

CHAPTER 30

Another one of my parents' parties and instead of hiding in the corner, I'm out on the patio sitting in a chair under the blue umbrella. Guests are trickling in. Their voices drift through the doors.

Boats crowd the lake. Some are moored to prepare for tonight's fireworks display. In a few hours, boats will fill the cove to watch the show. One year, an inebriated individual decided it would be a good idea to hop from boat to boat since they were floating so close together. He didn't make one jump and ended up in the lake. Good Samaritans dragged him out.

A water skier speeds by, jumping over the wake of the boat pulling her over the water. I've never been brave enough to try. My sister is an avid skier both on the snow and the water. Perhaps I should try it.

I glimpse blue out of the corner of my eye and spot Lucinda in a baby blue sheath being dragged around the living room by my mother to introduce her and perpetuate the sabbatical story. Mother is dressed in a royal blue dress with a red, white, and blue silk scarf tied at her throat.

I look down at my navy-blue maxi dress and white sandals and purse my lips. We almost match in a very generous description. We're all wearing blue anyway.

An older couple exit the doors and nod in my direction. I smile and nod in return. I don't recognize them, but my mother doesn't share her guest list with me. I wanted to invite Olivia, Monica, and the rest of the book club members, but she insisted it was too late and would disrupt her party.

Olivia and Sally are covering the bakery for me anyway, it's not like I can afford to close the bakery to attend one of my mother's parties. Although, I'm sure my mother wouldn't agree.

"Save me."

Lucinda drops into the chair next to me.

I chuckle and pat her on the arm. "I would if I could, but our mother is a force of nature."

She sighs, swipes my bottle of water and guzzles it.

"Thirsty?"

"I've been trying to get to the kitchen and get a drink for the past half hour, but she wouldn't let me. My throat is parched from having to smile and answer questions about the glamourous sabbatical she has dreamed up to tell everyone."

"Sorry Luce. How did you escape her?"

"Some emergency in the kitchen." She waves a hand towards the house.

"That could mean anything from ruined food to a glass with water spots."

Lucinda laughs and holds up the bottle of water. "I'm surprised she allows bottles at the party."

"She doesn't. I swiped that from the fridge."

"Uh oh, you better not let her catch you with it."

"You're the one holding it now."

My sister grimaces and then shrugs. "Oh well, what is she going to do to me?" Upending the bottle, she polishes it off.

"You really can ask that question about our mother?"

Shivering dramatically, she groans. "You're right."

"I have visions of that actress having a meltdown over wire hangers. I can see Mother yelling, 'No plastic bottles!'"

Lucinda snickers and cups a hand over her mouth.

"Ladies."

My heart leaps.

Mitch kisses each of our cheeks and then sits next to me. He's wearing a white button-down shirt with the sleeves rolled back to his elbows and navy-blue shorts. We could be a matching couple.

"How did you avoid my mother introducing you to everyone?"

He winks at me. "I didn't come in the front. I snuck around back."

"Brilliant." Lucinda sinks into her chair and crosses her legs. "No offense Mitch, but I may have to sacrifice you if my mother tries to abscond with me again."

Mitch looks at me and raises his eyebrow.

"Mother is telling everyone Lucinda is on Sabbatical," I say.

"I'm not. I quit, but that's taboo."

Reaching over I squeeze my sister's hand. "Only in her mind. You have nothing to apologize for or feel badly about."

She gives me a sad smile.

"Why don't I get us a round of drinks? What would you ladies like?"

Mitch stands and gazes down at us.

"I'll have a water please, Luce stole mine."

"Me too."

"Coming right up." Mitch strides to the door and, as he steps inside, the exclamations of surprise and greeting begin.

"He doesn't realize what he's in for."

I have a feeling he did and that he did it to give Lucinda a break. He has a caring heart. If I wasn't already madly in love with him, I'd fall again.

The aphrodisiacs I cooked for last night's dinner didn't accomplish my goal. Mitch is not seduced.

Yet.

I blame that photographer. My battery died on my phone while I was at Mitch's so I never got a chance to validate or refute whether Margeaux is claiming they're back together. It's been one thing after another today, rushing around at the bakery to prepare everything before I left and then dashing home to change for the party.

I'll find quiet time later and search until my mind stops worrying over it. I also need to come up with my next course of action to further along Mitch's seduction.

People wander on and off the patio, stopping to say hello to Lucinda and welcome her home. A server arrives with our waters and I glance towards the house.

Poor Mitch will never escape my mother's clutches. She'll be in search of Lucinda soon to parade them around together planting the seed in everyone's head they're a couple.

"I need to go use the bathroom."

"You're coming back, aren't you?"

I pat her on the shoulder. "As much as I'd like to disappear, I won't abandon you."

"Thank you. I'll come look for you if you don't."

Chuckling, I walk into the house and weave through the groups of people. Mitch is standing with my parents by the fireplace surrounded by a half-dozen people. He says something and they all laugh.

I catch his eye and smile, and he winks at me.

Avoiding the swinging door of the kitchen, I go through the foyer and up the stairs to use my bathroom.

"Scurrying away to hide as usual, Fanny. I'm sure your parents and the rest of the guests can now relax and not worry you will do something to ruin the party."

Vanessa is standing outside the guest room.

I look down the hall past her and then towards my room.

I walk towards her and stop a few feet away. "This is my home. I don't need to explain my purpose for being here to you. You, however, do not belong wandering around my parents' house. What are you doing up here?"

Her head rears back and a red tinge appears along her prominent cheek bones.

I am done being bullied by this woman.

"I was using the bathroom."

"There's a bathroom downstairs for the guest's use."

"It was occupied."

"Vanessa, I will give you the benefit of the doubt even though you certainly don't deserve it. You have been nothing but rotten to me our entire lives and I'm sick of it. Fair warning, I'm ready to fight back."

I swivel and strut down the hallway to my room.

A smile stretches across my face as I walk to the bathroom. My stomach is doing flip flops, but that felt good.

What if she tells Mitch I was mooning over him?

Finishing my business and washing my hands, I'm ready to run downstairs to intercept her.

No, so what if she does? She has no proof.

Would it be so horrible, anyway? I want him to see me in a different light.

Granted, I want him to realize he has feelings for me on his own with a little sexy prodding from me.

Opening the bedroom door, I shake my head. It doesn't matter what she says or does. I stood up to her and I survived.

Hell, I won that little battle. And I will win the war if she continues to wage one.

Vanessa has disappeared when I go downstairs. Mitch is still surrounded, but my parents are absent.

Stepping out on the patio, I glance over to where Lucinda was sitting. She's still there wringing her hands together in her lap.

My mother is standing next to her chair with a scowl on her face.

Riding high from my victory with Vanessa, I stride over to the table and sit next to Lucinda.

"What's going on?"

"Your sister is refusing to go mingle with Mitch." Her voice hisses out in a harsh whisper. "Stop this nonsense at once, Lucinda."

"Have you ever heard the expression no means no?"

My mother's glacial glare snaps to me.

"You may enjoy wallowing in that little hobby of yours, but your sister has the beauty and brains to accomplish great things. Stop trying to bring her down to your level. You've always been jealous of her. Is this how you get your revenge, ruining her life?"

I flinch. Direct hit. Yes, I've always been envious of her and what I perceived to be perfection, but I never wanted her harmed.

"Mother, that's enough."

Tears are welling and I can't look at my sister. She grabs my hand.

"If anyone has been jealous, it's me of Franny. She's brave enough to stand up to you and choose her own career and she has done so brilliantly."

I bite my lip and stare out at the lake willing the tears not to fall. My mother will only make a nasty comment about my drama if they do. I love my sister for defending me, but she's wasting her breath. Our mother will never see me as anything but a disappointment and a failure.

"Brilliantly? She lives in our house rent free and throws her life away in that tiny little bakery of hers. She will never find a husband worth a damn. Is that the life you want?"

Lucinda lunges to a stand. I reach for her hand to tug her back down. It's a waste of breath to argue with my mother. My hands are shaking, and I miss.

Mother's words hurt, but that's not why I'm shaking.

It's pure rage.

Screw her and her expectations.

I grasp Lucinda's hand and tug on it. She glances down at me and I give her a wobbly smile.

"You'll never change her mind, Luce, and I no longer care to."

My mother snorts and Lucinda looks from me to our mother and then drops into the chair.

"You're right. We shouldn't care."

"You're ungrateful brats. I threw this impromptu party for you to save your reputation from the horrible mess you've made of your life and this is the thanks I get? And you, you've corrupted your sister out of hateful jealousy. You're a disgrace to this family."

"Franny is a treasure and if you can't see that, it's you who are a disgrace."

Mitch's soft-spoken growl precedes his arrival behind me. He places his hands on my shoulders.

I cringe over what he may have heard.

My mother gapes at him and then gathers herself together. "Mitch, I don't know what you heard, but this is a private family discussion. It is a disagreement between us over Francine's intentions and actions towards her sister. I apologize you had to witness her outbursts. Why don't you take Lucinda inside for a drink?"

Mitch rubs my shoulders. My mother's gaze locks onto his hands.

"Ladies, why don't we find a friendlier location to enjoy the fireworks? I believe even a street corner would suffice."

"I would love to." Lucinda jumps up and pulls me up with her.

Mitch slides an arm around each of our shoulders.

"Goodbye Mother. It should please you to hear I will be moving out by the end of the summer."

She spins away and marches into the house.

The three of us walk around the side of the house and down the road to Mitch's truck.

Lucinda peeks over at me. "Did you mean it? Are you really moving out?"

"I'd move out today if I could. Mitch agreed to sell me the building so I'll be moving into the apartment when his house is ready."

"I'll move the process along. You can move in by the end of the week, I promise."

I can't decide whether to hug him, kiss him, or both. He stood up to my mother for me and is willing to get me into the apartment quicker.

I wrap my arm around his waist and lean into his side. He kisses the top of my head.

"Can I come to?" Lucinda leans her head forward to peek at me.

I smile. "It's only a one bedroom, but we can get a fold out couch if you're serious."

"Oh, I'm serious, and it won't be for too long. I'll get my own place when I figure out what the hell I'm going to do with the rest of my life."

"The two of you should move into my house and I'll stay in the apartment. The kitchen isn't functioning, but a couple bedrooms and bathrooms can be ready by the end of the week."

"Luce, you should see his house. It's spectacular. But, Mitch, we're not taking over your house. The apartment will be perfect for us."

Mitch opens the passenger side of his truck and holds it open for us. "The offer still stands."

Getting into the truck, I slide into the middle.

Mitch shuts the door once Lucinda climbs in and walks around to the driver's side. My thigh brushes up against his once he is settled.

"So, ladies, where are we going?"

I shrug. "You told Mother any street corner would do."

A snicker escapes me and then laughter rings in the truck as Lucinda collapses against me.

"It may have been a poor choice of words on my part. It was in the heat of the moment."

"We should go stand on a street corner and take a picture to send her. Won't she be proud of her daughters then?"

Lucinda shakes her head and straightens. "No, you were right, she'll never accept us making our own choices."

"Listen Luce, about what she said. I have been jealous of you, but I would never wish you any harm. I only want good things for you."

"Franny, I've been jealous of you too and I know what she said isn't true. She was deliberately cruel and hateful. I've never seen that side of her."

Welcome to my world.

"I'm sorry you had to witness it."

Mitch takes my hand in his and starts the truck.

Luce takes my other hand and squeezes.

My mother's words can't hurt me anymore.

CHAPTER 31

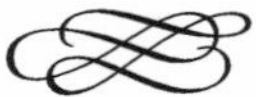

The fondant drapes over the layers of cake smooth and shiny, finally. I've redone it twice because of cracks and wrinkles that refused to cooperate. I carry the cake over to the cooler to set. It's already past five o'clock. I'll have to stop by tomorrow on my day off to finish up the decorations. It's a special order which needs to be delivered tomorrow afternoon.

Mitch texted me earlier and asked me to come up to the apartment after work. I'm guessing he wants to talk about the apartment and Lucinda and I moving in.

My mother is treating Luce and I to the silent treatment so there were no more outbursts when we went home last night. I was half afraid she would wait to ambush us.

I finish cleaning up the kitchen then use the bathroom to remove my hair from its bun and add makeup. My plan to seduce Mitch is still up and running after all.

Right after I show him the posts his ex has plastered all over the internet about their reconcile.

I finally found a few moments to do a search and the photographer hadn't been lying.

Mitch would have told me if it were true. I must believe that. So, it must be some sort of publicity stunt she is pulling. I just need him to confirm. He might not even be aware of what she is doing.

Staring into the mirror at my reflection, I whisper "I am beautiful —in my own way."

I squeeze my eyes closed and then try again. This is part of my new plan. No more negativity and insecurity.

Huffing out a breath, I try again. "I am beautiful. I am a great match for Mitch."

Okay, saying that a few hundred more times might make me believe it.

I walk out of the bathroom, grab my things, and lock the back door behind me. As I climb the stairs to Mitch's apartment, soon to be mine, he opens the door and leans against the jamb waiting for me with a smile.

"You're running late. I was just about to text you when I heard you on the stairs. Everything okay?"

"Yeah, I just had some work to finish up."

He steps back so I can enter. I inhale as I brush past him. The man always smells so damn good. I wonder if someone could somehow capture his unique scent and make it into a candle or something so I could light it and fill whatever room I'm in with *eau de* Mitch.

"Can I get you anything to drink?"

I shake my head and smile. "No thanks."

"I'll be ready to move out of here before Friday. Unless you need it sooner. How did it go last night with your mother?"

"Friday is great, really. I can't thank you enough. Mother seems to be punishing us with her silence. Little does she know it's a reward."

His mouth quirks to the side.

"Listen, there's something I want to talk to you about."

That sounds ominous.

And it's not about the apartment, he already mentioned that.

"Is this about Margeaux?"

He frowns.

"I saw some stuff she's been posting online. The photographer was telling the truth."

Mitch rubs the back of his neck. He doesn't look surprised.

I finger my necklace and wait for him to say something.

"It's hard to explain."

"Doesn't seem too hard, it's either true or not."

"It's not, she's impulsive."

I take a deep breath. It's not true.

"What about your crush?"

My back stiffens. "My crush?"

"Yeah, Bobby remember?"

"Oh, that."

He raises one eyebrow and continues to stare at me.

I swallow hard. "I never had a crush on Bobby."

Shit! I said it out loud.

I slam my eyes closed only to pop them back open. I pace the living area.

It's time for a full confession.

I rub my hand across my forehead and continue to pace.

"See, I panicked when you asked for a name and Bobby was driving by so that's why I said him. And then it snowballed from there and I didn't know how to explain what had happened."

I swing around to start another lap and ram into Mitch standing in my path. He grabs my shoulders to steady me.

Staring at the open buttons of his black polo shirt, my cheeks burning, and shallow breaths tightening my chest, I wait for him to say something, anything.

"Then who was that woman referring to?"

A part of me rejoices he doesn't remember Vanessa's name. Sheer terror drenches the rest of me knowing my day of reckoning has arrived.

Swallowing hard, I whisper, "You."

"So, all this time you were crushing on me? No one else?"

Still staring at his chest peeking through his open shirt, I nod.

The world tilts upside down as Mitch tosses me over his shoulder and strides toward the bedroom.

For a split second I marvel at his strength and then the terror returns and my mind spins wondering what he plans to do with me. I don't have long to imagine because he drops me in the center of the bed, and I bounce on the mattress and stare up as he looms over me and captures my lips in a devastating kiss.

There is no softness. No hesitancy. His mouth devours mine.

I fear I might melt right through the mattress as desire burns through every pore of my body.

One of his hands delves underneath the back of my shirt and clutches me closer to his aroused body. The other cups and shapes my breast, dragging his thumb back and forth across my pointed nipple.

Wrapping my arms around his waist, I yank his shirt up to touch his skin. The taut, hot muscles of his back bunch under my fingertips.

He wrenches his shirt over his head, baring his chest for my delighted gaze.

Instead of returning his lips to mine, he blazes a scorching path along my neck and shoulder. He lifts my shirt over my head and unfastens the front closure of my bra with a deft twist of his hand.

Embarrassment doesn't have a chance to encroach because his eyes worship me and his mouth and hands follow suit.

I comb my fingers through his hair and hold him close as the pleasure drenches me in sensation.

Mitch removes my skirt and panties in one quick tug.

My breath catches and holds when the rest of his clothes disappear. He really is a perfect specimen of man.

He kisses me deeply. Our tongues and breaths entwine. My fingers map every ridge of his abs and chest.

Mitch nips my bottom lip and kisses his way down my neck and shoulder. His hands cup and shape all my curves.

Heat races along my nerve endings. Perspiration dots my skin.

His mouth and tongue worship my breasts while his hands roam lower to open my legs. He slides down using his legs to open my body to him while his fingers work their magic.

Writhing in ecstasy, sharp exclamations of pleasure emanate from me as he wrings an orgasm from my oh-so willing body.

I pant as he grabs and opens a condom from the nightstand drawer and sheaths himself.

He returns to me and I loop my arms over his shoulders and revel over his body covering and entering mine.

His movements halt.

"Franny, are you a virgin?"

"Well technically no, not anymore."

He raises himself up and rests on one elbow as one hand cups my cheek. "Why didn't you tell me? I would have been gentler. Did I hurt you?"

"Only if you intend to stop now."

He closes his eyes and rests his forehead against mine.

Afraid he will stop, I clutch his cheeks in my hands and kiss him with all the pent-up passion my body has been hoarding for him and him alone.

When he still makes no attempt to enter me fully, I reach down and grab his ass cheeks and surge against him.

He lets out a harsh groan and thrusts. "God, Franny."

Pleasure climbs and throbs once again. I wrap my arms and legs around him exulting in the decadent sensuality of the act.

My body clenches in release. His hoarse groan of completion quickly follows.

Our sweat dampened bodies cool while we lay in each other's arms.

My brain regains the ability to function, somewhat, and a thought pops into my head and then straight out of my mouth.

"That was unexpected."

CHAPTER 32

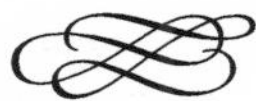

"It's time we finished that talk and make sure there are no misunderstandings."

Tension seeps in ruining the languid afterglow of our lovemaking. My hand stops petting his chest and I chew on my bottom lip.

"Maybe we should get dressed for this." I strain against his arms to pull away, but he holds firm.

"Hell no, I'm not letting you get dressed and take the chance you disappear on me again."

I peek up at him through tendrils of hair.

"Do you know why I came back here to Granite Cove?"

"Because you needed a break and you remembered a few happy summers here?"

He brushes the hair off my forehead and tucks it behind my ear. "I came back because of you."

My lip is now in danger of being permanently mangled as my teeth dig in. What does that mean? I'm afraid to ask. Afraid to hope.

"This isn't my first trip back. About a year ago I drove through town. I only intended to take a quick look around and reminisce a little. I didn't think you'd still be here, but I wondered because I had thought of you often over the years. Then there you were, waltzing down the sidewalk. I knew it was you instantly. This gorgeous hair was the same." He buries his nose against my hair and breathes deep.

Mitch thinks my hair is gorgeous?

"You were wearing jeans that showed off these mile-long legs of yours." His hand draws my leg over his and holds it in place. "You appeared to be in a hurry, striding down the sidewalk like you owned it. A car horn blasted at me because I had slowed to a crawl watching you. I made a U-turn and parked the car while keeping you in sight. You disappeared down the alleyway next to the building and, like a stalker, I got out of my rental car and trailed behind you and then watched you for a while through the window."

Euphoria fills my veins. Mitch came back to Granite Cove for me.

Resting my chin on my folded arms on his chest, I stare up at him. "Why didn't you say anything?"

"Because at the time I was still in a floundering relationship. It was at that point I knew without a doubt it was over." He cups a hand to my cheek and rubs my back. "I never felt a fraction of the emotion looking at her, or anyone, as I did seeing you. I planned to be back a lot sooner, but she started using again and I had to help her if I could before I left for good."

"So, you bought the building and the house?"

"Yeah, I saw the house was for sale and I remembered you mentioning it one summer."

"I did?"

"You described it and promised to show it to me, but then my parents left early a few days later."

I don't remember, but I had always loved that house. It makes sense I wanted to share it with him.

"Anyway, your parents sent an invitation to their Memorial Day party through my lawyer and I hoped it was from you."

"Mother only told me the morning of the party that you would be there. I was sure you wouldn't remember me."

"How could you think I wouldn't remember you?"

"Because we were kids and you're famous and I'm...well, me."

Mitch rolls me onto my back and looks down at me. “By that I surmise you mean you’re perfect in every way?”

Tears fill and over spill my eyes. He bends and kisses each one.

“I love you.”

I slap both hands over my mouth.

He stares down at me with one eyebrow raised and a smile lurking at the corner of his mouth. “Say that again, this time without the look of abject horror please.”

When I don’t comply, he tugs my hands away from my mouth and kisses me.

“Fine, we’ll work on that. Let me lead by example.” He kisses me again. “Franny Dawson, I love you. I love every single thing about you. I vowed I was going to make you mine. Nothing was going to stand in my way, not even when you declared you had a crush on someone else. I couldn’t stand the thought of not having you in my life. So, I plotted and hoped to show you the error of your affections. Your kisses nearly burned me alive. Each time I thought you must be feeling a hint of what I was, you dashed off or I’d find you with him. I wanted to drag you out of that restaurant when I spotted you there.”

I turn into a leaky faucet. Tears stream down my cheeks.

“Baby, please tell me those are happy tears.”

I nod and wrap my arms around him.

The tears subside as he holds me in his arms. Wiping my wet cheeks, I meet his gaze. “I love you. I’ve always loved you. It’s always been you, only you.”

“Thank God, because I’ve already told my parents all about you and that you’re the woman I’m going to spend the rest of my life with. They can’t wait to meet you.”

He laughs at the appalled look I am sure my face is showing. He wants me to meet his parents?

Well, of course he does, it is a perfectly logical step. Not that anyone ever accused me of being logical.

“I want to meet your parents. I’m sure they’re lovely.”

“They are and they will love you, I promise.”

I kiss him and nod.

"What do you think of having the wedding at the house once it's finished?"

Wedding?

I almost ask for whose wedding. The words are right on the tip of my tongue.

"Are you asking me to marry you?"

Mitch kisses me on the tip of my nose and grins. "I suppose that wasn't very romantic. Say yes, and I'll make it up to you."

"I…I can't."

Why the hell did I say that?

I scramble to a sitting position dragging the sheet with me.

Mitch frowns and scoots up to lean against the headboard.

"Franny?"

"Just give me a minute to think—please."

Tears fill my eyes and my chest feels like an elephant has plopped down on it.

I rub my forehead as if I can jump start my brain to help me make sense and explain.

"I love you. I think I've always loved you. But how can it last? You're surrounded by gorgeous women all the time with your job. Hell your supermodel ex is claiming you've reconciled. That stupid photographer thought I was your housekeeper."

Tears course down my face. I swipe the back of my hand under my running nose. "How can a marriage between us ever work? You're going to break my heart like you did before."

"Franny…we were kids."

"I know that damn it! I realize how stupid it must sound to you. How could you possibly understand? I lived for those summers! They were all I had. You weren't just my best friend—you were my only friend. You kissed me and disappeared. I suffered the whole school year just waiting for summer to arrive and you to return."

I wipe my cheeks with the heels of my hands and then throw them in the air. "But you never did. I never heard from you again. It devastated me."

I wrap my fingers around my necklace. "Then my grandmother

died and I truly had no one. She was the only one who understood and accepted me."

I choke on the sobs stuck in my throat.

"I'm just starting to make a life for myself. You have no idea how hard it is for me to trust someone to see the real me. I've been putting on this front for you trying so desperately to get you to see me as more than a friend, but the real me is a total disaster. I have anxiety attacks before social events. My instinct is to hide. What kind of wife to a famous director would I make?"

"Franny, I'm sorry. I never meant to hurt you. I was a thoughtless kid wrapped up in his own life. I told you about the rough patch my parents went through. I started acting right after that."

He rubs his hands over his face. "It boils down to trust. You don't trust me not to hurt you. Do you expect me to give up my career so I'm not around actresses? What's next? You'll be jealous of women in town? Do you see how silly that is? As for Margeaux, I already told you it's you I love and not her. Yes, she's been calling me saying she wants me back, but it will never happen."

Mitch stands and walks to the bathroom. He stops in the doorway and stares back at me. "I think it's you that you really don't trust. I wish I could make you see yourself the way I see you."

CHAPTER 33

The door shuts behind him and the shower turns on. I collapse on the bed sobbing.

He's right. I don't trust myself not to screw it up. I don't believe I'm enough to hold his interest.

Oh God it hurts!

I curl up into a ball with the sheet tangled around me.

What am I going to do?

I don't want to lose Mitch. I never thought he would propose marriage. I thought…I don't know what I thought.

I didn't plan beyond getting him to see me as more than a friend.

The hiccupping sobs constrict my throat and burn my eyes and nose.

What if he ends our relationship now? What if he leaves Granite Cove again?

It just might kill me this time.

The door opens and Mitch walks out with a towel around his waist. He stops when he sees me on the bed.

I bite my lips and try to hold back the sobs.

"Jesus Franny, you're killing me. Don't cry."

He climbs on to the bed behind me and wraps his arms around me.

"I'm so—so sorry." I'm blubbering and can't stop.

He kisses the top of my head. "We'll figure it out."

"We will?"

"You don't think I'm letting you get away after all this, do you? If you're not ready to get married yet, then we'll wait. I guess I'll have to shower you with love and compliments until you see how special you are."

I twist and throw my arms around him. "Oh Mitch, I was so afraid I was going to lose you. I love you so much."

He squeezes me. "I love you too, baby. I'm a patient man. I can wait until you're ready. You do think you'll be ready one day, right?"

"I'll make it my new goal in my life plan."

He chuckles and the sound reverberates against my head tucked against the hollow of his throat.

"Is it so hard to imagine marrying me? Trusting our love?"

The image of him dressed in a black tuxedo smiling down at me flashes through my head. We're standing on the back lawn of his house. My white gown glistens in the sun. Friends and family surround us smiling and laughing.

I look up into his handsome face and lift a finger to trace his eyebrows and down his perfect nose to his lips.

Fear.

Fear has guided my life for so long. I've been afraid of not being accepted, of being hurt, left alone, unloved.

"I can picture it."

He kisses the tip of my finger.

I stare into his blue eyes.

I don't want to live in fear anymore.

A calm washes over me. I love this man. I want to spend the rest of my life with him. He's my first love, my only love, and I want him to be the last.

I smile and lean up to kiss him. "I don't want to wait."

He leans his head back. "Are you saying what I think you are? Never mind. I need to hear the exact words. No more trying to guess what's going on in that beautiful head of yours."

"I'm saying yes. I want to marry you."

"Are you sure? I don't want to pressure you into anything you're not ready for."

"I'm sure. I was scared, but I refuse to make decisions based on my fears anymore. All that matters is we love each other. I want to marry you and someday have your babies."

He grins and leans down to capture my lips in a bone melting kiss. "How many babies?"

Laughing, I swat his shoulder. "That's up for discussion. At a later date."

"I can live with that. I suppose I should ask your father for your hand in marriage."

And the horror is back.

My mother will lose her mind.

The hard part is over. I have my Mitch and he loves me. Anything else will be a piece of cake.

And I know how to make one hell of a cake.

THANK you for reading *My First My Last My Only*! Continue the Granite Cove series with an excerpt from Olivia's story, *Covet thy Neighbor* .

A CRASH ECHOES across the yard from my neighbor's house. I startle, spilling ice coffee on my hand and shorts. *Crap, that's going to stain.* I place my cup on the patio table and stand, shoving the chair back. Two steps across my deck, I stop, chew on my bottom lip, and shift my weight from side to side.

The last time I set foot on his property he grunted, snatched the plate of welcome to the neighborhood cookies out of my hands, and closed the door in my face. Not an experience I care to repeat.

What if he's hurt? If I do nothing, and he's injured, what kind of person does that make me?

Damn it!

Standing around debating the issue wastes precious time if he's bleeding out or something. On TV, the ambulance always makes it to the hospital at the last possible minute before death or permanent disability occurs, but that's just drama, right?

I jog down my deck steps and across my yard into his. The line of waist high holly bushes separating our properties snag at my clothes and scrape against my skin.

Should I knock on the front door or go to the back? The crash came from his backyard. He's probably fine and simply dropped something, or maybe thrown it in a fit of rage.

Rolling my eyes, I veer towards the back of the gray colonial. Time is of the essence.

I reach the blue stone patio and jerk to a stop. A ladder is on its side and my neighbor is flat on his back.

I gasp and sprint around the low wall edging the patio.

Crap! Is he dead? Did I waste precious minutes debating when I could have saved him?

His eyes are open and staring at the sky. Is he breathing?

I reach for my phone in my back pocket as I step onto the stones. His blond head swivels in my direction and his dark gaze locks on me. I stumble to a stop a few feet away.

"Are you okay?"

"Who the hell are you?"

As charming as ever, I see. I point towards my house. "Your neighbor. I heard a crash."

He springs to his feet in a single flow of movement.

Impressive ab strength to accomplish that feat. My gaze drifts over his tall, rangy build. Yeah, there are serious muscles flexing under those jeans and T-shirt. They all appear to be in fine working order. No damage done. He isn't in need of my assistance. I shove my phone back into my pocket.

"Are you in the habit of barging onto private property?"

He braces his fists on his hips and scowls.

For real? Next time I hear a crash over here, I'll turn on the music and pour a glass or two of wine.

I huff out a breath and scowl right back. "No, like I said, I heard a crash and wanted to make sure no one was hurt."

"As you can see, I'm not in need of a Florence Nightingale."

I glance away. Okay, after our first encounter I tried to give him the benefit of the doubt. Everyone has a bad day, but this guy is a jerk.

Through the open patio door, I spot a gun, some type of rope, and an assortment of knives and sharp objects strewn across a table.

I snap my gaze back to his and swallow hard. "Yup, I can see that." I back up several steps. "I won't bother you again."

Grabbing my phone out of my pocket in case he decides to commit violence against me, I pivot and stride across his lawn as fast as I can, short of breaking into a run. The urge to glance back over my shoulder to see if he is watching me crawls up my neck, but I stare at the solace of my little blue cape.

Once I reach my back deck, I dart inside and lock the door behind me. I grip the doorknob in my fist as I sag against the door.

Okay, not going to panic, I'm sure there are many reasons for him to have an assortment of weapons on his kitchen table.

Just because I can't think of a single reasonable, nonviolent one, doesn't mean I should jump to any conclusions.

Thank God the boys are back at school. I might feel the need to bundle them close, pack up our stuff, and take off for parts unknown.

Imagination in overdrive, Olivia! Dial it back a notch or two.

I wipe the dots of perspiration off my nose with the back of my hand. Not sure if it was from the run, the heat, or the fear, but my clothes are sticking to my skin. One more summer where central air conditioning isn't in the budget. Fans and window units will have to suffice. Besides, it's already September and the heat should give way to cooler temperatures soon.

I push off from the door and walk around the corner to the bathroom and splash cold water on my face and neck and then wipe it off with a towel. I check the time on my phone, ten o'clock. My shift at the bakery starts soon.

Upstairs, I peek out my bedroom window at the gray colonial while slipping into a sleeveless pink sundress. My disagreeable neighbor is nowhere in sight. I walk back into the bathroom and comb my hair back into a ponytail, put on a few swipes of mascara to darken my pale lashes and rub a tinted lip balm onto my lips.

From the bathroom window I can see more of his backyard, but there's no sign of him. He probably went inside. I check the windows of his house. Nothing stirs. What if he's looking out one of his windows at my house like I'm doing to him? I jump back and shuffle backwards out of the room into the hallway.

If I couldn't see into his windows, then he can't possibly see into my windows, can he? Not without a pair of binoculars.

Great, now the image of him staring into a pair of binoculars at my house is stuck in my head. At least it's better than him holding one or more of those weapons.

Or worse, chasing me with those weapons.

"My neighbor is a serial killer."

"Umm...is that fact or supposition?" Lucinda's blonde eyebrows arch halfway up her forehead as she leans against the marble counter nibbling on a piece of muffin.

The aroma of freshly baked chocolate chip and oatmeal raisin cookies wafts across the kitchen after Franny opens the ovens. She puts the trays of cookies on the rolling rack in front of the ovens and props her hands on her hips. "You didn't go back there without me, did you? I told you I would go."

I shake my head and lift myself onto the counter next to the sink. "No—well, not intentionally. I was sitting on my back deck this morning enjoying my second cup of coffee while contemplating my life and what the hell I want to do with it when I heard a crash next door. So, of course, I went over to ensure no one was dying or anything."

"You went over there thinking you lived next door to a serial killer? Why didn't you call the police?" Lucinda drops the rest of her muffin into the garbage and brushes the crumbs off her fingers. "Have you called the police?" She glances at Franny. "She's not serious, is she?"

Franny holds up a finger to her sister. "Hold on, Luce. Olivia, what happened?"

"My neighbor was on his patio, lying on his back, just staring at the sky. There was a ladder on its side near him. To be honest, for a second, I thought he might be dead. Then he jumped up and yelled at me for trespassing. I was ready to give him hell right back, but when I noticed the large assortment of weapons littering his kitchen table, I left."

Franny frowns and glances at her sister. "This guy moved in next door to Olivia and was rude when she welcomed him to the neighborhood. She did a search for him on the internet and came up with nothing. She has her twin boys to worry about, so she's cautious. I told her I would go with her next time because there's plenty of reasons the guy might be unfriendly, but obviously her instincts were right in the first place. There's something fishy going on."

"I know I'm paranoid, but being a mother makes me worry about all sorts of things. So, when someone new moves into the neighborhood or comes into their lives, I do a quick search online and not only the predator lists, but a general hunt to make sure there are no red flags. Luke Hollister has no online presence whatsoever. No social media, nothing. That's weird, right? Now, coupled with his behavior and the weapon stash—I'm not crazy to worry, am I?"

Lucinda shakes her head. "Not at all, I can only imagine what you have to worry over as a parent. And, although there is nothing criminal about being rude or unfriendly, I admit the multitude of weapons is questionable." She raises her hand. "However, he could simply be a collector. Perhaps we shouldn't jump to conclusions just yet."

"Spoken like the lawyer you are." Franny smirks.

"A collector of weapons? I admit I didn't think of that. My mind went straight to murderous intent." I swing my feet and stare at the black and white squares of tile on the floor. All right, my paranoia for my kids' safety might be getting out of control.

"I'm simply throwing out other options. My firm in Connecticut had a private investigator on retainer. Would you like me to call him and ask for a referral for someone here in New Hampshire? Or we could ask our father to check with his former firm and see if they recommend anyone in the area."

"You think Granite Cove is big enough to have a private investigator?" Franny leans on the counter with folded arms. "I'd like to see Mother's face when you ask Dad for the name of a private investigator though."

"Ha ha."

"Thanks guys, but hiring an investigator isn't exactly in my budget." I cross my ankles and sigh. "I guess I'll just have to keep a close eye out and make sure my two devils don't go wandering out of our yard."

"Well, don't go back over there, no matter what you hear."

I nod at Franny. "I have no intention of setting foot on his property again. Maybe it's time I replaced the fence between our properties. There used to be a split rail fence, but it rotted in places so the former owner tore the whole thing out before listing it for sale. I could put in a tall solid fence with barbed wire at the top."

"That would certainly send a message." Franny grins.

Covet thy Neighbor

Sign up for my newsletter to be the first to hear about new releases, sales, contests, and read exclusive excerpts: Denise Carbo's Newsletter

ABOUT THE AUTHOR

Denise Carbo writes Contemporary Romance, Romantic Suspense, and Paranormal Romance. She is a voracious reader, loves to travel, is fascinated by the supernatural, and enjoys solving mysteries.

She lives in a small, picturesque New England town with her high school sweetheart and their three amazing sons.

Made in the USA
Middletown, DE
30 July 2021

45080954R00156